The Valkyrie's Sword

Warbler Peninsula series, Book 2

Siobhan Muir

ISBN: 1-947221-02-7
ISBN-13: 978-1-947221-02-4

DEDICATION

Dedicated to Liv Therese Dalin. Tusen takk.

ACKNOWLEDGMENTS

Good glory, this has to be the hardest book I've ever worked on, and not even for the usual reasons of lots of research or difficult subject matter. It should've been easy, but it wasn't. So I must thank Silver James, Suzie Quint, and George Varhalmi for reading the ugliness that were the first three drafts and helping me find the story within. Thank you to Sabrina York who gave suggestions on how to fix the "meh" storyline with a little zing. Thank you to Liv Therese Dalin, the keeper of the cookie recipe and my go-to for Norwegian language and names. Without you, this story wouldn't have been nearly as interesting. Huge thank you to my editor Paige Prince for snooping through the back alleys of this tale and finding all the pot (plot?) holes. Thanks to model John Dewall and photographer Wander Aguiar for producing such a magnificent image for the hero, Balder Templar. Great thanks to Kris Norris for creating this amazing new cover with John's image and the hot woman on the motorcycle, capturing the hero and heroine perfectly.

GLOSSERY TO NORWEGIAN TERMS

- Deilig – Delicious
- Drit – Shit
- Faen – Fuck (Literally "The Devil")
- Forsvarer – Defender
- Helvete – Hell
- Hjertet mit – My Heart
- Jeg elsker deg – I love you
- Kjære – Dear
- Kjekken – Handsome (masculine)
- Søta – Cutie (feminine)
- Tosk – Dimwit
- Tusen takk – Thousand Thanks.

CHAPTER ONE

"For the love of God, where are you dragging me now?"

Balder planted his feet in the mud along the side of road they'd traveled for the last two days and squeezed his hands into fists. Righteous rage rolled through him as he glared at his companion. Voices from his past, screaming and egging him on, filled his mind with fury and he wanted to roar across the rain-filled landscape.

Tiffany turned, stared at him with hollow eyes, and drifted straight through him.

Searing cold dismantled the hot fury and drained it away. Despair, shame, guilt and regret flooded in its wake, and Balder moaned as he dropped to his knees.

:You have no place to demand anything, Balder "Vengeance" Templar. We are only on this journey because of you.: Her words held the frigidity of her essence, but her eyes blazed.

"I'm trying to get better, Tiffany. I'm trying to help you." He mumbled it into his chest as the rain pattered down on his backpack, but he knew she could hear him.

:Trying to help me?: She scoffed with a deepening scowl. *:You're hoping to get rid of me so I can leave you to*

1

forget what you've done, to ignore the hurt you've caused, to dismiss the heinous acts you've committed. Oh no, Balder. I'm here until you've made amends.:

"I'm sorry, Tiffany."

She snorted. *:Not enough yet, you're not.:*

He squeezed his eyes closed as the memories of his past as an elite Blade to the Sword of God flashed through his mind. He'd infiltrated communities, seeking out the inhuman residents, and killed them, sometimes stealthily, sometimes violently. Tiffany Lupin, his erstwhile fiancée, had been the last one to die before he realized he'd made a mistake. And she never hesitated to remind him.

"I'm trying to change." He wanted to, but he didn't want to feel the pain, remorse, and guilt anymore.

:Shall I remind you what you said the night you murdered me and my family?: Her eyes grew cavernous and her face whitened out until she appeared like a wraith with nothing but blackened eye sockets. *:You said, and I quote, "My true name is Vengeance! You are the infection and this town must be cured. I will cleanse this town of your taint and humanity will be free." Cleanse, Balder, like the evil hadn't come to our town with you.:*

"I'm trying. I was wrong. The Sword of God is wrong. I don't want to be that way anymore." He dropped his head and cowered before her. Intellectually, he knew she couldn't do more than chill him, but she wielded fear and terror with remarkable aplomb when necessary, and the fire of his programmed fury flickered out.

:Be sure you remember that.: She faded back into her usual appearance of a pretty, young blonde woman with sky-blue eyes. *:Now get up and get moving. I want to make it to the next town by nightfall. If you're caught outside tonight, you might freeze to death. And I don't want to be stuck with you in the afterlife.:*

He agreed with her on that.

Balder took a deep breath and stood, his heart slowly

returning to normal as he scanned his surroundings. The wet, northern Michigan morning offered nothing but the soft patter of rain on the road, and the wind soughing through the pines overhead. The scents of damp summer forest and his own unwashed body filled his nose as his breathing leveled out.

The ghost faded from view as she headed up the road and he rubbed a hand over his face. The sooner he found a way to help Tiffany move on, the better they'd both be. He owed her at least that much. Balder pushed his body into motion and kept going to God-knew where.

He tried to keep his mind and thoughts on the present, but the rain and the dreary day sucked him back into the past. He shut his eyes and shook his head hard. He didn't want to face the guilt and horror of what he'd done. He couldn't. Regret, despair, and self-hate followed him around like baying wolves. *Wolves is right. Werewolves.*

Tiffany Lupin and her family had been good community members, but they shifted by the light of the full moon into glorious canines. He'd been sent by the Sword of God as one of their elite Blades to infiltrate and neutralize the "pack of mongrels" before they tainted more of the town. He'd posed as a young man interested in her as a woman. He'd even gone so far as to propose marriage to Tiffany the night before he planned to "cleanse" the world of her.

I was so stupid.

Tiffany snorted as she rematerialized beside him. *:Yes, you were. Still are as far as I'm concerned.:*

Balder growled and waved a hand at her. "Get away from me, ghost. Have done. You're dead and I'm sorry."

Tiffany cocked her head and scowled. *:You're sorry? Sorry? Not yet, you're not. Not until you make my death and those of my family right. The name is Tiffany, and I'll be right here with you every step of the way until you do something to help the very Elder Races you'd hoped to* *eradicate.:* She rose and drifted close enough to be nose to nose with him. *:You owe me and every other Elder Race you killed,* Vengeance.:

She spat the name he'd taken as a Blade and his stomach curdled as the guilt, pain, and regret ate at him from inside. Vengeance. Vengeance against those who'd ignored God and allowed the monsters to populate the world. That's what the Sword of God taught their members.

"That's not my name anymore." He'd thrown it away at Tiffany's insistence, and taken the one he vaguely remembered from his past. Balder meant "he who spreads the light" in his first language of Norwegian and she'd shot him a dry look, but hadn't argued. "I'm Balder Templar and I'm working on redemption."

Tiffany rolled her eyes. *:Work harder. I know you can. We have those places to visit on your map and one is close. So get your ass moving. Time to start spreading the light, Balder.:*

Balder growled, but pushed on.

They'd stopped for the night in the National Forest not far from a small town called Three Lakes, according to his map. Tiffany insisted they go there, but like all their previous destinations, she wouldn't tell him why they needed to visit. He suspected she didn't know. She seemed to be looking for something, but he couldn't fathom what she hoped to find. He just wanted to stop and sleep somewhere warm for once. Michigan hadn't figured out it was supposed to be spring yet.

The rain pounded on his head and pack, adding a new rhythmic sound to those already filling the wet forest. Tiffany made no noise at all and her white summer dress with the purple pansy pattern never got soaked. Sometimes he envied her, but how and why she resided in that state destroyed his covetousness.

He shoved the thoughts away and focused on the road. He had a little money left from the last time they'd panhandled and hoped to buy a hot meal and coffee when they made it to the next town. He'd either have to panhandle again or find a job.

"Do you think we'll stay in this town for a little while or move on immediately?"

Tiffany paused and frowned. *:I don't know. Something about this place feels different.:*

Balder snorted. "Different? You said that about the last town and it was no different than the four previous."

She gave him a flat look. *:This is a different difference.:*

His laughed. "A 'different difference?' Seriously?" *:Seriously.:*

She nodded and a grin curled her lips. It had been a long time since he'd seen her smile. *Since her death, in fact.* He much preferred it to her usual dour expression. She remained just as lovely as the day he'd met her, though he hadn't acknowledged her beauty at the time. But he'd missed her smiles.

"Well, all right, then. Let's check out this different town."

Balder continued his sodden trek toward the town, passing a service gas station on the way in. The repair bay doors remained closed against the rain. That was the first civilized place he'd seen along this road in two days of walking. A little more than a mile farther and the town came into view.

Welcome to Three Lakes, Michigan. He hoped he'd be welcome, but only if he hid who he'd been.

Despite the leaden skies, the town bustled with people out and about. Unease skittered up his spine, but he swallowed hard and kept going. The springtime migratory birds flitted beneath the deciduous trees lining the quaint avenues, their songs full of hope and renewal. He wished he could join in their jubilation, but new places made him nervous and the energy of this place sang along his nerves.

People joined them on the sidewalk, briskly walking to and from vehicles, ducking into storefronts, or pausing to talk to each other. Balder kept his gaze moving, but didn't allow it to connect with anyone. He didn't want to be noticed yet.

:Balder, I think I know what's different about this town.: Tiffany's voice held wonder.

"Oh?" He shot a look around him to make sure no one overheard him talking to a ghost. "What's the difference?"

:Most of the people here are Elder Races.: Her eyes grew round and she swallowed hard as she met his gaze.

Aw hell. An entire town of Elder Races? His gut sank. It had been three years since he'd been in the Sword of God, but the programming and indoctrination died hard. Most of the time he could ignore it, but periodically it would blare at him, trying to cage him in fear and sickness. Whenever it got the upper hand, Tiffany would rail at him for days until he broke free of its grip.

He'd really have to watch himself in this town.

The tension in his shoulders increased as Tiffany's demeanor lightened, her expression filling with curiosity as they passed the shops on Main Street. He kept waiting for someone to discover who he was and raise hell about it. But no one seemed to care and he forced himself to relax. *Maybe I can be normal here.*

Hope whispered with the sounds of the rain and he allowed it to plant a seed. The spring shower made the town shimmer with silvery light and his shoulders relaxed. He passed a grocery store where a giant of a man in a sheriff's uniform stood under the awning talking to a pretty woman with a laugh like tinkling bells. Balder dropped his head to keep from attracting the officer's attention.

He followed the sidewalk onward and passed the Three Lakes Library, the brass handrails lining the steps festooned with red, white, and blue buntings. A scent of fire and brimstone coupled with an ancient smell of old blood wafted from the front doors. *Dragon and vampire.* Once he'd believed they deserved to die, but Tiffany had taught him—beat it into him, actually—the weird and mythical folk were no different and no worse than humans. Still, vampires made him nervous and he hurried his steps onward.

"Why do you think there are so many Elder Races here, Tiffany?"

She paused beside a tall pine tree shading the sidewalk and shook her head. *:I don't know. The energy is powerful here. Maybe it's because there are so many Elder Races in one spot.:* She shot a look back toward the main road. *:We should go up the road a bit more.:*

"I can't."

Tiffany raised her chin and eyebrows. *:Can't?:*

"Yeah, can't. I'm tired, Tiffany, and I need a warm meal." He held up his hand before she railed at him for giving up. "I saw a sign for a homeless shelter here. Let's find a space for me to stay, and we can explore more after."

She opened her ethereal mouth to protest, but he sighed and shook his head. "I can't keep going. I'm exhausted and I need a break. I'm not giving up, but I need a day or two of rest."

:Balder—:

He scowled before he straightened his shoulders and marched through her. She growled her dismay and trailed after him. He rarely treated her like the ghost she was. Her cold touch felt uncomfortable on his skin, but she didn't have the needs he did, and he was no good to her dead.

"I promise to keep exploring once I'm dry. You don't feel the rain."

She matched his scowl, but said nothing as she trailed behind him. He followed the sidewalk past the Ironwood Café and the delicious scents wafting from it. Peach pie, minestrone soup, and garlic quiche hit his nose and he almost stopped. But the cold presence of the ghost pushed him on two more blocks to the sign for Little Hands Homeless Shelter.

He reached for the handles of the doors, but Tiffany laid a hand on his arm. *:Balder, wait.:*

"What is it?" Impatience to be out of the rain made him snap.

:This place has…unusual energy. Whoever stays here might not be human.: Tiffany bit her bottom lip. *:Are you ready for that?:*

Part of him wanted to tell her off for suggesting he had no control, but the more reasonable portion of him took her words into consideration. He could feel the energy, but it drew him closer rather than repulsing him. His gut told him he'd found a place where he needed to be.

"Yes, I think so."

:All right then.: Tiffany nodded and released his arm. *:Have at it. Your gut knows best.:*

It did. His gut was rarely wrong, and it had screamed at him to leave Tiffany's family alone when he'd slaughtered them. He shoved the thoughts away and pulled open the doors of the homeless shelter.

The scent of something delicious filled the foyer as a woman looked up from a desk reminiscent of a hotel registration counter. Her hair was short and silver, and laugh lines outlined her mouth. A set of reading glasses rested on the bridge of her nose as she offered a warm smile.

"Welcome to the Little Hands Homeless shelter. Can I help you?"

He nodded and met the warm brown eyes behind the glasses. A feeling of warmth, comfort, and peace hit him and he took a deep breath, releasing some of his earlier tension.

"Yes. My name is Balder and I need a place to stay."

She nodded in return, her gaze drifting over his gear. "Welcome, Balder. You're fortunate. We have several beds available in the men's dorm. My name's Angelina Burke and I run the place." She pulled out a ledger. "How long do you think you'll be staying?"

His first inclination was to mumble something about a few days, but something stopped him. A heart-wrenching yearning for forgiveness, acceptance, and redemption cut the words off in his throat. *Sweet Lord of Mercy, I don't want to be alone anymore.* To his horror, tears flooded his eyes and a great sob shuddered from his chest.

"I don't know, I just want to stop roaming relentlessly." His sorrow overflowed his lower lids and slid down his cheeks. "We—I was called to be here and would like to find a way to earn my keep so I can stay and find my place. If you have any jobs that I could trade for room and board, I'd really appreciate it."

:Balder!: Tiffany's exclamation mirrored the surprise shooting through him.

I want what?

Angelina scrutinized him for a few moments, rubbing her chin with one finger. Her gaze skittered past him toward the spot where Tiffany hovered, but it returned to him as she nodded slowly.

"I think you might be in luck. I happen to have an opening for a handyman. Usually it's small maintenance around the shelter." She tilted her head and tapped her lips. "Tell you what. I'll give you two weeks to see if it works out. If it does, you can stay on as a worker and trade for your room and board. Fair?"

Relief and gratitude relaxed his shoulders, and more tears decorated his cheeks. "Yes, ma'am. That sounds very fair. Thank you."

"Good. Shake on it, please."

Balder didn't like to touch people, but he needed to stay in this little town and he couldn't ask for a better arrangement. He held out his hand and Angelina grasped it, shaking firmly. Her touch soothed some of the raging emotions inside and he sighed with the release from their onslaught. She watched his face with focused attention as if looking for more than he wanted to show and he hoped she couldn't see the shame, disgust, and crippling guilt he carried with him. He tried to keep his expression bland, but her attention unnerved him.

She nodded sharply and released him. "All right then. Let's get you a room and a key."

He let out the breath he hadn't known he'd held and wiped the tears off his face. "A room?"

"Yep. I figure if you're gonna be working with me, you should have your own space." She stood and gathered a key from a little ornate wooden box set into the wall behind the desk. "If it doesn't work out, well, then we'll make new arrangements."

"Yes, ma'am." He shot a look at Tiffany, but she shook her head and shrugged as if to say, *This is all you, buddy.*

"Good. Follow me."

Angelina led him down the hall past the cafeteria to another hallway with doors on either side. "This used to be an old hotel before I bought it and renovated it. My apartment is the last door on the right. You can have this room right here." She opened the first door on the left. "Come on in."

The room looked like an ornate version of an extended-stay suite with a separate bedroom from the living space. A kitchenette opened to the left just inside the door and the bath stood opposite the kitchen. A few small paintings hung on the wall over a couch and TV stand, giving the space a homey feeling. One caught his eye.

"That looks like Lucifer." Six wings rose from the figure's back in a magestic warrior pose. Despite his innate hatred of the Lord of Evil, the painting evoked feelings of determination against all odds. *Like me trying to find a place in this town.*

:An effort that will in all likelihood be doomed to failure, Balder.: Tiffany shook her head.

"I do believe it is Lucifer." Angelina nodded, a half-smile curling her lips. "But I've always liked this picture."

Balder shook his head. "I'm pretty sure the devil never tried to be an angel in disguise."

"I don't know. I think Lucifer was asked to take the hardest job of all and does his duty to help people in his own way. Everyone deserves redemption." She shrugged and lost her smile. "That's why I built this shelter so I could give a helping hand to those who need one." She shot another look at the image. "Even him."

The old voices tried to break through his hold on them, raving at her faithlessness and demanding him to destroy such sacrilege. But Tiffany brushed her hand across the back of his neck before planting herself on the couch in front of the painting. The voices faded with a wailing protest and his breathing evened out until he could focus on Angelina again. Fortunately, she didn't seem to notice his lapse.

"So, as far as this being your room, will it do?" She held out an old skeleton key fitting the ornate deadbolt.

"Yes, ma'am. It's more than generous." He took the key and shoved it into one of his pockets. "Thank you very much." He dropped his pack in the sitting room.

"You're welcome. I have linens you can use for the sheets and bathroom, but it won't be five-star-hotel quality." Angelina smiled as she gestured for him to precede her out to the hall.

"I understand, ma'am. I'm just pleased to find a place with a door and a real roof."

Angelina nodded as Tiffany drifted up beside him. "You must have been traveling a long time, then. Good thing you made it here today. We're expecting a bad storm and it wouldn't do to be caught out in it."

"No, ma'am." Balder and Tiffany followed Angelina

back toward the front of the shelter. The sounds of children and other adults filtered into his awareness, but he didn't see anyone.

Angelina settled herself on her chair behind the desk and narrowed her eyes at him. "I'm thinkin' since you're new to town and it's only Thursday, you should take some time to visit Three Lakes a bit to get to know the place."

He raised his eyebrows. "You don't want me to start now?"

"Maintenance happens any day, but some of the busiest days are weekends, so it's better to explore now before something exciting happens." She winked and he couldn't help but smile.

"When do you expect the storm you mentioned?" He shot a glance at the water pelting the sidewalk outside. "It looks like it's already here."

"This is just the rain, but it's supposed to turn to snow tonight."

Balder shivered. "In May?"

Angelina laughed, a sound resembling cathedral bells. "This is Michigan, honey. Summer doesn't start until after Memorial Day."

:Are you sure you want to stay here?: Tiffany shook her head.

You don't even feel the cold.

:But I remember it well enough.:

"So should I start work tomorrow?" Balder returned his attention to Angelina.

"Yes. I'll show you the ropes in the morning. We'll work out a more permanent schedule as you got along." She tapped the ledger in front of her. "For now, explore the town a bit so you know where the hardware store, the library, and the grocery store are. You also should head out to visit Kate Blackamber today."

"Who is Kate Blackamber?"

"She's...our resident cookie baker and wisewoman."

Angelina paused and looked him over again. "She's a good person to know when a body is searching for healing and redemption. Plus, her cookies are really the local best."

"Yes, ma'am. How do I find her?"

"She lives in a farmhouse with a wrap-around porch up the main road to the northeast. Go back to the Gitchegumee Inn and turn left. Hers is the fifth house up the road on the left." She waved in dismissal. "When you get back, you're welcome to join the other residents for dinner from five-thirty to seven each night." She stuck out her hand again and he took it out of habit. "Good to have you here, Balder. Be welcome."

Gratitude and relief swallowed up his words until Tiffany nudged him by drifting through his right arm, effectively waking him up.

"Uh, yes, thank you. See you this evening, ma'am."

Angelina smiled. "Not if I see you first."

He laughed as he waved and headed back out into the rain.

:You're uncommonly lucky today.: Tiffany's mood had improved as she stared thoughtfully at the shelter. *:You have your dry place to sleep and directions to a wisewoman.:* She returned her gaze to Balder. *:Maybe that's the reason we were supposed to come here. And why there are so many Elder Races in this town.:*

Balder swallowed hard. "I don't know if it's a good idea to see her."

:I don't think you really have a choice, Balder.: Tiffany grew solemn. *:You said you wanted redemption and I have the impression she's the mistress of this town. If you want to stay here, you'll have to interact with her. You're going to have to face this at some point and now is the best time you have.:*

Fear bordering on pain filled his chest and he clenched his fists to fight it as the rain pounded on the sidewalk around him. "I'm scared."

Tiffany paused, surprise widening her eyes. *:You? You're admitting you're scared?:*

He grimaced and nodded, refusing to say the words again.

Her eyes narrowed as if determining whether or not he was playing her. But after spending time in Angelina's presence, he couldn't find the energy to lie and manipulate anymore. *And the fear is real.*

:Good. That's the first step toward being a better person.: She raised her chin thoughtfully. *:I think now is a good time to meet this wisewoman. You said you wanted to find a way to help me. If that's true, this might be the best option we have.:*

He met her gaze and she waited him out, holding his steadily. He didn't want her to be right, but experience taught him he couldn't fight once she'd made up her mind.

"Okay."

He threw his hood over his head and set off back the way they'd come. He passed the Ironwood Café and Gemini's Grocery before they took a left at the Gitchiegumee Inn. Balder's mind churned with unease and guilt, and his usual coping mechanisms of pushing them away no longer worked.

The town seemed to peter out, leaving long stretches of forested road between the few residences with large yards around them. Tiffany seemed to know which house they were looking for because she barely looked left or right as they passed the weather-beaten homes along the road.

I just hope this doesn't get me killed. The last time they'd visited a town with someone Tiffany wanted to meet, he'd been chased off by a furious woman brandishing a frying pan. He eyed the houses they passed. They didn't fill him with much hope.

CHAPTER TWO

"Somebody help me!"

Svanhild Bjørnsdottir pulled her Valkyrie motorcycle over to the side of the wet northern Michigan road and scanned the sopping forest. She'd heard the voice as if it had been inside her head, which didn't make any sense while she wore a helmet. But skid marks showed on the asphalt and left a scar in the dirt beyond it, showing where someone had gone into the ditch.

She hesitated. Her Valkyrie was on its last legs and if she turned it off now, she might not make it to civilization and shelter. But if someone had gotten in trouble, she couldn't leave them in the lurch. She hadn't passed anyone on this road in hours. If there would be a rescue, she'd have to provide it. *Son of a motherless goat.*

She sent a prayer to any deity listening that she could make it to the next town and turned off the bike. She swung her leg over the seat and pulled off her helmet before she followed the skid marks over the edge of the road. They led down into the gully running parallel to the blacktop. Despite the lateness of the year, the rain and wind in northern Michigan remained icy, and anyone exposed to them wouldn't last long.

"Halloooo!"

Svanhild scanned the streambed swollen with the spring rain. Downed trees slick with water lay like giant pick-up sticks across the gully's floor. The skid marks led directly to a mass of torn limbs, eddying water, and chrome. *Chrome?*

She slid down the bank toward the tangled mess and the twisted form of a motorcycle became visible. Somehow it had gotten wedged under an old uprooted stump and the swelling stream rose around it.

"Help! I'm down here."

A black-gloved hand rose out of the water be behind the stump and tree limbs, and Svanhild splashed through the stream toward it. A man in denim and leather with a red bandana tied around his head lay under the bike, half-submerged and slowly sinking.

"By Fenrir's balls, what the hell happened?"

The man scowled. "You're a woman."

"Thanks for the update. I'm also the only one here. Want help or not?" She matched his scowl as she steadied herself in the rising stream. "The water's rising and the current is getting stronger. You're running out of time."

He struggled to work himself free, but the tree and the bike had him pinned. "Fuck. Yeah, yeah, I want help."

"Fine. Tell me what happened while I work on dislodging some of this debris." She grasped some of the accumulated tree limbs and pulled them out of the tangle, throwing into the water to be carried farther downstream.

"Fuckin' deer's what happened." The man groaned as he tried to shove the stump away. "Came outta nowhere. I swerved to miss the damn thing and wheels lost traction. I had to ditch in the gully. I woulda been okay except this fuckin' stump chose that moment to fall on top of me and my bike. I got pinned and with the rain, the stream just kept risin'."

Svanhild nodded and stood back a moment to survey

the situation. The stump lay across the bike with the man under it. The old trunk was a good half meter in diameter and solid wood. She'd be able to move it, but only if she tapped into her Valkyrie essence that she'd long forsaken.

Ja, because Odin banished me from Asgard.

She thrust the thought away and shot a look at the pinned biker. He still scowled, but he appeared more concerned with his current state of submergeance than whatever she chose to do.

"Be ready to drag yourself away from your bike." She strode toward the other side of the stump. "I'm going to shift the stump enough to get you free."

"How the fuck are you gonna do that? And what about my bike?"

Humans—always worried about their toys. She sighed as she made sure her footing was solid before she grasped the downed stump. "Your bike is secondary and we'll deal with it once you're out. Ready to move? On the count of three."

"Hold on...okay. Ready."

Svanhild closed her eyes and ignored the icy water soaking into her jeans. She released some of her Valkyrie essence, just enough to be imbued with the strength of a berserker warrior so she could move the trunk. She'd haul the man out then work on the bike.

"One." She steadied her grip on the stump. "Two."

"You sure you can move this?"

She ignored him. "Three." She yanked and lifted the stump. The waterlogged wood moved sluggishly as if a great hand held it down. But Svanhild increased her effort and a wet, sucking sound tore through the rain-soaked air as the thick trunk moved. If she'd completely taken on her true form, she would've been able to toss the waterlogged tree across the stream, but she was only able to shift it a little to the side, freeing the bike and man.

"Holy shit." The man groaned as she sloshed back to

him, the water already up to her thighs. "How the fuck did you move that?"

"It's not important at the moment. Let's get you out of the stream. Do you think you can walk?" She held out her hand to him, her feet braced. He reached out to clasp her wrist and her world grayed out around the man touching her.

Her Valkyrie senses roared to life, screaming with the wrongness of the being holding her wrist. *Unworthy! Defiler! Forsaken!* Her eyes widened as she met his brown gaze and the edges of her mouth pulled down as she bared her teeth.

His eyes filled with dread and he swallowed hard. "Oh shit."

She yanked him close to her chest until they stood nose to nose, her fury mounting. "You are a butcher."

"Now, now, let's not be too hasty. I haven't done anything—"

"Today. You haven't done anything today." She scowled and thrust him away from her, wishing she had her sword in her hands. "I shouldn't have saved you. I should've let the water take you." She clenched her hands into fists. "What's done is done. You're safe now."

"Yeah, but what about my bike?" He shuffled to the bank and stared at his motorcyle slowly disappearing under the rising stream.

She tightened her fists and wished they could be wrapped around his throat, but she held back the berserker's rage. *Five hundred years!* Odin had exiled her from Asgard to the mortal world because she'd dared to disagree with him. *I was right, dammit.* The warrior she'd been sent to collect during the Ottoman-Hungarian War had been a butcher, a murderer without honor or conscience. Seeing his actions and choices in life laid out before her turned her stomach and she refused to give him a place of honor.

And now I've saved this butcher from death. I am a fool.

With a snarl, she reached down into the water and grabbed the bike's handlebars. She heaved the heavy Harley painted with red and orange flames out of stream and let it drop on the bank closest to the road. She would've flung it to the ground, but she had too much respect for the machine to take her fury out on it. He'd survive. That was more than he deserved.

"Thanks a lot." He sounded sullen.

"Be glad I didn't leave it in the water. You'll survive to walk it to town." She stomped her way up the bank to her bike and hoped she wouldn't have to slog with him.

Come on, søta. You gotta start for me and take me to safety. She didn't trust herself with the dishonorable biker. In all her cursed years of living among the humans, she'd never come across anyone quite as horrific as the man in the gully behind her.

Thank Odin I don't have to take him to Valhalla.

Not that she could. She jammed her helmet on her head and kickstarted the bike. The engine turned over, but didn't catch. *Oh please, søta, start for me.*

The bike chose to grant her wish and she sighed in relief as the engine caught. She didn't gun it, just eased the throtted and let the bike move under her own power. The Valkyrie motorcycle coughed and whined as it puttered along the wet Michigan road, but Svanhild was just glad to be moving at all.

The story of my life.

Ageless and purposeless, she usually drifted wherever—*It's not like I don't have time on my hands*—but this time the need to be somewhere specific had buzzed in the back of her head until she'd pointed her Valkyrie north from Detroit. She hadn't felt the sensation since Odin exiled her from Valhalla.

And I have the misfortune to save the kind of man who

got me exiled. I'm an idiot.

Thank Freyja she'd been alone. No one saw her mistake. She was used to working alone, but she'd always had sisters, the other Shield Maidens, to watch her back. Until the day she defied the All-Father. None of them had backed her up.

Cowards.

Her bike coughed as if in agreement. *Just a little farther. We're almost there.* She prayed to any deity listening to let her get close enough to a town to make walking in the rain not too miserable. The cold seeping into her from her stream-soaked clothes already made her irritable. *Or more irritable. How could I have saved such a dishonorable being?*

A service station appeared out of the woods in a clearing beside the road and she sent a prayer of thanks to her bike and Freyja for giving it the strength to get this far. The pavement had enough of a slope she was able to coast the bike into the parking lot before it gave up the ghost. It sputtered a wheezing cough and a protesting squeak as she gripped the brakes, sliding to a stop under the overhang in front of the service center door.

Thank you, kjære. You can rest now.

Svanhild sighed and rolled the bike onto its kickstand, pausing for a few moments to form a plan of attack. *And to calm down after meeting that...drit.* She closed her eyes and took a few deep breaths to calm the derision and fury at having touched such a being. Especially when the same kind of bastard had caused her exile. But she couldn't take her frustrations out on others.

While places like this didn't faze her, she knew how men of this world looked at women, and most mechanics were male. They saw tits and ass, something to fuck rather than respect, and they often upheld that stereotype. Being a Valkyrie helped, but she always had to endure some testing at first. Fortunately, she knew her skills, she just had to

20

educate the men.

And now I'm calm enough not to kill anyone. I hope.

She swung her leg over the seat and strode for the door of the station, the rain pattering on the roof of the overhang. She left her helmet on as she pulled the door open. Originally she'd seen the head gear as silly and constricting, but she'd found them useful when it came to entering a building among men. They didn't rush to judgment until she took her gear off.

Inside, the building smelled of used oil, rubber, wet cardboard, and metal. The proprietor came in from the service bay, wiping his hands on a dirty rag. He stood a little shorter than her own height, but he had shoulders broad enough to carry her bike across them and hands the size of serving platters from Odin's table.

"Can I help you?"

Moment of truth. She pulled her helmet off her head and tucked it under her arm. His bushy brows rose up to his non-existent hairline and he tipped his head, but his expression remained curious.

"*Ja*, my bike died, and in this weather, babying her isn't going to work. Not sure if it's the fuel pump or carburetor. But she lost power about halfway here to nowhere and I've been coaxing her until I could find a town."

The man nodded slowly. "Yeah, you got lucky, you did. Ain't much up here for at least fifty miles. Good thing you made it to Three Lakes."

"I'm glad I made it anywhere." She shrugged. "I can fix her myself, but I needed parts and money, and I'm short on both." She spread her hands. "So I need your help. Maybe you can direct me to a junkyard and let me use your shop for a bit, and I can get her running again."

He shook his head. "No junkyard close by. But maybe we can work out a trade."

Ah yes, here it comes. Her irritation rose and she

waited for the come-ons. She expected him to lick his lips and fondle himself in hopes of getting some carnal activity.

"What kind of trade?"

"Sounds like you need a job and a bike fix. Why don't you work for me for a short time?"

Svanhild raised her chin and narrowed her eyes. "Work for you how?"

He shrugged. "I have more business in the shop than I can handle at the moment, what with tourist season coming on, and I could use the extra help." He ran his semi-clean hand over his bald head. "You help me work on any of the cars and bikes that come through, and I'll trade you parts and help on fixing your ride. Deal?"

She blinked and her irritation gave way to surprise at his offer. "You're offering me a job?"

"Yes, ma'am. Completely under the table, but still something to get you on your way and helps me get my shit done. Whadya say?"

Svanhild opened her Valkyrie senses and found her prospective employer to be more than a typical mechanic. Swirling earth energy flowed over and around him. He had deaths in his past, but they'd been honorable and in defense of those weaker than him.

Honorable and worthy.

But not human. If she'd remained in the Shield Maidens, she wouldn't have paid attention to his species, but she'd learned to be more aware. *I should've been more on guard along the road.* The being waiting for her response only wore a man's shape. In reality, he was more bear than man.

But still honorable and worthy.

She nodded sharply. "*Ja,* I say that's fair."

"Great." He flashed her a wide smile and held out his hand. "The name's Bart Fisher. Welcome to the Fix-It Cave."

She grasped his forearm above his wrist and stood

silent a moment as shifter energy wafted over and through her. The image of a powerful bear filled the space around him for a few seconds before dissipating as if he'd pulled it back into his core. She grinned. The bear had always been her spirit animal, her guide and totem, to use the vernacular of the First Peoples in this part of the world. And here Ursus stood again, to help and guide her.

"Honored to meet and work with you, Bart Fisher. I'm Svanhild Bjørnsdottir." She inclined her head out of respect. "Thank you for this opportunity. Could you direct me to a place to stay? I haven't actually seen the town yet and I'm not familiar with this part of the state."

Bart tilted his head and narrowed his eyes as if assessing her worth. She held her breath, wondering if she'd have to fight him after all.

"I got this old cabin. It ain't much, just a great room, a bath and a couple of bedrooms, but it's well insulated with a good fireplace, quiet, and halfway between here and town." He shrugged. "It'll need some cleaning and airing out, but if you're interested you could stay there."

She shot a look back out the windows of the garage to the cascading rain and nodded. "That sounds agreeable. How much is rent?"

"If you do all the cleaning and upkeep while you're there, I'll let you have it for two hundred a month."

She had a few dollars stashed in her saddlebags, but not enough to repair her bike or pay for lodging and she preferred to have a job to bring income steadily. Five centuries of survival had taught her to be frugal, especially when someone decided women couldn't earn a living. She nodded again. "I can agree to that. Can we take it out of my first paycheck? I'm short now."

"Yeah, that sound fine. Lemme get the keys to the place and show you where it is."

Svanhild hesitated, not comfortable with leaving her bike, and the bags it carried, anywhere.

"What should I do with my ride? She's not moving until I fix her."

"Bring it into the garage. We'll lock the place when we go into town. No one will bother it." He walked with her to the door. "Just put it in the back near the tool cabinets. We'll move it to a better place when we get back."

She stepped outside under the overhang and took a deep breath. *What in helvete am I doing?* She rarely made plans to stop anywhere, much less work and stay. *It's only temporary.* But her gut told her otherwise. Something was different about this place. She'd roamed all over the globe, in the old world and the new, but nowhere had felt like this small town in northern Michigan.

Stop woolgathering.

She clipped her helmet to the handlebars and kicked the stand just as Bart opened the garage bay doors. She pushed it in past him, the chrome still steaming from their last-ditch ride.

"Whoa, is that a 1997 Honda Valkyrie 1500?" Bart whistled with appreciation as his gaze slid over the black with turquoise pin-stripes scratched and scarred by long use. "She's gorgeous. Did you get her new?"

Svanhild rolled the bike over to the back wall, smiling her affection at her old companion. "Nearly. I bought her when she turned two. She's both powerful and steady, but she's been suffering lately, poor *søta.* I haven't had the time to stop and care for her properly."

She stroked the double leather seats, wiping off the excess water. *I promise to take better care of you now, kjære.*

"We'll get her fixed up right, I promise." Bart seemed to know the direction of her thoughts and Svanhild gave him a grateful smile.

"Thank you." She unzipped one of her carryall panniers and pulled out the last of her cash for groceries and toiletries. "I'm ready to go."

"Good, we'll take my truck." He pulled the bay door closed and headed back to the office. "I need to go to the post office and the grocery store anyway, so I can show you around a bit, Ms…" He trailed off with a frown. "What name can I call you? That last name of yours is pretty impressive."

She laughed. "Call me Svanhild. It's easier."

"Sounds good." He gave her a relieved smile as he gathered up his keys. "You're a Valkyrie, aren't you?"

She lost her smile and swallowed hard. While she didn't actively hide what she was, she didn't go around broadcasting it, either.

"*Ja*. I used to be, but haven't done a Shield Maiden's work in a long time."

Bart nodded as he locked up the shop. "You'll always be a Valkyrie, Svanhild. No one can take it away from you just 'cause you don't do the work anymore. It's who you are, not what you do." He gestured for her to follow him out back. "I have to say it's a real treat to meet you. Never met a real live Valkyrie before."

"Can't say as I've met any bear-shifters either, so I guess that makes us even."

He rumbled a happy sound. "I'm happy to be your first. Just don't let on. Not all the folks in Three Lakes are Elder Races, although we do have more than our fair share."

"Good to know."

Despite the run-down appearance of the shop, a shiny forest green Dodge RAM sat parked under the lowest boughs of a fir tree.

"Nice truck." Svanhild appreciated the sleek lines illustrating power.

"Thanks. It's a good way to move shit and stay dry." Bart grinned as he unlocked the cab and walked around the hood. "Get in. We'll hit the post office and Gemini's General Store before I show you around Three Lakes."

"Fair enough." Svanhild didn't mind the tour. It would give her a sense of how long she'd be staying.

Long enough to fix the bike at least. But it was good to stop. She already liked Bart and the Fix-It Cave, and she was so tired of roaming forever. She'd had wistful spells before where she'd hoped to stay in one place or another, but none of them had held her interest long and she'd move on.

There's something different about this place. Maybe it was the energy, although she hadn't detected anything when she arrived. *Ja, all fucked up from dealing with that drit-face biker.* But the air had a taste she almost recognized, like broiled salmon with rosemary. She mentally shook her head. *Air doesn't taste and I probably won't be staying.* She just hoped the man she'd rescued didn't bring his bike to the Fix-It Cave. She couldn't be around him long and not kill him.

"So what brought up all the way up here to the Warbler Peninsula?" Bart started the conversation as they headed off in the direction she'd been riding.

Svanhild shrugged. "Been traveling around the US for a long time and thought this might be a good way to see the northern parts before I crossed into Canada to explore there."

"There's the driveway to the cabin. I'll take you there on our way back." Bart pointed out a gravel road leading into the trees. "You been ridin' around on that bike the whole time?"

She shook her head. "No, before then I had an old 1969 Dodge Charger."

"Nice. Was it orange like the car from Dukes of Hazzard?"

"No, orange would've been an improvement. This thing was light green, you know the pale color people turn when very sick?" She raised her eyebrows and Bart chuckled. "But it ran for twenty years so I can't argue with that."

A gas station attached to the Gitchegumee Inn came into view just as Bart turned left into town past a sign that read *Welcome to Three Lakes*. The post office stood next to Gemini's General Store so Bart parked between them.

"I'll meet you back here after you do your shopping."

"Thanks, Bart." Svanhild nodded and took measure of the town of Three Lakes. Again, the air smelled good. Hearty, cozy, even joyful. *I've been sniffing too many fuel fumes.* The rain sheeted down and the place resembled pretty much every small North American town she'd visited. But she had the odd sense she'd come home.

She snorted and headed for the grocery store. Home didn't exist, not since her exile. But she couldn't shake the feeling.

The world twisted a moment as she stepped over the threshold, shifting on its axis then settled back into normalcy. Svanhild blinked and scanned the interior of the store. It appeared to be like any other general store with one side being groceries and food, and the other for clothing and hardware items. But the building on the outside couldn't match the inventory.

It's like the tent in Harry Potter.

She grabbed a basket and perused the shelves, listening to the sounds of other shoppers. Most were quiet, but a few chatted with the clerks or a companion. She kept to herself until she'd found what she wanted and took it to the check stand. The cashier positively sparkled, and not euphemistically. Swirls of magic curled off her shoulders and fingers, and Svanhild's Valkyrie powers responded.

"You must be new here. Welcome to Three Lakes." The cashier smiled and her lavender eyes twinkled.

Svanhild inclined her head. "Thank you, I am. This store is…curious."

The woman laughed and the world brightened around her. "Yes, very curious. I'm Gemini." She held out her hand.

"Svanhild Bjørnsdottir."

"Oh, that's a pretty name. Where is it from?" Gemini rang up her purchases as she tilted her head like a curious bird.

"Norway." Svanhild liked Gemini for all that she was a fairy. A big one, too, at about human-sized, but she kept a wary eye on her. Fairies were notorious for being mercurial. Friendly one moment, raging terrors the next.

"Oh, Norway. I think my good friend Kate Blackamber has family up that way. Have you met Kate yet?" Gemini's voice, while still friendly, had a serious edge to it and Svanhild eased back a step.

She shook her head. "I don't believe so."

"Oh, you really should. That'll be sixty-five forty-one." She took Svanhild's money, counting out the change. "She lives up the road a bit and she's a big fan of meeting newcomers to our town."

"What, is she the mayor?" Svanhild snorted as she tucked the change away.

"No." Gemini sobered. "*Morukai*."

Svanhild blinked and swallowed hard. A *Morukai*? She thought they were myths. *Helvete, they're more mythical than Valkyries.* She nodded slowly. "Thanks, I'll be sure to drop in. I'm working with Bart Fisher at the service station down the road."

"Oh, that's wonderful." The sunshine returned to Gemini's voice and Svanhild breathed a sigh of relief.

She could take Gemini in a fight if need be, but she'd rather not. Fairies were unpredictable when riled and their magic could be powerful. Peace seemed the better part of valor.

"Thank you so much for coming in today, Ms. Bjørnsdottir. It was lovely to meet you. Don't be a stranger, now."

Svanhild grabbed her bags, cloth she noted, and

inclined her head again. Stepping out the door had less of an impact than stepping in, but she felt inexplicably better. *So there's a* Morukai *here.* That explained the energy she'd felt in town. Maybe the delicious air she'd inhaled was a byproduct of it. The *Morukai* were a magical, holy race said to speak directly to their Goddess. She'd never met one and relegated them to stories much like the Loch Ness Monster. But she'd heard the Elder Races flocked to them whenever they made a residence.

"Find everything you needed?" Bart's voice recalled her to the present and she jumped.

"Ah, *ja.* Thank you." She gave him a chagrinned smile and nodded. "Hey Bart, you wouldn't happen to know where Kate Blackamber lives, would you?"

His dark brows rose. "Yeah. Why?"

"Gemini told me I should go meet her since I'm new to town."

"Yup, I was thinkin' that myself. Our next stop." He gestured to the truck and they climbed in. "Did she tell you who Kate is?"

Svanhild nodded. "*Ja. Morukai.*"

"Ever met one before?" He put the truck in gear and pulled out into traffic.

"No. Heard of them, but never met one."

"Good. Kate ain't like the others, all stuffy and what have you. Ever asked anyone who's met one how they are?"

"No." Svanhild raised her eyebrows.

"I have, and you'll get all sorts of answers. But Kate's pretty down-to-earth." He snorted. "She should be, she's got Cree ancestry in her. But she used to think she was human so she's not all full of herself."

"How in Fenrir did she ever think that?"

Bart shrugged. "Dunno. It was before my time here, but she knows who she is now and she's damn good at it. She married a werewolf. I wish she'd picked a bear, but

29

nobody's perfect." Bart winked as they turned left at the Gitchegumee Inn.

Svanhild laughed. "Are there a lot of Elder Races here in town?"

"Yeah. Some have been here for generations, but more started showing up after Kate figured herself out." He paused as they waited for someone to turn left into a parking lot. "They ain't the only ones who've shown up, though. You ever heard of the Sword of God?"

She thought back to the biker she'd rescued and nodded. *He definitely could have been Sword of God.* "*Ja.* Fanatical religious group who've made their members brainwashed assassins. They claim to be saving mankind from the darkness of the Elder Races."

"That's the ones. They've been here twice now, once to take out Kate and another time to take out our archivist."

Svanhild raised an eyebrow. "What had the archivist done?"

"Don't know the whole story, but he's a vampire, so I figure that was enough to get him on their Most Wanted list." Bart eased the truck forward. "The thing is, the archivist hooked up with the doc in town, who just happens to be a dragon. Pissed her off somethin' awful and she dealt with the assassin. It didn't go well for him."

Svanhild barked a laugh. "*Ja.* I bet it didn't." She'd met a few dragons on her travels and had made a point not to irritate them. Oh, she could've fought them, but it would've hurt like hell.

She turned her head to look out into the rainy forest. The whole place dripped like the lake had emptied out over the top of them, but she found she liked it. Up ahead, two people walked at the edge of the road heading in the same direction as Bart's truck.

Correction: One person and one ghost.

She idly wondered if the man was aware of the ghost just as he looked up to meet her gaze. *Sweet Freya!* Her

Valkyrie powers kicked in before she could blink and the inner voice of the gods roared through her. *Vengeance! Wicked death of innocents! Unworthy!*

Svanhild grasped the door of the truck to keep from launching herself through it to take out the misguided warrior walking in the rain. The berserker fury rose again and she gritted her teeth. *He's unclean.* She closed her eyes and shook her head. How the hell had she managed to meet so many unworthy butchers in one day? *I'll set you ablaze to cleanse your evil.*

"Hey, Svanhild, you all right?" Bart's voice intruded on her thoughts and she opened her eyes.

They'd parked in front of a pretty two story house with a wrap-around porch and some of the glorious fury faded away. *Yeah, well, if the room starts shaking, blame the gods.* She nodded, but gave herself a few moments to breathe.

"Are you sure? You looked like you were gonna leap out of the truck back there."

He wasn't wrong, but she nodded again and got out, sucking in deep breaths. Despite the rain, the air tasted sweet and comforting rather than dank and wet.

"I'll be okay. Is this the *Morukai*'s house?"

"Yeah. Come on." Bart motioned her to follow him up to the porch and he knocked on the door.

A pretty woman with golden-brown hair and wise hazel eyes pulled it open with a wide smile.

"Hey, Bart. Good to see you. What brings you out this way? Everything good in the Bear community?"

To Svanhild's surprise, Bart blushed. "Yeah, everything's good. Thanks, Kate. But I wanted you to meet Svanhild. She's gonna be workin' with me for a time and I figured I should bring her by."

The hazel gaze met Svanhild's and for the briefest moments, she swore she looked into the eyes of Freyja. Yearning for acceptance and belonging hit her so hard, she gasped. *Here is where I need to be forever more, serving Her.* She dropped to one knee and bowed her head, crossing her hands palms up over her upraised knee.

"My lady, it is an honor. I am here to serve."

Silence greeted her statement for a few moments, but eventually a hand rested on her head and a small sigh echoed over her.

"The honor is mine, Svanhild. Welcome to Three Lakes. We're grateful you're here. Your strengths and abilities are needed."

Svanhild raised her gaze to meet Kate's. One hazel eye winked at her and a grin curled Kate's lips.

"Come on in. Would you like some coffee or tea? It's pretty blustery out there."

The incongruence of the Goddess asking her if she'd like something to drink made Svanhild blink and scramble for an intelligent reaction. Instead, she ended up gaping like a fish on the beach and Bart clapped her on the shoulder to get her back to her senses.

"Uh, *ja*, thanks. Tea, please." She followed the bear shifter into the house and tried not to knock anything over. *I might as well be the bull in the china shop.* She felt too tall in the comfortable space, but Kate only waved her to sit down on the settee.

"I had the feeling someone would be dropping by today, but I had no idea I'd get to meet a Valkyrie." Kate grinned as she brought a teapot full of fragrant tea and a plate of cookies into the sitting room. "My Aunt Sue told me about them, tall, beautiful, fierce women. You definitely fit the mold."

Not hardly. Svanhild barely held back her grimace, but Kate noticed, and would've said something had Bart not said something.

"You know of Valkyries, Kate?" Bart raised his gaze from the cookies on the plate beside the tea. "They're pretty nice bikes, but I'm still a Harley man, myself."

Kate and Svanhild shot looks of surprise at the bear shifter just before he winked. "Gotcha."

"You're so bad, Bart." Kate shook her head and laughed as she sat down beside him. "So, you'll be working with this rascal. How long are you planning to stay?"

Svanhild shrugged one shoulder. "I was just passing through and my bike broke down here. I guess it depends on how long it takes me to fix it." The answer had been accurate when she first arrived. Now it felt off.

Kate nodded. "That makes sense, I guess. Have a place that's home to get back to?"

Not anymore. Svanhild grimaced and shook her head. "Not really. I'm kinda a roamer."

Kate tilted her head. "Huh. I wouldn't have guessed that. You look like someone who knows where she belongs and sticks close to home for the most part." She shrugged. "I've been wrong in the past, though. Remember when I thought I was human, Bart? Surprised the hell outta me when I found out I wasn't."

Svanhild smiled along with the *Morukai* woman, but the assessment shook her to her core. She desperately wanted a place to call home. A place where she was safe, secure, and someone had her back. It had been too long since she'd found one.

"It's a good thing you're here now, though. With all the increased tourist traffic we've had in the last year, Bart's been up to his eyeballs in work." Kate nodded as she poured the tea into three cups. "He can definitely use the help."

Bart grunted as he stuffed a whole cookie into his mouth.

Kate laughed. "Nice, Bart. Bears. Friendly, full of heart and love, and will eat everything in sight in preparation for winter. Even in May."

"Hey, winter lasts a long time up here in Three Lakes, Kate. I'm starving." Bart swallowed and reached for another cookie. "Besides, your cookies are the best. I look forward to them at the shelter bake sale."

"Good to know. I'll be sure to make extra this year." Kate swung her gaze back to Svanhild. "Will you be staying for the festivities?"

"Festivities? I wasn't aware there'd be any." *Helvete, did I forget a holy day?*

"Yes, this coming weekend. I hope you'll stay for them." Kate nodded then grimaced. "Hopefully the weather will cooperate and we'll get sunshine rather than more of this rain." Her gaze swung back to the windows of the front of her house. "Something's coming and it would be better to have clear weather for it." She shook her head. "Wow, listen to me. I sound like some sort of crazy soothsayer. I'm glad you're here, Svanhild. Thanks for bringing her to visit, Bart."

The bear shifter nodded, crumbs sprinkling his beard. "Yeah, well, I needed to stop by anyway. My cousin Theo is having a bit of trouble with some out-of-town folks. I don't suppose you could help him with that?"

"Sure, Bart, I can give you advice, but it would be better if Theo came to talk to me." Kate nodded with a smile.

"Yeah, that's what I told him, but he's old and grumpy, and obstinate as, well, a bear." Bart grimaced and shrugged. "I was hoping to get some advice that might convince him to see you, or at least light a fire under his ass to realize he should."

Kate laughed. "This is Theo we're talking about, right?"

"Yeah." Bart snorted. "But if anyone can help him, it's you, Kate."

"I can give you some privacy if you prefer, Bart." Svanhild stood, needing to get some air and consider the odd feelings of loneliness and the need to serve surging through her.

34

"Thanks, Svanhild. That would be great." He nodded with a rueful smile.

"Not a problem. I'll be outside on the porch." She headed for the door as Bart turned his attention back to Kate.

Svanhild took a deep breath and gathered herself before stepping out the door of Kate's house. She wanted to stay and bask in the *Morukai*'s company. *She's Freyja's emissary.* There was no question of Kate's divinity. It radiated from her and warmed everyone near her. Svanhild's heart thundered with the need to find her place in the *Morukai*'s world. *This is what I've been searching for all these centuries. I could be useful again.*

Joy and contentment flooded through her. She'd been hit with a punch-drunk kiss of connection she hadn't experienced since she'd first become a Valkyrie in the Goddess's service. And she wanted more, more time with Kate Blackamber, serving her specifically. *This is where I'm meant to be.*

The door closed behind her while Bart conferred with Kate—something about his cousin and the local hunters. She took another deep breath and damn near ran over the person who'd just stepped up onto the porch. The creeping hiss of awareness that someone stood too close coupled with the smell of rain-soaked wool brought her up short and she braced for evasive action.

By the time her gaze had sharpened on the man in front of her, he'd shifted to the side and taken a defensive stance, his own expression tight with wariness. Her Valkyrie senses roared to life, gearing up for battle with the black and poisonous taint surrounding him. *Butcher! Unworthy drit-monger!* Her berserker rage rose once more.

Her fists clenched at her side and she missed the feeling of her sword and hatchet. She realized she'd stepped into his space and throttled back the urge to carry the fight to the enemy.

"Excuse me." The words came out more snarl than conversation. But she'd been more or less polite.

He dipped his head in acknowledgement and took another step back. "It's not a problem. I didn't mean to get so close."

His own words were clipped and tense, and his hands clenched on his pant legs as if he needed something to hold on to. She raised her chin and stared him down, asserting her strength and height over such an unclean apparition. *I will destroy you.*

He met her gaze, holding his ground without openly challenging her.

"Why are you here?" The audacity of her question shocked her, but she'd learned to hide her surprise over her own unintentional actions.

His chin jerked as if he wanted to meet her blow for blow, but he inhaled slowly and released his breath with measured effort.

"I'm here for the *Morukai*."

"In what capacity?" Something about the guy suggested his visit might be more ambush than social call. *I won't give you a chance, bastard.*

Again he took a long slow breath. "For...help."

The words were forced, thrust between clenched teeth and riddled with reluctance. He shook as if he held something back. Then his whole body stiffened and his eyes rolled back in his head before he crumpled to the floor of the porch.

CHAPTER THREE

The walk through the rain seemed to go on forever, but Balder kept going. He had no idea how far out Kate's house sat, but he knew Tiffany wouldn't let him give up. Balder had slogged on, filled with a curious hope. *Hope for what? That she won't condemn you on sight?* At one point, a truck had passed and he'd met the gaze of the passenger, a blonde woman with fire in her eyes. He hadn't seen her before, but she stared as if she knew him and he wasn't on her favorites list. He'd shivered at her projected animosity and kept going.

They'd come to a clearing in the trees and found a beautiful two story white house with a wraparound porch and a detached garage behind it. Flowers and shrubs filled a garden-like space in the front yard, and a long driveway stretched from the road to the garage.

:This is Kate's house.: Tiffany gazed at the farm house, a dreamy smile curling her lips.

"How can you tell?" Balder raised his eyebrows.

:Can't you feel it?: She closed her eyes and inhaled as if sniffing something delicious. *:The positive energy is off the charts.:*

He took a deep breath and tried to feel anything

coming from the house, but nothing but dread hit his awareness. Some deep-seated panic built up as he closed in on the property around the house, and he stopped at the edge of the road.

"I don't know if I can do this." Bile rose as the voices of his past screamed in warning. He gritted his teeth and clenched his hands into fists as the rain beat down on his head.

:You have to, Balder.: Tiffany swung back to him, her expression implacable. *:Angelina said you needed to meet her. If you want to stay in this town for any length of time, you have to face the wise woman of Three Lakes.:*

"I don't think I can." He willed his feet to move forward, but they remained stuck to the road.

He expected Tiffany to rail at him, shifting into her gruesome aspect to get him to move, but she shot a look at the house before she nodded slowly.

:You have a choice to make, Balder.: She fixed her pale blue eyes on him. *:I suspect this wise woman is the reason we were drawn here to this town. She may be able to help us both—you with your redemption, me with my state of being. You said that's what you wanted. So you have to choose. Either you stay the way you are or you make real, if frightening, strides toward change. The choice is yours.:*

He swallowed hard as the panic continued to build. "How do you know she won't kill me?"

Tiffany shook her head. *:I don't. But most wise women are healers and spiritual advisors rather than warriors. I suspect she won't resort to violence unless you do something stupid.:*

He wiped the rain out of his eyes and bit his lip to contain the fear. *I can't guarantee I won't do something stupid.* But he nodded and deliberately picked up his feet to stepped onto the wise woman's land.

A ripple of energy flitted across his view as his feet hit

the ground beyond the road and motion caught his eye near the trees boxing in the property. A man dressed in black with the same hard look of his brother assassins watched him approach the house. Balder stopped and focused on him. Why was he here? Had he already come for the wise woman? What had made her a target of the Sword of God?

When the man flitted between the trees to get a clearer view of him and Tiffany, Balder realized the assassin was another ghost. He shot a look at Tiffany, but she apparently couldn't see the other apparition. When he returned his gaze to the ghost, the man in black nodded and Balder had the feeling he'd passed some sort of test.

Thanks be to God. I don't need to placate another ghost.

:Balder, I think this is the home of a Morukai.*:* Tiffany laid a hand on his arm and the voices retreated a little.

"What's a *Morukai*?" He groaned as he swallowed against the rising bile produced by the programming in his head.

:Another Elder Race, but one devoted specifically to be the shamans of the Goddess. I think the Sword of God referred to them as the Antisaints.: She gave him a significant look. *:If this is the house of a* Morukai, *you better be on your best behavior, because I'll kick your ass if you make any stupid moves.:*

"I'd like to see you try." He tried to sound snarky, but he knew she could make him writhe with pain and fear until he lost consciousness. She only snorted and waved toward the house.

Balder approached the porch steps and the voices screamed at the sacrilege of the place. An Antisaint lived here and the urge to destroy it locked his muscles. He groaned and pushed through the rising fear.

:Just a few more steps to the door, Balder. Don't stop now.: Tiffany's words broke through the indoctrination warbling in his head and he made it to the first step. *:That's*

it. Take another step. Don't give up.:

He gritted his teeth and forced himself to move. Each step made the voices in his head scream louder, shrieking and wailing as if they knew their deaths were imminent. *Sweet mercy, let me make it to the door so I can say I've done my duty.*

He reached the doorway and raised his hand to knock just as someone stepped out onto the porch.

The woman must have been over six feet in height and had a glorious mane of golden hair woven into a thick braid. She wore a leather jacket, jeans, and boots up to her knees. She smelled of aromatic cedar smoke and leather, and she had eyes the color of storm-tossed gray skies. *Good God, it's the woman from the truck that passed us.*

She jerked when she realized he stood beside her and he backed up to give her space.

"Excuse me." Her expression said he could go jump in the lake for all she cared, but she strove to be polite.

"It's not a problem. I didn't mean to get so close." Her scent teased him as he dipped his head. The voices in his head raised hell over her proximity, and he grasped his pant legs in an effort to keep from throwing a punch at her. *No, I'm done with violence.*

He had the odd sensation of wanting to get closer, but not for the reason the voices suggested. *She's so beautiful and strong.* Her strength and fierceness were seductive, and he wanted to bow to her even as he stood his ground.

"Why are you here?"

The voices shrilled a warning, urging him to take her on, and he jerked in an effort to resist. They screamed that he'd come to a den of sin and decay, the home of a creature so heinous, even his standing here was a sin.

No, Tiffany and Angelina said this is a wise woman, a healer and a spiritual advisor. They helped people with their problems. They helped everyone. *Including bastards like me, I hope.* He inhaled and exhaled slowly, trying to find his words.

"I'm here for the *Morukai*."

The woman bristled. "In what capacity?"

At that moment, the voices overran his ability to fight and he sank beneath their fervor. But before they dragged him down into the howling abyss, he threw two more words out. Words that held more truth than anything he'd ever said before.

"For…help."

He would've said more, but the screaming of the voices drowned out his resistance to their urges and sucked him down into insensibility before Tiffany could curb them again.

Somebody help me!

When his awareness resurfaced, the voices were gone and blessed silence ensconced him. He lay on a sofa in a parlor, the room sparkling as if pixie dust filled the air. He lay with his head in someone's lap and the warmth of their hands on his cheeks seeped into his skin. Uncertainty rippled through him, but fear remained notably absent.

Taking a chance, he glanced up at the person holding him. A woman smiled at him with hazel eyes full of wisdom, wearing an ornate breastplate decorated with wolves.

"There, now. Feeling better, Balder?" Her voice held the music of the stars, ancient and seasoned, and some of his uncertainty faded.

"Yes, ma'am."

"Good. I see you've made it here to start the final push toward your redemption. Good job. I'm very pleased."

He didn't know why her pleasure should mean anything to him, but it warmed his heart and threatened a blush across his cheeks.

"Where am I?"

"A safe place beyond time and consequence." The woman tipped her head to the side. "I brought you here because you asked for help. Do you know who I am?"

He frowned. "The Holy Mother?"

She laughed and his heart warmed. "I have been called that a time or two, yes. Close enough. But I need you to do something for me."

Wariness filled his gut. "What?"

"I need you to stay here in this town and put down roots. You need to make your family right here."

"I don't have a family."

She nodded. "Not yet, but that will change. Or rather, it can. I'm asking you to devote your considerable willpower to the people here. All people, including the Elder Races. Can you do that for me?"

He clenched his jaw. "Do I have any choice?"

"You can always say no." She tilted her head and shrugged. "But each choice, yay or nay, comes with prices and consequences. And you did ask me for help. This is my help."

He thought about all the choices that had led him to this moment, this place, and wondered if he was doomed to follow the same lonely path forever. His gaze drifted around the room, searching for answers in the comfortable furnishings and homey knickknacks. He almost missed the warrior standing in the corner, watching and waiting.

He immediately recognized the woman who'd been on the porch. She wore her own breastplate, but hers had bears molded into the metal and looked like it had seen some action. Despite her forbidding presence, her brows pulled together in the middle and her jaw clenched as if she feared for someone.

Probably the Goddess holding me. He didn't know why he knew she embodied the divine, but certainty hit his gut along with the comfort she provided.

"And if I say no?"

She shrugged again. "You'll continue on your path as you are now. You'll get help and you'll eventually heal.

But, it will take longer, be harder and lonelier. And there are people who need you." She nodded her head toward the woman warrior in the corner. "The Valkyrie is alone, too."

She's a Valkyrie? He swallowed hard. *Why would a Valkyrie need me?* That didn't make any sense. *Oh wait. Maybe she needs me on my knees, with a sword in my gut.* She didn't look like someone who'd take kindly to his help in any case.

But he wanted things to change. He wanted to be free of the indoctrination that had damned him to this hideous existence, and he wanted to belong again. But most of all he wanted Tiffany to be free of his horrible actions.

"She needs me? To do what?"

The Goddess winked. "I can't let every secret out of the bag. Where's the fun in that?" When he sighed, she rubbed his cheeks with her thumbs. "I will say you're not the only one who needs to find redemption and family. And the town needs you to show them not everyone can be painted with the same brush."

He grimaced. "How can I help her, or anyone, find redemption? I haven't found my own and I'm former Sword of God. I don't think I have anything to teach."

"Oh, Balder, you have so much to teach and to offer, it would take centuries to write it all down." She gave him a compassionate smile. "And I've met the Sword of God before. Most of you aren't bad guys, just terribly misguided."

"Oh no, ma'am, I believe we're very bad guys." The admission sat like poison on his tongue, but he had to own up to his actions. "I've committed so many heinous acts—"

"I know, Balder. But you're facing them and taking responsibility. That's why I'm offering you help. You deserve redemption, too."

"Yes, ma'am. Thank you." He didn't believe her, but it wouldn't be polite to argue. "Will you help Tiffany, ma'am? Will she be okay if I do this?"

The Goddess raised her eyebrows. "You're worried about Tiffany?"

"Yes, ma'am. It's my fault she's stuck like this and I promised I'd help her out. Especially because she's pulled my butt out of the fire more times than I can count. I owe her." He shoved away the memories of how she became a ghost.

She nodded slowly. "I'll keep that in mind. But now it's time for you to make better introductions." She gestured to the warrior with her head. "Time for courage and hope rather than rage and fear. Ready?"

"Ma'am, I don't know—"

But the Goddess didn't give him time to decide before she shoved him out of the comforting sitting room into the light.

****

Svanhild lunged for the haunted man to keep his head from slamming into the wood as he fell. She caught his body and eased it to the boards, just as a ghost materialized beside him, shaking her head in exasperation.

"What's wrong with him?"

The ghostly woman jumped and turned wide eyes on Svanhild. "You can see me?"

"Yes, I can see you. Hear you, too. What's wrong with him? Does he have epilepsy?"

The ghost shook her head. "No, well, not really. Deep programming. He's got this message on replay that demands he kill any Elder Races he finds, and the *Morukai* are at the top of that list." She scowled at his pasty white face. "But every time he makes any strides toward overriding the programming, it overwhelms him and he faints."

Svanhild added her own scowl. "Programming from whom?"

"Sword of God."

She recoiled as if he'd turned to rotting meat and released him. "He's Sword of God?"

The ghost snorted. "Recovering...more or less."

The berserker rage rose again in Svanhild's chest. She resisted the urge to pull out her knife and plunge it into the assassin's back, ending the threat to herself and Kate. But while she fought dirty when in battle, she refused to kill someone who couldn't fight back. She had no doubt she'd be able to overwhelm him either way, but it was cowardly to kill him while insensible.

"Why is he really here at the *Morukai*'s door?" Svanhild rose to her full height, the scowl tightening on her face.

"He's here because we were drawn here and sent by Angelina to visit the 'wise woman'." The ghost's chin rose in challenge. "I didn't know a *Morukai* lived here. It just felt right to come."

"Are you a fool? You could've endangered the *Morukai* with your insistence."

"No, I'm not a fool, Valkyrie. He's no longer an assassin. He's trying to recover."

"How do you know? He could snap at any time." Svanhild crossed her arms over her chest.

"I've haunted him a long time. I know him well enough to say if he's dangerous or not." The ghost met her stare.

"What the hell happened out here?"

Kate's question made both Svanhild and the ghost jump, but Svanhild recovered first.

"He had some sort of fit."

"And you just let him collapse on my porch?" Kate knelt as Svanhild's confidence slipped. "Jeez, did it ever occur to you there might be something really wrong with him?"

"He's a Sword of God assassin, my lady." Svanhild

shrugged.

"That doesn't mean he doesn't need help. Shit-oh-dear, he probably needs more help than the rest of us."

Kate checked the man's pulse and Svanhild wanted to snarl a warning, but she sealed her lips as Kate rose.

"Bart, give me a hand here. We need to move this guy onto the couch."

Bart hesitated, his gaze on the fallen assassin as the corners of his mouth turned downward. "Are ya sure, Kate? He looks like trouble and not worth the effort."

"Oh, for the Goddess's sake." Kate bent down, hooked her hands under the man's armpits, and dragged him through the door. "Sometimes the best solution is counter-intuitive. Bart, get his legs and help me lay him on the couch. Svanhild, put the kettle on to boil. And tell the ghost lady she can come in. I suspect he'll need her, too."

After his initial hesitation, Bart jumped in to assist and Svanhild couldn't lollygag. She waved to the ghost in invitation and headed for the kitchen. The warmth of the living space enveloped her and her concerns melted away. She frowned as she turned the knob under the burner, trying to hold onto the worry she'd felt when she realized who the man was. But the click and whoosh of the gas lulled her rage and fear, and she returned to the living room with calm.

She found Kate seated on the couch with the man's head in her lap and her hands on either side of his face. The *Morukai*'s eyes were closed and she barely breathed. The ghost stood to the side in the shadow cast by the wall while Bart watched with tension wreathing his shoulders. No one said anything and Svanhild stopped, her body naturally relaxing into parade rest as she waited for orders.

The seconds lengthened into minutes and the silence continued. Svanhild's concern built as nothing happened. But more disturbing, her concern lay with the man in Kate's lap rather than for Kate herself.

I've lost my mind. Why would she worry for his welfare? He'd once been the worst the Elder Races would ever face. She scowled. *He doesn't look like much now, but that doesn't mean he deserves my concern.*

But the unease wouldn't leave and the more minutes passed, the greater the concern grew. *Sweet Freyja, please let him be well.* She didn't understand her need to pray or why she should offer it to the assassin, but she couldn't stop herself.

When the panic hit a screaming pitch in her head, she strode to the couch and knelt beside it, laying one hand on the man's arm and the other on his chest. The moment she touched him, he gasped and his eyes opened wide, locking on her face. She met his gaze, as surprised as he, and time stopped.

She fell into the pale blue depths and swore she was looking into a mirror of herself. She recognized the loneliness and desolation. Her heart broke for the desperation and fear she read in his eyes, but she grudgingly admired the determination to keep going in a search for something better. Her heart went out to him despite her mind screaming that he was beyond redemption.

"I'm sorry." His whisper cut her like broken glass shards, sharp and painful.

"No apology necessary. Just don't give up."

Where were these words coming from? She didn't know this man or why he needed encouragement to keep going. *Hellfires, he's Sword of God, for Freyja's sake.* But she wanted to make sure he stayed among the living, and no logic could deter her heart.

"Yes, ma'am. No giving up." He nodded before his gaze rose to Kate's. He froze and swallowed hard.
"Ma'am? I was going to say I don't know if I'm ready, but I'll do my best."

Svanhild frowned while Kate raised her eyebrows.

"That's all anyone can ask for. Why don't you start with your name and we'll get some hot tea into you. It's pretty damp out there today."

He blinked at Kate's words as if they didn't quite make sense. "Balder, ma'am. Balder Templar."

"Very nice to meet you, Balder." Kate helped him sit up and patted his arm. "Who's your quiet friend in the corner?" She nodded to the ghost hovering beside an old Singer sewing table.

"Friend?" He followed her gaze. "Oh, that's Tiffany. She needs your help, ma'am."

"She needs my help? Or you do?"

"We both could use a hand, I think, ma'am."

Balder's gaze returned to Svanhild and she tried to wear her most forbidding mask, but she couldn't quite bring it up. He still blushed and looked away as if she'd made goo-goo eyes at him.

"Hmm, right. Let's start with tea in a to-go cup so I can make sure to get Svanhild and Bart on their way." Kate smiled as she rose.

"A to-go cup, ma'am?" Balder stood as well, much steadier than he'd been on the porch.

"Yep. Tiffany, you can stay here with me and tell me what's going on with you while Balder goes with the others." Kate's voice grew distant.

Or Svanhild's hearing was going because she swore the *Morukai* shaman just said she was supposed to take the former Sword of God assassin with her.

"But I just got here, ma'am." Balder's eyes widened and he shot a look at everyone in the room. "I was told I needed to meet you."

"Yup, that makes sense. And we've met. Good job and welcome." Kate leaned through the doorway of her kitchen with a grin before she disappeared back inside.

Svanhild raised her eyebrows at Bart, who scowled but shrugged, before she made her leaden feet move toward the kitchen.

"I'm sorry, my lady, did you say the Sword of God assassin would be coming with us?"

Kate paused in pouring a big paper to-go cup of tea. "Yes. Well, more specifically you rather than Bart, but Bart's driving, so yeah."

Svanhild gaped at Kate. "Why?"

Kate laughed as she fit the lid to the cup. "Because it's raining out there and he needs a ride back to where he's staying." She handed the cup to Svanhild who took it without thinking. "And he needs your help."

"My help? What for?"

"For adjusting back into a community." Kate lost her smile. "He's been alone for a long time, and wants to belong."

"So have I, my lady." Alone, but not necessarily wanting to belong. Right?

"I know. This will be the perfect opportunity for you both to make a new friend in a town of strangers." Kate gestured for her to go back to the living room. "Think of this like when you marry someone who you've only known for a few hours. People do it in Vegas all the time. It can turn out to be the best relationship ever."

Svanhild gulped. "Marry? As in vows before the Goddess?"

"No vows needed. Just the willingness to help each other." Kate patted her shoulder as they rejoined the others. "Now then, Balder. Svanhild has your tea and will drop you anywhere you need to go."

Balder looked like he'd seen a ghost. Well, another, more surprising ghost, maybe. His gaze switched between Svanhild and Kate, tension holding his shoulders.

"I'm to go with her, ma'am?"

Despite sharing his reservations, Svanhild couldn't help feeling a little hurt at his hesitancy.

"Yes, it's a long, wet walk back to town and she and

Bart are headed that direction." Kate nodded and gestured for him to follow Svanhild and Bart as she pushed them out the door. "Don't worry about Tiffany. I'll make sure she gets back to your place."

"But—"

"You can get better acquainted since you'll both be here awhile. You can trade non-vital statistics like if you drink your whiskey neat, or make your bed every morning, or prefer Coke to Pepsi. That sort of stuff." Kate grinned despite the blank look on Balder's face. "Off you go now. Have fun, you crazy kids." And she shut the door behind them.

CHAPTER FOUR

Balder switched his gaze between the Valkyrie and the big bald man, and wondered if the Goddess was granting him release from his life early. He recognized the man as something more than human, a shifter probably of the bear variety. Neither Elder Race being looked particularly pleased to be saddled with his ass and he had to agree the arrangements weren't what he would've chosen, either.

They might have stood there staring for a lot longer if the bear shifter hadn't grunted, shrugged, and ambled for the large extended-cab truck parked beside the house. The Valkyrie refused to take her gaze off him. She wore threat like perfume and Balder had no doubt she could carry through on it. Where had the concerned woman who'd knelt beside him gone? It didn't matter. She definitely wasn't present now.

"Get in the truck." Her voice could've frozen liquid mercury.

"Yes, ma'am."

Remarkably, the programing voices that usually screamed at him when in the presence of Elder Races remained silent. Or severely muffled. Whichever, he climbed into the backseat of the extended cab and scrounged around among the old rags to find a seatbelt. *Safety first. Yeah, right.* There wasn't likely to be much safety in the presence of the huge man and a Valkyrie.

"Where can we drop you?" Bart started the truck and glanced at Balder in the rearview mirror.

"I work at the Little Hands Shelter."

"Really? What do you do there?"

The tone of his question suggested Bart thought Balder might be frying the residents up and eating them.

"Angelina hired me as a handyman for maintenance in the shelter in exchange for room and board."

Bart grunted. "Yeah, she's always willin' to give folks a second chance."

Thank everything that's holy for that.

"Are you planning to stay long in this town?" Svanhild didn't turn her head to look at Balder, but his gut tightened with all her attention.

He shook his head. "I haven't made plans for a long time, ma'am. I just arrived today and Angelina insisted on us visiting...this house. But it looks like I'll be here for a while at least. How about you? Planning on staying?"

The silence in the truck as Bart drove back to town became glacial. Balder didn't know Svanhild's story but he suspected she had little faith in people, and in Sword of God specifically. *I wish she could have faith in me.* Hell, he wished he could have faith in himself.

But though they left the Goddess' residence, the usual presence of the voices remained absent. Balder's shoulders loosened and his breath evened out. He hadn't been this relaxed in years, and the two people in the front of the truck were liable to kill him just for being there.

"I'm here until my bike is fixed."

Bart shot her a look with raised eyebrows, but said nothing.

Disappointment thumped Balder in the chest, but he ignored it. He owed these folks nothing except for the ride back into town, and Svanhild didn't appear to want any reparation.

"Oh, right. That makes sense." Balder nodded as the truck slid through the rain and turned onto Main Street. "Maybe I'll see you around town then."

What in the name of all that was holy was he saying? See her around town? Valkyries were warriors of legend, and had little interest in men except to take them someplace to die.

She paused, her shoulders taut before she turned her head to look at him, her own eyebrows up. She opened her mouth to say something scathing, if he read her expression right. But all that came out was, "Yeah, maybe."

Surprise filtered through her face and hit him in the chest. *Maybe? There's hope, then.* He almost shook his head in amazement, but curtailed the motion before he did more than move his chin. He was supposed to help her connect to the community, to find family. *How the hell am I going to do that?*

"I think Angelina is going to have a bake sale this coming weekend. The proceeds benefit the shelter." Bart rumbled the statement to the windshield as if answering Balder's internal question.

Balder nodded. He'd seen the flyer on the bulletin board in the lobby of the shelter. "If you have time off from the shop you could come down to help her out." Where the hell were these words coming from? He'd never been particularly chatty or social, but now he couldn't seem to stay quiet.

"I might be able to drop by to set up and take down." Bart nodded as he pulled up in front of the shelter. "You let Angelina know I'm available. Won't be able to stay all day or all weekend, but I can help move stuff around."

"I don't know if I'll have time—"

"Aw, come on, Svanhild, you can't be stayin' home instead of helpin' out the shelter. The whole town pitches in for the kids and the homeless adults." Bart threw the truck in park. "Besides, it's Memorial Day Weekend and it becomes a party in town. You can't miss that."

"Memorial Day? What's that?"

Bart blinked in surprise as Balder gaped. She didn't know about Memorial Day?

"Memorial Day, you know, when we honor those military service members who've made the ultimate sacrifice?"

Svanhild frowned. "You mean honoring dead warriors for their actions in battle?"

"Yeah. I figured you'd know that holiday better than anyone, bein' a Valkyrie and all."

She sat back in her seat and raised her chin. "Why do you say that?"

Bart blinked. "Uh…"

Balder decided it would be a good time to exit stage right. "Thank you for the ride into town. I'll see you later."

He ducked out of the truck into the rain, preferring the sting of icy droplets to the ferocity of Svanhild's outrage. He didn't know why she wouldn't expect the bear shifter to know what she was, but Balder certainly didn't want to be there when she directed that same fury on him.

He strode for the entrance without looking back, but he could feel her eyes on him the whole way. *And I'm supposed to make friends with this woman?* More likely he'd make friends with her sword in his heart. He ducked past the front desk and headed for his room without speaking to anyone. He wanted to be alone to figure out what was happening and why he'd changed from being taciturn to downright gregarious. Plus, it was one of the very few times when Tiffany had something else occupying her. The realization froze him at his door.

I'm really alone.

He blinked as he let himself into his room and closed the door. It had been so long since he'd had time to himself he had absolutely no idea what to do. He let his gaze slide over the furniture and walls until it stopped on the picture of Lucifer. For some reason the image didn't fill him with loathing or fear. Instead, he got the impression the artist had focused on Lucifer's solitude and resigned loneliness. The more Balder contemplated the image the more he swore the dark angel knew he'd be reviled, but took the job anyway.

I'm a lot like that. Except the job he'd taken was redemption, even if everyone in town and the surrounding countryside hated him for it. Three Lakes seemed to be a magical place and he suspected a lot of the residents were much like Bart and Svanhild. Elder Races who knew the Sword of God, and had no compunction about destroying them.

Balder braced himself for the scream of the indoctrination he'd sustained, but though the voices were there, they seemed diminished like a scratchy record playing on an old phonograph in the next room. They remained in the back of his head, allowing him to think around and through them.

I guess the Antisaint—He checked the thought and shook his head for good measure. *The* Morukai *really did help me.* And if he could think around the voices, maybe he could get to know the town a little better. Maybe he wouldn't have to keep moving, searching for peace. *The Goddess did say I needed to put down roots and make a family here.* That seemed like an impossible task.

Everyone deserves a second chance. Angelina's words came back to him as he gazed at the picture of the lonely dark angel. *Maybe she's right, Lucifer.* Maybe they more than their past actions. He hoped so. And he hoped the Valkyrie could see it.

Wait, what?

He thought back to the glorious woman with the fierce beauty and for the first time in years his body reacted. His

cock stiffened against his fly and his balls grew taut.
Arousal and need boiled up and he moaned as he ran a hand
over his tight jeans.

Oh my God, what the hell is wrong with me? The
Sword of God had trained their operatives to use sex as a
tool, but ruthlessly eradicated all arousal from the
responses. He'd learned how to get hard and feel nothing.

But the image of the Valkyrie set his arousal on fire.
Her glorious hair, her magnificent strength, her tall, athletic
body made him yearn for physical connection. He reached
between his legs and opened his fly, whimpering as his
fingers brushed his taut shaft. *Holy hell, I'm hard.*

He retreated to the bedroom and shoved his pants and
boxers off his hips before he lay down on the bed. He
didn't have any lube, but his cock already wept a bead of
pre-cum so he didn't need anything else. He ran his palm
over his cockhead and hissed as the rough calluses scraped
the glans. *Fuck, I'm horny.*

It had been decades since he'd felt such erotic
pleasure, but the vision of the Valkyrie with a smirk on her
lips and her hand around his shaft elevated his arousal. He
could see her smirk turn sultry as she bent down and slid
her mouth over his cockhead.

"Oh, God, yeah. Fuckin' suck me." He'd never used
such vulgarity during sex, but the crass speech sent lust
flashing though him as hot, wet heat encased his shaft.
"Harder, Svanhild."

He couldn't explain why her, of all the women he'd
met over his life, filled him with such aching desire, but no
one else captured his attention like her. He imagined
unravelling her hair from the confining braids and riffling
his fingers through it while she bobbed up and down on his
cock.

Slick, tight, heat warmed his shaft and his balls
tightened up with a warning of his building release. God,
the feeling of her mouth on his cock and her hair in his

hands made him moan with ecstatic abandon. But he wanted to enjoy this, to prolong it, if only to have the vision of pleasuring the Valkyrie stay with him a little longer.

He tried to hold back, tried to picture something else, but his mind's eye saw only Svanhild, her head in lap and her lips around his cock. The friction from her lips and tongue over the edge of his cockhead set up an unstoppable ripple effect. Each hot, wet caress sent pleasure ricocheting through him, building on the previous sensations, and building his arousal higher.

He thought he could fight it, but the moment she used her teeth, he was lost.

"Oh yeah. Fuck yeah, Svanhild. I'm going to come in your hot mouth, *kjære mit.*"

His cum erupted in great gushing spurts over his hand and belly as he groaned his pleasure. He hadn't used his first language in a lifetime, but it felt right as the orgasm flooded his body with ecstasy. He lay on the bed and floated with the after-effects of his release, his mind offering images of Svanhild's satisfied smile.

But I didn't pleasure her.

Oh yes, you did. He could see her lick her lips like the proverbial cat who'd eaten the canary. *And now I have you right where I want you.* She winked and faded from view.

That's exactly where I want to be.

The thought was so alien it jerked him out of his euphoria and back to the reality of cooling cum on his belly. *Bet they never write about that in erotic stories.* Probably not, but reality rarely followed a storyline anyway.

Balder rolled to his feet and headed for the bathroom to clean up, glad Tiffany had been otherwise occupied. Jerking off had never felt that good before, but doing it in front of Tiffany would've made it damn near impossible.

He tried to remember if he'd masturbated with her around before as he stripped and turned on the shower. He couldn't recall a time he'd relieved the pressure in his balls with Tiffany there. The water heated quickly and he stepped beneath the spray, allowing it to rinse the cum off his body. God, he'd never been so turned on in all his life.

But why would I get hot for a Valkyrie?

He wanted to think about it more, but he didn't want to set off his programming. Tiffany wasn't around to calm him down and he could hurt someone inadvertently. He finished showering quickly and dried himself with the towels provided by the shelter. He didn't want to dress in his dirty clothes, but he didn't have much choice. He glanced at his pack and grimaced. The clothes and gear would need to be unpacked and aired out. He hoped the shelter would have laundry machines so he could wash his limited wardrobe. *Maybe when I get paid I can buy some new socks and underwear.* He shook his head. *I'm really splurging there.*

He unloaded the pack and draped the wet things on various pieces of furniture to dry. He even brought out his sleeping bag and hung it on the bathroom door, and unrolled the tent he'd slept in the last three nights. The musty wet scent of damp cloth hit his nose and he grimaced. *Tiffany's gonna hate this.* Her nose, even as a ghost, was far superior to his.

When he was satisfied with the state of his gear, he threw his coat back on his shoulders and grabbed his new key. Nodding to the picture of the lonely dark angel, he let himself back out into the hallway and headed for the street. First stop? The library to learn about the town since he had no money to buy new underthings. He waved at Angelina as he passed through the lobby and she nodded, giving him courage to face the other residents of Three Lakes.

The rain had let up, though the clouds weren't letting go of their grip on the sky. Balder hunched his shoulders and headed away from the lake he could see in the distance. Despite the cold and wet, the air still smelled good and he let it fill his lungs with sweetness. For the moment, life was edging toward good. He had a place to stay and work, Tiffany had the *Morukai*'s attention, and the voices in his head remained quiescent for the moment.

And I came.

To the vision of the Valkyrie. *I'm totally insane.* He couldn't argue with that.

Gusts of wind periodically blasted his back with rain, but Balder enjoyed the walk down Main Street. The shelter sat across from a building housing a steampunk art gallery, a clock and watch repair shop, and the Ironwood Café. On his side, he passed a plumber, an electronics store, and Sweet Summer Blooms flower shop. The doors of the florist stood open despite the rain and the fragrance of various flowers wafted onto the street.

He passed a park and crossed the driveway to a pharmacy. The Three Lakes Medical Clinic stood across the street with the Three Lakes Post Office and the Sheriff's Department. Balder scrupulously avoided the police. They either treated him like a homeless beggar or a threat to security. He didn't want to give the sheriff any reason to be interested in him. *Especially in this town.*

Gemini's General Store sat beside the Sheriff's Department and the library across from that on his side. He liked the welcoming feel of the steps and entrance, and despite its size, the inside of the library felt open and modern. A young woman behind the front desk smiled at him and some of his tension fled. A studious silence welcomed him as he scanned the interior for a card catalog or computer terminal.

He found an empty computer and typed in his search parameters. Some of the books he wanted were in the Archives section of the library, but there were a few in the general stacks under local history. He wrote down the call numbers on a scrap of paper provided and headed for the book shelves.

He passed a room filled with little plastic chairs and low polka dot tables where several children sat listening to an older man who read a story about a donkey named Sylvester and a magic stone. A few of the children looked up, but one boy about five or six years old stared at him with narrowed eyes as if trying to place him.

The voices in his head stirred with warning. *Not human, must be destroyed.* Balder swallowed hard and gritted his teeth, but tried to smile as he headed for the adult books. The boy didn't smile back and Balder could feel his gaze on him long after he stepped out of sight.

Deep breaths, focus on the books.

The stacks provided silent protection as he gathered the titles he sought and his shoulders slowly relaxed. *I'm safe and relaxed and alone.* He ignored the spike of sadness at the last thought and retreated to a reading nook overlooking a garden. Flowers and leafy shrubs took advantage of at the rain. The vista soothed him and he settled into a chair, opened one of the books and started reading.

Balder had read only a few pages when the young boy who'd noticed his entrance appeared at the end of the stacks with the distinguished man who'd been reading aloud.

"That's him, Papa. I smelled him when he came in."

Cold unease zipped down Balder's back at the look of fury settling across the man's face as his eyes flashed red for just a moment. *Saints preserve us, that's a vampire.* The man stalked toward Balder, keeping himself between him and the boy as he advanced, and the voices shrieked another warning. He tightened his hands on the book and prayed for calm.

"What are you doing here?" The question came out in a furious whisper and menace wafted off the distinguished vampire.

Balder breathed deeply a few times before he was calm

enough to respond. Though not without sarcasm.

"Uh, reading?" He held up the book as he raised his eyebrows.

"Have you come to finish what your erstwhile compatriot started?" Fury laced each word and the man's hands tightened into fists. "It won't work. We stopped him and we'll stop you."

Balder set the book down and focused all his attention on the man. The voices of his programming squealed in the back of his head about the evil vampires and their blood-sucking ways, but he studiously ignored them. This man had age and experience, and no matter how good Balder had been as a Blade in the Sword of God, he suspected this man was better. *And neither Tiffany nor Kate are here to calm my ass down.* He desperately needed something to look at to ground him in safety, but he didn't want to look away from the furious vampire.

He settled for focusing on the edge of the book. He studied the binding and the black letters on the page without losing sight of the man in front of him. He beat the voices back behind his thoughts, but some of his own ire rose to the fore. He didn't like being accused of anything, particularly when he'd been minding his own business.

"And who exactly do you think I am, sir?" Balder added the honorific to blunt some of his own hostility. *I didn't do anything. Yet.*

The vampire shot a look around to be sure no one overheard him. "Sword of God."

Hell and damnation. The anger ramped and his shoulders tightened again, but the fury settled on himself. He didn't want to fight any of the Elder Races, but he couldn't change his past. *I'm trying to get better, dammit.* He didn't believe the *Morukai* woman would take kindly to violence in her town, but he also wouldn't be driven off for doing nothing but existing. *Even if that's what I used to do to the Elder Races.* Chagrin ate at him, but he tried to keep it out of his expression.

Balder nodded. "I used to be. I left them and am recovering from such indoctrination."

"Recovering?" Incredulity flared in the man's expression and voice. "There's no such thing with the Sword of God. Why are you really here?"

Balder shrugged, trying to push away his anger. "I was called here. To the *Morukai*."

The vampire reared back as if he'd been slapped. "You stay away from her."

"Too late. I visited her this morning." He shouldn't bait the old blood-sucker, but he couldn't stop himself as his anger surged. Anger from the accusation of past actions.

The vampire hissed and Balder's blood ran cold. "If you've harmed her, there will be no sanctuary for you in this life or the next."

Balder clenched his teeth and rose to his feet, nose to nose with the man. "I've harmed no one in this town." Not strictly true while Tiffany's ghost remained with him, but it felt good to say. "I told you I was called to visit the *Morukai*. I'm no longer part of the group that you named and she has given her blessing for me to stay here. If you have a problem with that, take it up with her."

"I don't have a problem with that, I have a problem with you." The words would've sounded simply belligerent if the vampire's eyes hadn't glowed red at the same time.

"Oh, dear. Is everything okay here, gentlemen?"

Balder kept his gaze locked on his adversary as the vampire turned his head to scrutinize the woman who'd spoken.

"Yes, yes, Angelina. Nothing to worry about." His voice belied the words.

"Nothing to worry about?" Angelina snorted. "You looked like you were ready to do bodily harm, Drake."

"Just finding out what this man is doing here." Drake's gaze returned to Balder's. "Letting him know violence and harm to anyone in this community won't be tolerated."

Balder raised his chin, but said nothing. *Follow your own edict, buddy.*

"Uh-huh. Well, when you're done having an anatomy-measuring contest, I hope you can get along with Balder as he's my new maintenance man at the shelter."

Drake shot her a look of incredulity. "You can't be serious, Angelina."

"Perfectly serious. He came here looking to start over and I'm giving him his second chance." She tilted her head with a half-smile. "Some folks come looking for redemption. You know what I mean?"

The vampire gave a sharp nod and stepped back out of Balder's space. "Yes, I know. But saying it and living it are two different things." Drake glared at Balder. "Make sure it's the latter rather than the former."

Drake grasped the young boy's hand and dragged him away, leaving whispers and raised eyebrows in his wake. Balder let out the breath he hadn't known he'd been holding and flexed his shoulders to loosen them.

"Thank you, Angelina. He's intense."

She nodded and ushered him toward the front of the library. "He has reason to be. He's met Sword of God before and it didn't go well. If he could, he'd run you out of town."

Balder shook his head. "He's gotta kill me first."

Angelina rolled her eyes. "He might just do that. Are you going to check out that book?"

Balder looked down at the book in his hands. He hadn't realized he still had it. The others remained in the nook where he'd been reading.

He shrugged. "I don't have a library card yet."

"Let me check it out for you until you get one." She grasped the book and took it to the computer kiosk. "Just give Drake some time. Oh, and his lady, too. She's a doctor at the clinic, and she's not very understanding, either."

Balder sighed. "How many people in this town are…" He shot a look to those still in the library. "Not strictly human?"

"Why? Are you planning to take a run at them?" She waited for the computer to produce the checkout receipt her expression serious.

"No. I just need to know how many people might take a run at me."

She laughed, but there was little humor in it. "About thirty-five percent of the residents here are other than human, but most of them blend in pretty well unless you're looking for them." She handed him the book. "The majority of them know what the Sword of God is because they've come here twice. Once to kill Kate Blackamber and once to kill Drake whom you just met."

Guilt slapped him on the back of the head and some of his earlier anger faded. "I'm sorry. It wasn't me. I've been out of the game for several years now. And I'm trying to make up for my own mistakes, Angelina. I can't take blame for the whole group."

"I know, Balder. But to everyone else here, you are the embodiment of those people, and once bitten, twice shy." She gave him a rueful grimace.

"Why did you give me a chance, then? For all you knew, I could still be in that group, planning violence." That's exactly what the Sword of God did. They "protected" the human race by all means necessary and available, including extermination.

Angelina stepped out the door into the rain and waved to a woman herding the children into a fifteen passenger van. The kids chattered and laughed as they climbed into the vehicle. Balder had never experienced happy children, especially at an orphanage or shelter. But these children acted as if they were on a school outing and life was good.

"You're right, Balder. I took a chance on you. But I meant what I said to the archivist. Those striving for redemption should be given the opportunity to achieve it." She headed for the van. "I'll let you in on another secret. I'm not 'strictly human' either." She winked. "Can I give you a ride back to the shelter with us?"

He stood in the rain on the sidewalk for a few moments, taking in her words as she climbed into the front passenger seat. *She's not strictly human.* In what way? Did it really matter? She'd been nothing but kind to him and she'd known him all of five hours. The voices ranted in the back of his head about sin and vile monsters, trying to secure most of his attention, but he shoved them aside.

"Yes, thank you." He scrambled to find a seat with the kids in the back of the van.

The children eyed him curiously, but no one said anything.

"Alrighty. Let's get a move on. We'll be just in time for lunch." Angelina closed the doors and off they went.

It didn't take long to reach the shelter in the van, but the cacophony of the kids all talking at once made Balder grateful for the shortness of the trip. He was the first one out the door to help the little ones down and Angelina winked at him when he gave a sigh of relief. He had no idea how she managed to survive such sound.

At least it kept his mind off the churning anger left over from the encounter with the vampire.

After the kids had been herded inside, Angelina accepted the keys from a tall woman with a thick afro of black, curly hair. "Thanks, Shania."

The woman nodded and barked a couple of orders to the little hooligans about taking off their shoes and coats.

Angelina grinned. "Shania's our resident cat-herder, bus driver, and pediatric nurse. Thank goodness for her, otherwise I'd lose my mind." She shrugged and handed him the keys. "But since you're here, how about you take the van in for service at the Fix-It Cave out on Route 2?"

"You trust me with the van?" Surprise and gratification

swirled in his chest.

"Yeah." She gave him a half-smile. "I figure you can handle something easy like this. Besides, Bart can give you a ride home after you drop it off. I won't need it for a couple of days, but don't tell him that or I won't get it back for a week."

"I think I've met Bart. Big guy with a bald head and beard?"

"Yep, that's him. Where did you meet him?"

"He was at Kate's house with a Valkyrie when I arrived."

"A Valkyrie? Here in Three Lakes?" For some reason Angelina frowned and shot a look toward the back of the shelter's garage. "She must be new."

"I guess. I met them both at Kate's house." *And Kate told me to watch out for Svanhild.*

"She was with Bart?"

"Yes."

"Does she ride a motorcycle?" The question came out breathy as if Angelina was nervous.

"I don't know. Why?" Balder frowned. "Is everything okay?"

"Oh, yes, it's fine." She gave him a bright, patently fake smile and shrugged. "So the way to get to the Fix-It Cave is you take a left onto Main and take a right at the T. The Fix-It Cave will be on your right as you head southwest. Bart's a good guy and if the Valkyrie is with him, it means she's okay, too. He's a little rough around the edges, but honest as they come. Take your book with you. He's thorough, which means it could be awhile."

"Yes, ma'am." He wanted to ask more about her unease, but the moment passed and he didn't feel it was his place.

"Good. I'll probably see you this evening for dinner. Just let Bart know you need a ride if he doesn't finish it tonight." She waved as she headed inside.

"Yes, ma'am."

Balder took the keys to the front of the van and climbed in the driver's seat. It had been a long time since he'd driven any vehicles, but the gear shift came out of the steering column and most of the gauges looked about the same as he remembered. He turned the key and shifted the van into reverse to back out into the street. Maneuvering a large vehicle took some careful focus, but eventually he waited at the stop sign to head out of town.

He wondered if the Valkyrie would be at the Fix-It Cave. If so, he might be dead sooner than he expected.

CHAPTER FIVE

"Are you out of your ever-loving mind?"

"What's the big deal, Svanhild?" Bart blinked at her as he dropped her off at her cabin.

"Why would you expose what I am to that former Sword of God assassin?"

Bart snorted as he put the truck into park and leveled her with a dry stare. "He was at Kate's house and she let him inside. I'm pretty sure he knew we weren't human. Hell, he's traveling with a ghost. And he knew what Kate was. She probably told him what you are."

"*Ja*, but you didn't have to confirm it." Anger and unease swirled through her gut in equal measure. She didn't like Balder knowing what she was. *Because he's former Sword of God.* It certainly wasn't because she worried it would scare him off. *Don't be foolish.*

Bart shrugged. "He might be former Sword of God, but he didn't look like he was in any condition to fight. Hell, he collapsed on the front porch, for the Goddess' sake."

"I know, I caught him."

Bart sighed. "Look, my point is, I don't think he's a concern. He was there to see Kate and get help."

"A lot of help she was. She hustled his ass out the door

ten minutes after he got there."

"Maybe it wasn't her help he needed, yeah?" Bart shot her a meaningful look. "All I know is I got a feeling about this guy. I don't trust him—"

"*Ja,* that makes two of us." Svanhild grimaced.

"But I trust Kate, and I trust her to know what's best for all of us, including a former Sword of God assassin." Bart patted the console between them. "Give him a chance to be a real person instead of his past."

"But that's how they hurt people. They get the Elder Races to trust them, then they massacre them." Svanhild shook her head. "How can you be so relaxed about this?"

"Because I trust Kate. She's dealt with these people before and has a pretty good idea of what to look for. Plus, Angelina hired him. She's got a nose for people and she wouldn't have let him work for her if he was still Sword of God." He shook his head. "No use borrowing trouble. All of us will be keeping an eye on him, but I think he's legit."

Svanhild shook her head. "It seems like a good way to welcome the wolf in sheep's clothing."

"Just think about it. I'm gonna head back to the garage. I'll see you there once you get settled in."

"*Ja,* I'll be there in an hour or so." She nodded and slid out of the truck, pulling her purchases with her.

Bart waved and backed up so he could turn around retreat down the road. She didn't watch him go, choosing to get started on her home. *What's done is done. Can't change it, will just have to deal with it.* And if the former Sword of God assassin showed his true colors, she'd unpack her sword *Forsvarer* and show him what an enraged Valkyrie looked like.

Svanhild unloaded her groceries into the cupboards of her new-to-her cabin before grabbing the broom from the closet to viciously attack the overgrown dust bunnies inhabiting the floor. She still seethed at Bart's choice to reveal what she was to Balder, but tried to let it go. *No point crying over spilt milk.*

She worked on her new home with the same attention and effort as she would clean her weapons. They probably needed a good cleaning and honing, but given her current state of mind, she left them alone. Instead, her home became so spotless she wouldn't have a problem eating off the floors. *I never had to clean when I was an honored Shield Maiden.* She shoved the sorrow and loneliness away.

Svanhild worked the edge off her anger until the cabin stood clean and smelled good. She cracked one of the windows to allow for circulation of fresh air. It was frigid, but it helped cool the rest of her ire. She shot a look at the clock and figured she'd been in her home long enough. She donned her jacket and locked the place behind her before heading out toward the Fix-It Cave. The rain continued to soak everything and she considered getting herself a woolen toque. At least her ears would be warm.

When she arrived at the garage, a large van sat in the open bay and voices carried from the front office. She recognized Bart's gravelly growl, but the other was male and sounded familiar. She put up her jacket on a peg to drip dry and sauntered to the office.

"Angelina needs it back by the end of today, right?" Bart typed something on the greasy keyboard cover as he peered at a small flat screen.

"She didn't say tonight, but she did mention she needed it tomorrow or the next day." Balder's clear tenor wrapped around her ears and an odd sensation tightened her gut.

Is this fear? Fury? Unease? None of those words seemed accurate. *This can't be excitement.* There was no way she was pleased to see him.

She stopped in the doorway of the office and scanned Balder's body. He didn't seem to be carrying any weapons, but she wouldn't put it past him to have at least a knife somewhere. He matched her in height, but he had an athletic build, strong and gracile. Red hair shaved along the sides of his head but long on top, draped over his left eye in a shaggy, satin mop. A roughly trimmed beard covered his lower face and jaw with auburn scruff, and she had the audacious urge to test its softness.

Handsome.

The word was as foreign as the urge, and she made an abortive movement that attracted his attention.

Eyes as blue as the summer fjords met her gaze and she damn near swooned. *What is this foolishness?* She raised her chin in challenge, but to him or her own odd reactions, she didn't know. Instead of challenging her, Balder dipped his head without lowering his gaze, and she found the graceful retreat arousing. *What is wrong with me?*

"Hey Svanhild. I was just tellin' Balder here we'll get on Angelina's van ASAP." Bart nodded his bald head. "You think you can do the simple tune-up while I finish up on Mr. Tisdale's car?"

"Of course." Anything to get away from Balder and the unsettling feelings he engendered.

"Great. Here are the keys. Bay two."

She snatched them and bolted out of the office as if dodging an arrow. *Just fix the van and he'll be gone back to where he came from.* The thought spurred an odd combination of relief and sorrow, and she shoved them both aside as she opened the van's door. She released the hood latch and returned to the front to check on the engine.

Unlike the emotions swirling through her at the moment, the engine's lines, while dirty from use, seem clear and simple. She understood where the oil went and how it coursed through the engine, making the pieces move smoothly during operation. She followed the lines, testing their fit and continuity. Everything seemed in working order, but she'd have to run diagnostics to be sure.

"Everything look all right?"

Balder's question came from her shoulder and she jerked upward, slamming her head against the little hood.

"*Helvete!*" The oath came out as pain sparked through her head from the impact.

"Are you all right, Svanhild?" Concern filled his voice as he took a step closer.

"Yes, fine. Isn't there something you need to be doing rather than hovering over me?"

Her words came out harsher than she intended, but she stuffed her chagrin under her anger. Why was he hanging around, anyway?

He blinked at her, tipping his head as if listening to a voice only he could hear.

"Actually, no. This is the task I'd been given and so here I am." He shrugged, concern still in his eyes. "Are you sure you're okay? You hit your head hard." His lips shifted into a sardonic smile that transformed his face from merely average to gloriously handsome. "I know Valkyries are hard-headed, but there's no need to prove it to me."

She wanted to be angry, to tell him off, but the smirk burrowed under her armor and she laughed as she rubbed her head. She gave him a rueful snort.

"I wasn't trying to prove anything, but I definitely proved I'd misjudged the distance to the hood." She grimaced. "If you really have nothing to do, perhaps you could help me by moving this lamp where I need it when I ask."

What in Freyja's name was she saying? She'd never needed help holding anything when she worked on a vehicle. But Balder nodded with that sexy smirk of his and the world seemed a little brighter.

That's because of the lamp, you fool.

"How long have you been working on engines?"

Svanhild shrugged. "Years now. Ever since I came...here." She didn't want to talk about her banishment. "There wasn't much use for women in the military when I arrived. Apparently my gender made me soft and weak to the powers-that-be." She snorted. "So I learned something I was interested in."

"You didn't encounter derision for that?" Balder raised an eyebrow.

"Oh, I did, but they couldn't argue with my skills." She shot him a grin. "Besides, I was a strong and as big as some of those 'men'"—she used air quotes—"who suggested I was too weak. I swear egos bruise far more easily than bodies."

It had taken more than words to convince the men she was capable, especially when they took one look at her breasts and lost all coherence. But they tried to force her to leave twice before the boss decided to fire her. Unfortunately for him, her skills were such that she took his business with her when she left.

Balder nodded. "Men are stupid."

"What?" She almost bumped her head on the hood again.

He chuckled. "Men in general are stupid when it comes to women. They either can't think beyond the anatomy hanging between their legs or they believe in some outmoded idea that women are damsels."

"Anatomy. You mean their cocks?"

He blinked at her choice of words, pink tingeing his ruddy cheeks. "Yes, ma'am, their cocks."

Svanhild laughed as she went back to the engine. "I worked with mechanics, remember? Rough language never bothered me. Most of the time my thoughts are far more crude than my speech."

He didn't say anything to that so she focused on tuning up the van. She checked oil levels, antifreeze, and power steering levels. She rotated the tires and checked the brakes. Balder followed her around, helping either with the light or handing her a tool or two. He seemed fascinated with her ability to fix anything mechanical, but not derisive.

"Can you hand me that wing nut please?"

"Hey, I resemble that comment." He smirked as he gave her the nut.

It took her a moment to realize he'd made fun of himself. She barked a laugh of surprised amusement and his smirk widened into a grin. *I shouldn't be charmed by him.* But she was. He easily fell into conversation and had enough intelligence to make thoughtful and insightful remarks.

And Goddess forbid, she actually liked him.

At one point while she turned the engine over to check the gauges, he noted the crank for the window on the passenger side rattled. He grabbed a screwdriver and tinkered with the handle until it rotated smoothly to move the window.

"Where did you learn that, Balder?"

He replaced the plastic cover on the crank and shrugged. "I've always been good with fixing things. In the orphanage where I grew up, stuff was always breaking and there wasn't a regular maintenance man to repair it. So I would tinker with things until they worked better."

"You learned this all on your own?" She checked the air in the driver's side front tire.

"Yeah." He nodded as he closed the passenger door and came around to the driver's side. "To start. When I got older, in between training...I would...read...books on..."

Balder shook like having an epileptic fit and his eyes rolled up in his head as his body sagged.

"Balder!"

Svanhild dropped the air hose and caught him before his head slammed into the concrete floor. *What in helvete is wrong with him?* This was the second time she'd seen him collapse and it frightened her more than a full company of Berserkers. She hated the Sword of God and Freyja knew the assassins were the worst. For hours she'd been thinking of this man as yet another fanatic, but she'd learned different while he'd waited in the garage for the van.

She'd definitely grown to like him.

"Balder? Can you hear me?" She held him tight as his body shook and his eyes fluttered. "I have you, warrior. You're safe. Come back to me."

Seconds passed as he trembled in her arms and her gut clenched tight with unfamiliar concern. *Please, Freyja, protect this warrior from harm, keep him strong and true, give him the courage to continue.*

Only hours ago she never would have prayed for the man in her arms, but seeing him helpless filled her with sorrow. As much as she hated the cult he'd be a part of, she preferred to beat them into submission rather than have them fall at her feet.

Fall at my feet in supplication is a completely different matter.

The thought was so absurd she laughed aloud, and Balder settled into boneless silence. His breathing evened out and his shoulders relaxed in her grip. At first she feared he'd given up the ghost, but he remained breathing and his hands flexed as if searching for purchase. She grasped one of them to give him an anchor.

"I'm here, *kjære*. I've got your back. Breathe easy." The endearment slipped out and her cheeks heated with her chagrin, but Balder didn't seem to notice.

"Holy shit, what happened?" Bart lumbered to a halt as he came around the front of the van.

"He had another fainting episode, but I caught him before he hit the floor."

Balder opened his eyes and stared up at her with an intensity she'd only seen on the faces of warriors going into battle.

"Don't let me go." His whisper resembled the rumble of avalanches coming off the glaciers of Asgard, but urgency underlay his words. "Please don't let me go."

"I won't." She squeezed his hand with emphasis.

"You better take him somewhere to lay down to recover." Bart tipped his head and frowned. "I'll call Angelina and tell her she'll get her van tomorrow. Her maintenance guy, too."

"Where exactly do you suggest I take him?" Svanhild raised her eyebrows.

"You're almost done with the van, right?"

"Yeah. I was just filling the tires when he fell." She waved at the discarded air hose.

"Put him in the passenger seat and take him to the cabin. He'll be able to drive the van back tomorrow after he's rested."

"Take him to...where?" Svanhild couldn't help but gape. She was supposed to take him home with her?

"To the cabin where you're staying so you can keep an eye on him in case he needs anything." Bart nodded slowly. "You'll be doing us both a favor. Angelina will get her man and van back, and I'll have less to work on."

"But, I thought you needed help with this." How could Bart suggest she take an ex-Sword of God assassin to her sanctuary, however temporary it was?

"He needs your help more than I do."

"Don't let me go, Svanhild. Please." Balder gripped her hand tighter and begged her with his blue gaze.

"There, y'see? Go on and take him to the cabin. I'll let Angelina know what happened and tell her not to worry." Bart gave a decisive nod and ambled back toward the office.

"Wait. Bart...no, I can't..."

"Please, Svanhild."

She met Balder's gaze and some part of her melted. In her home, no one ever turned down a plea for help. The weather and the country was too severe to leave anyone out in the cold. And Balder had charmed her despite her better judgment. Besides, he begged her. She'd be heartless to turn him away.

I used to be so much better at that...

"All right, fine. Can you get up and get into the passenger seat of the van on your own or do you need help?"

"I can make it." Balder levered himself up, paused to take a breath, and scrambled to his feet.

He swayed a moment and she feared he'd topple to the floor again, but he managed to brace himself on the van. Using the vehicle as a support, he worked his way around to the other side and pulled open the passenger door.

"Here are the keys. Make sure you both eat something hardy. A rainstorm's due in tonight and it's gonna be a rough one." Bart handed them to her and gave her a significant look. "And that's only if the Ice Demons don't get involved. Stay warm and dry."

She raised an eyebrow, but he ambled away and opened the bay doors.

Guess I'm going home...with a man. The thought made her laugh out loud as she climbed into the driver's seat. She turned over the engine and backed the van out into the rain. The drops came down so hard it sounded as if a child poured gravel on the roof. Balder didn't move from his slouch in the passenger seat and she wondered if he'd fallen asleep. *How can he sleep through this racket?* She turned onto the main road and headed for her cabin.

The drive took less than five minutes. When they reached her home, she threw the van into park and turned it off before sitting a moment. Was she certifiably crazy to let this man into her sanctuary? *I don't think that's even the question.*

"Right, let's do this." Shaking her head, she left the vehicle and hurried to her front door. Bart had built a small vestibule to keep the rain and snow off, but it wasn't large enough to shelter two adults her size. She threw open the door then went back to help Balder out. He remained where he was, but he watched her come and was ready for her to pull the passenger door open.

"Balder? Can you walk on your own?"

"Yes, ma'am, I think so."

He slid his feet out of the van and sort of fell onto them from the seat. She hovered in case he needed her help to stay upright, but he managed to make the safety of her front step on his own. She hurried to lock the van before racing back to the house, her hair plastered to her head from the downpour. *At least it's dry inside.*

Balder found the couch and settled into it as she closed the door behind her.

"Let me turn on some lights and start a fire in the hearth. Are you hungry?"

"A little. Can I help with anything?" He struggled to rise and she had to help him up.

Svanhild hesitated. She knew how frustrating life became when she couldn't do simple things, but she didn't want him to end up falling on his face into the flames.

"Do you think you can start a fire without killing yourself?" A reasonable request.

Despite his unsteadiness, he laughed. "Yeah. I think I'm capable enough to do that."

"Okay then." She helped him over to the hearth. "The tinder and kindling are there, and the matches are here." She reached up on the mantle and handed them to him. "I'm going to start some tea and make some sandwiches."

"Sounds good."

He bent to set the fire and she waited a few moments, afraid he'd topple over. But he kept himself upright and she had no excuse to stay around. But the curve of his back filling out his coat and the breadth of his shoulders enticed her in spite of herself. *Don't be a ninny. Go make tea and food.* She finally retreated to the kitchen to do something useful. She filled her kettle and set out two mugs with teabags. She preferred loose leaf, but hadn't picked any up at the grocery store.

She pulled the bread out of the bag and grimaced. *I'll make bread the next time I have a few free moments.* She prepped the sandwiches as best as she could as the kettle heated up, but kept an eye on Balder. The last thing she needed as him to fall over. *And I'm not enjoying his broad shoulders at all.*

She rolled her eyes at her wanton side and told herself to focus on the food. But she kept stealing glances toward the hearth. She shouldn't want him, but he'd piqued her interest when he joked with her in the garage.

But he's an assassin from the Sword of God. Except he seemed to be trying to change. And she admitted, she rather liked the man he was becoming. *If it isn't all an act.* She bit her lip and shot another look out at her living room. Could he be that good an actor to hide his true intent? She frowned as the kettle whistled and she pulled it off to fill the mugs. She hoped Bart was right about the *Morukai*'s assessment of Balder. *I want him...to be okay.*

The thought sounded as hollow as an old log. Svanhild rubbed her hands over her face and shoved her confusing thoughts aside. She'd never been one to fawn over a man, but then few saw her until the end anyway. She sighed and shook her head. Maybe she should just use him for sex and get her fix. No connection, just a simple release. But the idea didn't sit well with her and she shoved it aside. No point borrowing trouble.

She carried the plates into the main room from the kitchen just as Balder sat back on his heels, watching the new flames lick up through the wood in the fireplace. A sigh of satisfaction tripped across her lips about the same time as his own sigh, and they shared a grin.

"Is the fire strong enough to go on its own for a bit?" She set the plates on the table and added some paper towels for napkins.

"Yes, I think so." Balder used the fireplace to lever

himself up.

"Good. Come sit down to eat. The tea's ready."

Damn, their conversation could be considered domestic, like an old married couple. Pretty soon he'd be calling her *kjære* and she'd be responding with *kjekken*, and they'd be worried about having enough wood chopped or something. Pleasure and comfort unfurled in her chest.

She barked another astounded laugh. *What's wrong with me?*

"Everything okay, Svanhild?" Balder settled himself in one of the wooden chairs.

"Yeah. I'm just bringing the tea." She took a deep breath and tried to get her head back in the game. Whichever game they were playing.

Why is he here again?

She brought the tea to the table and set a mug down in front of him. Unfortunately, it hit the edge of the plate and wobbled. They both gasped at the same time and he reached out to stabilize it before it tipped over.

When his hand touched hers they both froze and her gaze locked on his. Desperate need to connect and touch swamped her and she gritted her teeth.

I want him.

Valkyries weren't forbidden from sex. It was understood they were a lusty lot, full of passion and vigor, but romance never entered the equation. Svanhild had slaked her sexual thirst many times in her long life, but she'd never wanted more beyond a one night stand. She'd scratched an itch and they both moved on.

But Balder held her attention far more intently than any man she'd met before, and all he'd done was touch her hand. *And laugh with me and is currently sharing a meal.*

"Svanhild?" He never looked away, his gaze boring into hers.

"Yes?" She swallowed hard. Did he want her as much as she wanted him?

"You can let go now."

She blinked and dropped her gaze to their joined hands. "Oh, yes. Sorry. The tea's all yours."

She jerked her hand free and sat down, trying to ignore the flood of embarrassment suffusing her cheeks. Anger followed swiftly behind. *Why am I embarrassed? I've done nothing wrong.*

Somehow she had to make it through the night and get him back to his place. One night. They'd share food, a little bit of fire, and wait out the rainstorm. She'd watch over him, make sure he was all right, and send him home on the morrow. That shouldn't be too hard, right?

CHAPTER SIX

Balder blinked as Svanhild sat down and fixed her gaze on her sandwich. Her expression had been an odd mixture of intensity and yearning, something he'd never expected to see on her face. *Maybe I imagined it.* But her current studied avoidance suggested otherwise. What would she yearn for? He didn't believe she might be interested in him sexually. God knew he wasn't the most handsome or even in great shape after his breakdown. Did Valkyries even have sexual interests?

He tried to remember what he knew about Valkyries, other than the drivel the Sword of God had taught. They were definitely lusty in battle, and warriors hoped one day to have one bring them to Valhalla. But he had no idea what they were like in life. Hell, he didn't even know what ordinary folks experienced in life.

His cock filled out the space in his jeans and he shifted his legs to relieve the pressure. He definitely wanted her in a non-platonic way. He stole a quick glanced at her and wished he hadn't as his shaft swelled more. He wanted to see if her hair felt as heavy as it looked and if she blushed the lovely shade of rose everywhere, not just on her cheeks.

He frowned down at his sandwich, trying to get his

wayward body under control. *I took care of this in the shelter*. Surely he'd assuaged his urges enough to make it until the next day. But he wanted Svanhild in all her ferocity. *Fuck, I just want have her ride me into oblivion.* If she killed him after, he'd die a happy man. His mind painted delicious images of her face flushed with pleasure of his making and he almost moaned.

I want her.

Now there was an impossible desire. He rarely regretted his past more than when he interacted with Tiffany, but he hated it now. Svanhild didn't trust him, rightly so, and she'd kill him if he acted out of turn. But his heart and his arousal urged him to make the first move.

Start with the tea.

"The tea's tasty. Which kind is it?" It was an inane question, but he needed something to break the ice.

She blinked. "Uh, I don't…it's just something I picked up at Gemini's store. Sweet and something."

"It's good." He nodded, hoping his next words wouldn't set her off. "Thank you for letting me stay. I'm sure you think of me as pond scum."

She tilted her head. "I've met pond scum, just today, actually. You aren't quite that bad. So you have that going for you."

He blinked, staring, and her lips curled into smirk. "Just today? And it wasn't me? I'll have to work harder."

She lost her smile. "Don't work harder. I'm starting to like the person you are."

He raised his eyebrows, trying to ignore the happy skip to his heart. "You are?"

"*Ja.* You're growing on me."

He laughed. "As long as I'm not a fungus, that might be an okay thing." He took another bite of his sandwich and wondered why she didn't seem worried about him. "I know they've had trouble with Sword of God in this town before, so I'm not surprised they aren't thrilled to meet me. But you don't seem to have the same problems. Why is that?"

She shrugged. "I've heard about the group and seen some of the aftermath, but never actually met one of the assassins." She frowned as she eyed him. "Were you really one of the elite warriors?"

And here's where I lose all her regard. His gut sank, but he shoved his unease away.

"Yes, ma'am."

She nodded, betraying nothing in her body language or her expression. He sipped this tea, knowing what was likely to come next. He had so much blood on his hands she'd probably cleave him in two with a sword or axe.

After a few moments she grunted. "Did you believe everything they say about the Elder Races? That killing them is necessary for safety of the human race?"

An old dread soured his stomach despite the sweet tea. "It wasn't belief so much as indoctrination. The assassins are programmed, brainwashed and gaslighted, into being effective killers of anything 'different'. The target of the Sword of God is anything sentient and not human."

"Humans aren't particularly virtuous or better than the Elder Races. I've met several who weren't worthy of honor."

"No, I know. Sometimes they're worse." He nodded, gripping his tea like a lifeline. "I was worse. I killed so many in the name of the Sword of God, it now sickens me." He shook his head. "I couldn't do it anymore, and Tiffany made sure of it."

"Tiffany's your ghost, right?"

"Yes." Balder rubbed the back of his neck, grateful for the reprieve from Tiffany's company. "She was the last werewolf I killed. In fact, I killed her whole family. It wasn't until after their deaths I realized they were innocents. But Tiffany made sure I remembered. She's haunted me ever since."

Svanhild sat back, her eyes hard. "You killed her and

her family?"

"I did." He didn't bother to look up. He knew what would be written on her face and he couldn't bear to see it. "When I realized what I'd done to innocents, I left the Brotherhood and tried to lose myself in drugs and alcohol."

She snorted. "Did it help?"

"No, they only made Tiffany louder and clearer." He grunted. "Great way to cure alcoholism."

Svanhild chuckled. "I can see that. Did Tiffany drag you up here to this little town, then?"

"Not just here. We've been moving constantly across the country for years. Something drives her and we move on to the next place."

"Will you be moving on from here, too?" For some reason, her voice sounded tense.

He sat back a moment and rubbed his chin. "I don't think so. Something feels different about this place, like we're meant to stay for a while." He shrugged. "I can only guess it's because of the *Morukai*. Perhaps that's who Tiffany has been looking for. Who *we've* been looking for." He grimaced as he met Svanhild's gaze. "This is the first place I've been in a long time where I don't want to leave. But that's why I'm still here."

"Do you think it's the *Morukai* that makes you want to stay?" She sipped her tea, her expression more thoughtful than anything.

Balder rubbed his chin. "I don't know. I've never met a *Morukai* before, though they are on the most wanted list of the Sword of God. There's definitely something about this town." He tilted his head and took a gamble. "Of course, I've never met a Valkyrie before, either."

She chuckled again. "That's because you're not dead."

"Not yet." He grinned as she took a bite of her sandwich. "So why are you here? If men don't see Valkyries until they die, why am I so lucky to have your company?"

She shot him a half smile before she sipped more tea and swallowed. "Many years ago I was sent to collect someone I found unworthy of Valhalla, but Odin didn't agree. Our differing…perspectives resulted in my being banished to the human realm."

The flatness of her voice suggested she felt stronger than the words she used, but she tucked into her sandwich as if she hadn't eaten in months.

A Shield Maiden defying Odin? He'd never heard such a thing, but Svanhild didn't strike him as someone who doubted herself or refused to speak up when something was wrong. If she found someone unworthy of Valhalla, he suspected there was a damn good reason. *I'd never qualify for the sacred halls of warriors.*

He shoved the morbid thoughts away and sat up straight. "I'm sorry. That's a hard place to be, separated from your confederates." He knew the feeling well, yet didn't regret the change. "Would it be untoward of me to say I'm rather glad Odin sent you here to this world?"

Her brows lowered. "Why?"

"So I had the chance to meet and share this meal with you."

She blinked slowly. "Balder, are you flirting with me?"

He swallowed hard and nodded his head. "I think I am."

"Why?"

"Uh…" He'd never expected that question. "Because you're beautiful and I like your company." He added a half smile. "Besides, I already swooned twice with you. Surely that means we're meant to be like in some old romantic tale, right?"

She stared for a few more moments as if she didn't quite understand his words. Eventually, she shook her head and snorted.

"You did swoon, but I'm not convinced it was my beauty that made you do it."

"Oh come on. Chalk it up to being so breathtaking as to make all the men fall at your feet." He'd never flirted for himself before, but he enjoyed the hell out of bantering with Svanhild.

"This is the most surreal moment of my life. And I'm a Valkyrie."

"What's surreal? Me flirting with you?"

She nodded as she finished her sandwich and brushed the crumbs off her hands.

"Hasn't anyone ever flirted with you before?" Balder gaped at her.

She shook her head and gestured to his mug. "Do you want some more tea?"

"Yes, thank you." He handed her the mug, but didn't try to touch her. *More than likely she'd lop off my hand.* "Come on, seriously? No one, ever?"

"No, not ever, Balder." She threw the comment over her shoulder as she took their mugs to the kitchen.

Not ever? What the hell was wrong with those men? *More than likely she lopped off more than their hands.*

He levered himself up and shuffled over to the fireplace. The heat increased as he closed in on the hearth and he sighed with pleasure. He'd always enjoyed a real fire in a hearth. He settled himself near the grate and shook his head, both at his temerity to flirt with Svanhild and at her lack of experience in it. Perhaps she'd been too intimidating, but he found her intelligence and sharp wit intoxicating. He didn't expect her to respond favorably to a former assassin offering her something as tender as flirtation, but he couldn't seem to stop. *I don't want to stop.*

Emotions are dangerous, a weakness easily exploited to cripple and distract.

The voice blared out its warning in the back of his head and he gritted his teeth against its ferocity. He closed his eyes and tightened his hands into fists, holding back the howling fury and insanity. *Shut the fuck up. I'm done listening to you.*

Emotions weren't dangerous or crippling. Instead, they gave people drive. He'd seen the ferocity of people fighting to save or protect their loved ones, and the love made them stronger, more determined. He wanted someone to fight for him, someone he could defend and protect. He'd once been able to feel something other than anger and righteousness, but the negative emotions had taken all his energy and focus for decades.

I'm so tired. Tired didn't begin to cover his exhaustion. Anger took so much energy, he wanted to curl up in a ball and sleep. The voices increased in volume and drowned out all the lovely emotions, making him swallow against losing his meal.

"Balder, are you all right?"

He opened his eyes and stared at the most beautiful woman he'd ever seen, her expression creased with concern. *I need her.*

"Help me please…"

The voices shrieked, demanding he fight and kill the warrior woman who crouched beside him. She set the mugs aside and grabbed one of his hands, drawing him into her embrace. His back hit her chest and fire seared through their clothes, burning through his chest. *Oh sweet mercy, what's happening to me?*

He might have whimpered as Svanhild's arms tightened and the fire between them flared higher. He couldn't move, yet he wanted to writhe against the intense pain in his core.

Begone! A new voice thundered the order and a vision of a warrior woman with wild hair and leather armor filled his mind's eye. *You have no place here and no one will mourn your passing. Leave this man in peace or face me. He is under my protection.* She slammed her sword against her round wooden shield and raised her chin.

The voices retreated, taking the fiery pain with them

and Balder came back to himself, panting and sweating in Svanhild's embrace. She was singing a tune he almost remembered. Something soft and comforting, yet with a Viking edge to the words. Norwegian sounds flowed over him and he sank into the familiar syllables.

Balder tilted his head back and looked up at her. Winter-gray eyes met his, but instead of cold, he found the heat of hearth fires and the comfort of thick woolen blankets. He wanted more. He freed one of his arms and reached for her face, brushing his fingertips over her cheek.

"You're beautiful."

She snorted softly, but there was no heat behind it. "Flatterer."

"No, not flattery, truth." He swallowed and took a deep breath. "Thank you for your help."

She shrugged. "It was nothing."

"No, not nothing. Not to me. No one's ever defended me before." He looked down at her arms around his waist. "I'm not…" He stopped and shook his head. "Just thank you."

Svanhild squeezed him gently. "You're welcome."

He loved being in her arms, her breasts pressed against his back. The heat from her body and the curves made his cock stand up and take notice. *What is up with you?* He'd never experienced the rush of arousal so quickly before and wondered if regular men had such raging lust. *Maybe it's just me because of Svanhild.*

Balder rolled his head back and took another gamble. "May I kiss you?"

"Kiss—?"

He slid his hand behind her head and tugged her face down to his. Her breath smelled like the tea and their meal, but the brush of her lips against his sent his heart into overdrive. *Oh, God, I want this.*

At first, she did nothing as if testing the sensations of the kiss. But after a few seconds, she moaned and pressed her lips harder on his.

Balder sighed, relief tumbling through him. She hadn't rejected his offer and he refused to lose her favor. But he couldn't resist trailing his tongue over the seam of her lips. Svanhild stiffened a moment and her arms tightened around him, but not in a comforting way. He didn't press his luck, but nibbled at her lips, tickling them with his tongue.

When at last she opened her mouth, he slid his tongue between her lips and caressed hers. She jerked in surprise, but didn't pull away, and he kept tasting her. Eventually, her own tongue made forays into his mouth and he swore his cock would burst through the fly of his pants.

He moaned and tried to deepen the kiss, but she pulled back and met his gaze. They both panted as if they'd engaged in a much more strenuous activity than mere kisses.

Mere kisses? Nothing 'mere' about it.

"What are you doing, Balder?"

****

Emotions crashed inside Svanhild. Arousal, need, desire, yearning, all in equal force and all at once. She wanted more. More kissing, more touching, more connection. And that scared the hell out of her.

"What are you doing, Balder?" She sounded breathless. *Because I am.*

"Flirting?" He gave her a cheesy grin.

She raised her eyebrows. "That seems more active than flirting." *And I want more. What's wrong with me?*

Balder sat up and turned his body to face her, his expression becoming cautious. He scanned her body and licked his lips as if he wanted far more than only kisses.

Or maybe I want far more than kisses.

"We could call it high-impact flirting." He waggled his eyebrows.

She chuckled at his feigned innocence. But he sobered and cleared his throat. "I like you, Svanhild, and I'm enjoying this time with you. I'd like to pleasure you in any way I can, but only if you want it."

She tilted her head even has her heart thundered with illicit hope. "Why?"

He blinked. "Why, what? Why do I like you, or why do I want to pleasure you?"

She nodded. "Either. Or both."

He opened his mouth to say something funny and flippant, but stopped himself when he met her gaze.

"I don't know if there's a way to explain why I like you. Maybe the best explanation is you gave me a chance and a place to stay tonight. And you caught me when I fell." He rolled his eyes and shook his head with a grimace. "Three times now. Maybe it's good old fashioned hero-worship."

She snorted and some of her humor returned. "Are you always this collapsible? I need to know if you require crutches or a walker."

He laughed and she grinned. "I might. But in the meantime, we could diffuse the situation by moving this to the couch or bed."

Overwhelming desire surged through her, but she shoved it back behind her eyes. She bit her bottom lip. "You're really suggesting intimacy between us? Why?"

"Because you are beautiful and sexy, and I want to worship your glorious body."

Every word he uttered warmed her more and more, and her pussy tightened with arousal. She wanted connection. She wanted to believe he wanted her for her, but the warning wouldn't be silenced. *It could all be an act.* The Sword of God were master manipulators and she didn't want to open herself to ridicule. *I will not be made foolish.*

She raised her chin and narrowed her eyes. "I don't think that's a good idea." She pulled away from him and searched for something to distract him. "Here, your tea is getting cold."

She handed him the mug of steaming, fragrant liquid, but her hands trembled. *Hold it together, woman.* Balder took the tea and sipped, his expression thoughtful. Her good sense warred with her need to touch and find solace in physical connection. *I refuse to be another one of his marks.*

"Are you well, Svanhild?" He kept his hands to himself, watching her carefully.

"I'm fine." A blatant lie, but the best answer she could come up with. She wanted him, but not if she'd be sleeping with someone who didn't care. *No pleasure is worth indifference.* Not this time.

Balder was different. Something about him made her yearn for more. But his past made any connection difficult, especially with someone like her. She had mastered the skills of fighting and strategy, but her heart remained her most guarded treasure, especially after Odin cut her to the quick all those centuries earlier. She wouldn't be tricked into sleeping with the enemy.

The wind howled and rattled the windows, giving a welcome distraction. She shot a look outside. Snow blew in horizontal lines past the glass. She was glad they'd made it to her home before it shifted to snow. This kind of weather was perfect for snuggling with a lover. *The sad fact is I have a man who wants to and I'm too afraid to make the move.* Cowardice never sat well with her.

"I'm sorry I pushed too hard. Thank you again for giving me a place to stay for the night. It sounds like the storm is picking up." Balder drank some tea and she heard the resignation in his voice.

"It's not that. It's..." She sighed and set her mug down to rub her face. "You're welcome. It's not a good night to be outside."

"No. These are the kinds of days it's best to be inside

with friends and lovers. I'm fortunate to be able to share it with you."

She gaped at him. Had he read her mind? She shook her head and regrouped, trying to discern what he really felt. "I don't understand you, Balder. Is this a male thing? You must have carnal relations with anything female?"

He blinked. "Is that what you think men are like?"

She snorted. "I've lived in this world a long time. Human men put a lot of stock into their cocks and getting pleasure. Isn't that what you're attempting right now?"

Balder nodded slowly. "I haven't spent a lot of time around typical human men, to be honest, so I don't know how they are. My own cock and I aren't that close." He winked and she laughed. "I know my past associations make my current actions suspect. But I don't want to have sex with you as an objective or to solely scratch a sexual itch. I want to share pleasure and intimacy with you because I like you."

"We don't know each other very well and we've only just met." She tried a different tack as her resistence to him started to crack. "And there are our pasts to consider."

"You being a Valkyrie and me a recovering assassin with PTSD-like symptoms."

"Exactly." Svanhild laughed again. "How do you know about PTSD?"

He shrugged. "I might be a wandering vagabond, but I read newspapers and listen to the radio. The information is out there even if I'm not always plugged into it. From what I understand, some of the flashbacks and dazes I've experienced are similar to what soldiers feel."

She nodded, her heart going out to him. "I've seen some of them react like you, although you tend to collapse."

He snorted ruefully. "Hey, I have to be original somehow."

She barked another laugh and some of her unease

retreated. "You're definitely that."

"From what I understand, connection to the familiar helps with those who suffer from PTSD." He sat back with his tea in front of him. "Unfortunately, I don't have anything familiar in my life except a ghost. Not much connection to the physical world."

She raised her eyebrows. "No past lovers or friends?"

"No, none. The last person I had intimacy with was Tiffany, and there was no sex involved."

"No sex? Seriously?" Svanhild gaped. That didn't make any sense, not with the Sword of God's reputation. She rubbed her thumbs over the mug as she considered his words.

"Honest. Our relationship was a courtship...for the worst reasons." He waved that story away. "But you're the first woman I've been attracted to in years."

"I'm not an ordinary woman, Balder. I'm a Valkyrie." She dropped her chin and eyed him from under her brows. "I don't need flattery like a typical woman."

"And I don't only think with my dick like a typical man."

Sweet Freyja, I want that to be true. Would it be so bad if she took a chance on him? *I'm so lonely.* She hadn't realized it was true until he'd kissed her. She'd had sex plenty of times, and even enjoyed most of her encounters. But she'd never risked her heart. Each sexual partner had been a one-night-stand and easily abandoned. But something in her gut said she wouldn't be able to simply walk away from Balder if she let him in.

She wanted him, more than she'd ever wanted another man. And from the looks of his jeans, he wanted her, too.

"You don't?" She gestured at his crotch. "That says otherwise."

"Not usually, but my body definitely reacts around you." He sighed and smiled. "I'm attracted to you, Svanhild, but it's not just your body that interests me. I like talking to you."

She sighed. "There isn't much talking during sex."

"There is if you do it right." He smirked.

"Oh?" She raised her eyebrows. "How would you know?"

He blinked. "Are you suggesting I'm not skilled at sex?"

She shrugged, lifting her chin in challenge. "How much skill can you have gotten in a cult of assassins?"

He chuckled. "More than you'd expect. We were taught all sorts of things to accomplish our missions."

"You were taught the art of sex?" Her eyes widened and she licked her lips. *Goddess of all, he might be the best lover I've ever had.* And she wanted him, but she tightened her hands around her mug to keep from grabbing him. *He's former Sword of God.*

"I was, but that's not where I learned all my skills. I have had some practice since the initial training." He set his mug aside and shrugged. "I've learned a few things about giving pleasure, and about pleasing my partner. But I've never had a partner I wanted please until you. Hell, this is the first time my dick has shown any interest in a woman since I was a teenager."

"Oh, come on. I'm not buying that, Balder."

"I've gotten hard, but you're the first woman to engage my mind as well as be physically attractive." He took a deep breath and leaned forward, his blue gaze serious. "I want to please you, Svanhild. For our mutual satisfaction. Let me show you the joys and comforts of snow-days."

"You really want to give me pleasure? Seriously?" She shot him a dry look, her last defense against the temptation of him. "Sounds like a good line."

"It would be a good line with anyone but you." He nodded. "But it's the truth. I don't know if there's any way to prove it to you beyond showing you." He reached for her hand and held it against his chest so she could feel his heartbeat. "But nothing would give me more pleasure than to ensure yours."

Balder met her gaze and held it along with her hand. Sweet glory, she wanted him and wanted the connection he promised with every beat of his heart under her palm. Could she take the chance? And if he turned out to be fooling her, could she walk away?

Svanhild studied him for several moments before she fisted her hand in his shirt and hauled him close to her face until their breath mingled. *I'm lost for sure.*

"All right, fine. Pleasure me, Balder." And she sealed her lips to his.

CHAPTER SEVEN

Excitement and jubilation weren't emotions Balder commonly experienced, but they flashed through him like a starburst as Svanhild kissed him. He fell into it with abandon. He allowed her to take the lead, but he guided her tongue, sliding his over hers. She tilted her head and whimpered, but tugged him closer to her body.

When they both came up for air, he pulled back and took one of her hands.

"We need a bedroom now."

"We do?" She stared at him with glazed eyes as she licked her lips again.

"Aw mercy, yeah, we do." If she licked her lips again, he'd come in his pants.

His cock would've pointed the way if his clothes hadn't covered him. As it was, he still tented his pants as he dragged her down the hallway to the single bedroom in the back. The room held a simple double bed with several quilts draping its surface and a six-drawer bureau and matching bedside tables. The bed appeared clean, but unused and he wondered how long Svanhild had been in Three Lakes.

Balder shoved the thoughts aside as he drew her to the

bed and turned her until she stood with her back to the quilts.

"Do you trust me, Svanhild?"

She shook her head with a smirk. "Not remotely."

He laughed at her blunt response. "I mean do you trust me not to hurt you physically?"

She eyed him for a few moments before she nodded. "Yes, in that I trust you."

It's a start.

"Then let's see if we can make that grow." He ran his hands over her shoulders and brushed as kiss across her cheek. "Let me help you undress."

She raised an eyebrow along with her chin. "You want to help me undress?"

"Yes. Would you let me? I want to discover your body as it becomes visible." He met her gaze, waiting to see what she'd do.

His heart thundered in his chest and he forced his hands to stay at his sides. He needed her to know he would wait her out. *Sweet God in heaven, that's the truth.* He'd made the decision to reach out to her. Now the ball was in her court and he'd wait for her forever. He wanted to share something real with Svanhild, something not tainted by hatred or religion. He wanted to simply be a man loving a woman.

The seconds ticked by as he waited. Did she want the same? It was hard to imagine a Valkyrie agreeing to such tender interactions. They were known as fierce warriors, strong and powerful. But he'd never heard how they were as lovers.

Hell, if she kills me with pleasure, I'll die a happy man.

"All right." She nodded and allowed him to pull her shirt over her head.

Balder almost forgot to breathe.

She's not wearing a bra.

Her breasts were full and round with pale pink nipples, and Balder's mouth watered. *Holy God, thank you for this gift.*

His cock, already happy with the direction of his thoughts, flexed and stiffened even more. He tossed her shirt aside and ran his fingertips over her shoulders. Her skin was soft and supple, and she moaned with the light touches he offered. He trailed his fingers down her back to her hips and skimmed her waistband, stopping at the button.

"How 'bout remove these jeans?"

He set to work on her pants and he held out hope that she'd gone commando as well. If so, he might come in his shorts. He slid her jeans down off her thighs, enjoying the toned muscles. A few scars marred the pristine skin and his cock flexed. She'd seen battle and it was so sexy. He raised his gaze and caught sight of black cotton bikini-style underwear. It hugged her sleek curves and he knelt at her feet to pull the pants off her legs.

"You're glorious, *kjære mit.*" He urged her to sit on the bed as he lifted each leg to tug off her socks and pants.

"Your words are sweet, Balder, but I'm skeptical of them."

He paused and met her gaze. "Why?"

"You said your masters taught you well and you learned how to seduce and cajole. But the flattery isn't needed. I know my own worth."

He stood and set her clothing aside, considering her words. "I'm glad you know your own worth, but I wasn't handing you empty compliments. I truly think you're glorious." He skimmed his hands up the outsides of her thighs. "I haven't had much opportunity to give compliments to a sexual partner." He dropped his gaze to her legs. "To be honest, I've never wanted to."

Svanhild reached out and tipped his head up until he met her gaze. "Never?"

He shook his head, falling into her storm-gray eyes. "Not until you."

A smile curved her lips and more blood shot to his cock, straining against his clothes. *Sweet mercy, I'm crazy for this woman.* The sensations coursing through him were new, unusual, and strong. He'd seen women without clothing, their breasts and hips and butts in lovely curves, but none had ever captured his attention as much as Svanhild.

And she's a Valkyrie. An old memory, one from before the Sword of God, filled his mind with words from another woman. His mother, perhaps? *Freyja's warriors are passion incarnate. May a Valkyrie bestow her blessings on you, and you shall have all the luck in the world.* He could only hope this was such a time.

"Then it pleases me to be the first." She crawled onto the bed and settled with her back to the rustic headboard, her glorious breasts pointing at him in generous swells.

Sweet mercy.

She had small areolas around large nipples and he wanted to suckle them to see how high they'd point. They were the color of a spring sunrise over the mountain peaks, pale pink and rosy against her lighter skin.

"Are you going to strip, Balder?" Svanhild sounded amused, watching him with sultry interest.

He gave her a lazy smile and set his coat aside before jerking his shirt over his head. Her eyes flashed with interest as his chest came into view and his smile broadened. He liked her appraisal of his body. While not ripped like the models in work-out magazines, his body was hard and flat, without much fat lining the soft sections.

He bent at the waist to take off his boots and she gasped.

"What in Freyja's name happened to your back, Balder?"

He kept working on his boots to gain some time to

explain the scars on his back. They'd come from pain-training, a way to compartmentalize pain so it wouldn't stop a Blade from doing what must be done. Especially when facing creatures like dragons or goblins that could project intense heat through their claws.

"Pain training." He shrugged as he rose, leaving only his pants on. "It was a long time ago and I've forgotten about them." Most people never saw his bare back, but the few times someone had, they'd been unnerved.

"They did that to you for training?" She shook her head. "That's barbaric, and I'm from a barbarian people."

He laughed, nodding. "You are. My mother's people as it turns out."

"Your mother was a barbarian? I like her already."

He laughed again, the unease over his back fading away. "You probably would. As I recall, she was strong and blonde, like you."

"You don't know?" Svanhild raised her eyebrows.

He shook his head. "I was about four when I was taken from my family and I haven't seen them since."

Her expression settled into impassiveness. "I'm sorry. Have you looked for them after you got out?"

He shook his head as he unbuttoned his pants. "I don't remember their names. I have nothing to research."

Sadness filtered into her gaze. "I'm sorry."

He shrugged as he crawled onto the bed to pause on all-fours in front of her. "It's been a long time and I suspect they'd be very disappointed in what I became. It's probably better that I'm dead to them."

He settled belly down between her legs and looked up her body to her eyes. "But I'm not here to talk about my past. I'm here to give you pleasure." He ran his hands over her thighs and she inhaled slowly, her eyes glazing over. "You're beautiful. So strong and sleek. Have you ever been tasted, Svanhild?"

She blinked a couple times before finding her voice.

"Tasted?"

"Yes, here." He dragged one finger over her cotton-covered mound and she shivered.

"No." Her sharp answer held yearning and curiosity.

"Then it pleases me to be the first."

She chuckled as he threw her words back to her, but it changed into a moan when he ran his nose over her cleft and inhaled her delicious scent. Musky, tangy woman with a hint of ginger spice filled his senses. His cock flexed against the covers and he nuzzled her nether lips through her panties.

"You smell so good." Balder skimmed his fingers along the edges of the elastic at her groin. "I think we should take these off. May I?"

"So polite." She snorted, but lifted her hips so he could slide the cotton briefs off her hips.

He grinned at her as he tossed the panties away. "I've found it pays to be polite." He dropped his gaze to her mound and almost swallowed his tongue.

Golden curls the same color as her hair covered her groin and glistened with the juices from her slit. Her clit peeked out from between her labia and his mouth watered with the need to suck on it. He'd always thought women beautiful, from their luscious curves and soft skin, but he'd never seen such beauty as the woman in front of him. Svanhild had strength and sleek lines to go with her feminine curves, and he wanted to lick and touch all of them.

"Your beauty is…" Words failed him. He couldn't think of anything that would encompass what he saw in front of him.

"Is what?"

Yeah, she would ask an answer of him.

"Beyond compare." He leaned forward to nuzzle the soft, fragrant curls and lost himself in her musky aroused scent. "Oh, Svanhild, you are glorious. Let me taste you."

He extended his tongue and licked along her lips, pausing only at the hood of her clit. She gasped and arched her back, but he held her in place with his hands as he savored her. He took his time, enjoying the flutter of her muscles under the soft skin and the increasing flow of her arousal on his tongue. Hot ginger spice.

He hummed against her flesh and licked each labia he could find, tickling her folds. She whimpered and writhed, her hands tightening on the bedcovers. He took her responses as a good sign and continued to savor her magnificent pussy. Each time he tasted her flavor, he needed more.

His cock agreed and stiffened as she moaned deep in her throat. She wriggled her hips as if she couldn't get enough of his touches and pride rippled through him. He continued to suckle on her clit as he pushed one finger into her clenching slit.

"Oh holy Freyja!"

If she was shouting gratitude to the Goddess, he whole-heartedly agreed. He worked his finger in and out of her pussy in time with the licks he gave her clit. She grew so slick he added a second finger and increased the frequency of his thrusts.

"Sweet glory, Balder. Don't stop."

Music to his ears. He continued to hum as he curled his fingers to rub the magic spot inside her pussy. Svanhild's whimpers deepened and her inner muscles squeezed his fingers hard. He tickled her clit with the tip of his tongue before he sucked hard on it as he thrust his fingers inside her.

"Oh, sweet Frreeeeyyjjaaaaah..."

Her pussy clamped down on his fingers as she bathed his tongue with her hot release. Sweet and tangy with a ginger finish, she gave Balder his first taste of her and he found himself addicted. Addicted to her flavor, to her sounds, and to her erotic motions of pleasure.

Thank all the saints for this gift.

He drank down her release, humming his approval so she'd know he accepted her offering. At last when she settled onto the bed, he wiped his mouth and crawled up her body to settled on the mattress beside her.

"Are you all right, Svanhild?"

"Give me...give me a moment. I wish to enjoy this feeling." She lay beside him breathing hard, but a smile curled her lips.

"You are magnificent when you come, *kjære mit.*"

"I can't imagine that to be true, but since you've made me feel so good, I won't argue." She took a deep breath and opened her eyes. "Thank you, Balder."

"It was my pleasure. Perhaps you'd let me do it again some time?" He stroked his fingers over her breasts, enjoying the silken skin and her delighted tremors.

"Yes, I believe if I have you in bed again, it'll be a requirement."

He laughed and rubbed his aching cock against her thigh. She paused and tilted her head so she could look down their bodies at his determined anatomy.

"Your penis seems to need some attention." She reached between them and closed her hand on his hard shaft. "Maybe I can help you with that?"

Pleasure swamped his brain at her touch and his breath caught in hot ecstasy. She could touch him forever and he'd never say no. Her weapon-callused hand sent delicious sensations ricocheting up his spine, eliciting a groan and his cock jerked.

"Saints above, don't stop." He had no idea where the demand came from, but he'd never felt anything so good as her hand wrapped around his shaft.

"I'm not going to stop, but I want to be sure you're ready."

"Ready?" His mind couldn't quite make the connection to meaning. "Ready for what?"

She released his cock and straddled his thighs, rubbing her wet pussy against his balls and shaft before she stood him upright.

"This." She sank down on his cock, impaling herself to the hilt.

Balder's eyes rolled back in his head as her hot, slick sheath squeezed him tight. *God have mercy, I want more.* She trembled, wriggling as if testing his girth within her, and he saw stars.

"Now, warrior, I'm going to ride you until we both scream with pleasure."

He opened his eyes and grinned up at her, her perfect breasts rising and falling with her breath. "I'm game for that, *kjære mit.*"

She rocked her hips, pulling her pussy off his cock. The head dragged along her inner walls and sent spikes of pleasure straight to his balls. When she reversed, heat and pressure enveloped him, and he couldn't resist the urge to grab her hips. She kept up a steady rhythm for a few strokes, but the need to move faster gripped him and he thrust up harder.

"Oh, yes, Balder. Fuck me."

She rose and fell with a rhythm that stole his breath but built his arousal up higher. He moaned and thrust, matching her motions as his balls tightened against the base of his cock. He'd never experienced such tight heat in all the years of his sexual life. Svanhild took him higher than he'd ever been and when she slammed down onto his cock, squeezing her muscles around him, his release exploded through him.

"Holy God in heaven!" He roared his pleasure as he slammed her hips down on his, his cum shooting into her welcoming pussy.

"Freeeyyjjaaah!" Her matching roar sounded triumphant and her sheath tightened on his cock with erotic relentlessness.

He'd never seen anything so beautiful as Svanhild in the throes of passion and ecstasy. Her full breasts bounced and trembled as she soared with her release. His own pleasure ramped up with watching hers. *I did that. I made her feel good.*

He rarely brought pleasure, only pain. To see Svanhild in erotic ecstasy of his making did something funny to his insides. It produced a craving to see it and do it again. *I want her and to be with her. I want to love her.*

The voices so long a part of his adult life stirred, trying to intrude on his joy. He almost turned his attention to them, but Svanhild shifted on his cock and sighed with delight, and the voices lost the battle.

"You're magnificent, Svanhild." He couldn't help but compliment her. If he could, he'd spend hours looking at her and coaxing her smile out from behind her fierce scowl.

She dropped her gaze to him, a languid expression suffusing her features. "Perhaps my magnificence comes from your own bearing, Balder." She tilted her head. "Your expertise in loving shouldn't be wasted or allowed to molder. I'm happy to keep you in peak condition."

He laughed, delighted she wanted more pleasure. That aligned with his immediate concerns. "Would it be arrogant to say I would hope so and I'm more than willing to accept your proposal?"

She grinned and leaned down, pressing her lips against his as her pussy squeezed his shaft. He let himself fall into her kiss, tangling his tongue with hers and something loosened within him. Bliss and ecstasy flooded his soul, washing away more of his anger, fear, and the hold the Sword of God indoctrination had on his mind.

She sat back up, her hands braced on his chest, and smiled. "Not arrogant if I'm in agreement."

"Fantastic. Give me a half an hour and I'll be happy to practice my skills on you again." He squeezed her hips in his hands.

Her eyes blazed with renewed arousal. "A man with stamina. I'm game."

Sweet Heaven, she'd kill him. But he'd die a happy man indeed.

CHAPTER EIGHT

Morning sifted into Svanhild's awareness with the cotton silence of a new snowfall. She loved these kinds of mornings when she lay toasty warm under thick blankets. Except one on of the blankets wrapped around her had a heartbeat and breathed. *Holy Freyja, who's in my bed with me?* It took her several breaths to identify Balder's callused hand stroking her breasts, and a few more to understand what that meant.

I let him stay the night.

Most of the lovers she'd had in the past had either left before she woke up or she'd retreated from them before they roused. But she'd fallen asleep in Balder's arms after her fifth orgasm and had no inclination to kick him out. In fact, she'd slept better with him than she ever had alone.

"Good morning, Svanhild."

She shifted onto her back and met his gaze. Only one blue eye opened, but the edges crinkled with his smile.

"Good morning. You're still here."

It was an inane thing to say, but it completely expressed her astonishment at the situation.

"I am. After you wore me out completely last night, I thought it better to wait out the storm wrapped around your warm body." He blinked, but with only one eye visible it came across as a wink. "I didn't really want to leave anyway."

"I didn't want you to leave, either. I still don't." The words surprised her again.

"You don't?" He lifted his head off the pillow and met her gaze fully. "I don't know how long I can, because Angelina needs her van, but I'll stay as long as you want me to." He rolled over enough to turn his head toward the window. "It's still snowing."

"A perfect day to stay inside with a lover." The words were unusual for her, but they tasted good in her mouth.

He met her gaze again. "Will you allow me to be your lover, Svanhild?"

Would she? Could she take a chance on more than just a one-night-stand?

"Yes, I would like you to be my lover."

A broad grin transformed his merely handsome face into glorious beauty, and she shivered with delight and desire. She could see how he'd been an effective infiltrator. Women would be drawn to his magnificent smile. *Probably gay men, too.* She wasn't ready to trust him with her heart, yet, but she'd definitely trust him with her body.

"That's excellent news." Balder cuddled up to her again and took the opportunity of the shifting blankets to nuzzle her breast and suck on the nipple. "Want me to start right now?"

She opened her mouth to answer, but her stomach rumbled with its emptiness and Balder laughed.

"Sounds like you need fuel to make up for last night's workout."

"*Ja,* I'm hungry. You were insatiable." She grinned to show him that wasn't a bad thing.

"Only for you, *kjære mit.*" He stretched and the blankets fell to expose his ripped chest covered in copper-colored hair.

Her mouth watered for another taste of his tangy cream and his tiny nipples, but he rolled to the side of the bed, searching for his clothes. She rested in the bed and watched him, enjoying the play of muscles in his back and buttocks. *The man is beautiful despite the scars.* She appreciated the hard lines of his thighs and ass. Not much extra fat on him, but he'd endured a hard nomadic existence and it had honed his body into hard lines.

He pulled his jeans up and buttoned them before turning around to give her an amused smile. "Liked what you saw?"

"*Ja.*" She didn't need to say more. He was what she wanted and at the moment, their pasts didn't matter.

"Nice to know." He nodded toward the kitchen. "Want me to start coffee or tea?"

"I don't have a coffee maker so it'll have to be tea."

His eyes widened in mock-horror. "No coffee maker? We'll have to remedy that."

"You're a coffee fan?" She slid out of bed and pulled on a soft woolen nightdress that tied in the front. "I thought you preferred tea."

Balder shrugged as he marched toward the main room. "I like tea for many things, but coffee was the only controlled substance that didn't make Tiffany's haunting any worse. And she liked the smell of it, so it calmed her somewhat."

"Smell?" Svanhild frowned as she followed him into the main room. "She's a ghost. How could she smell anything?"

"She remembers the scents. I think it comes from being a werewolf and having such a great nose." He turned his back and filled the kettle with water at the sink. The scars on his back, though extensive, gave her an impression of his strength, rather than his damage. He'd endured a lot.

Ja, to become a horrific assassin. The truth soured her stomach. *But he knows his faults and is trying to correct them.* Another truth, only more hopeful. Humans had a remarkable capacity to harm their own species and others, but they also had the ability to admit their mistakes and work to reverse the damage of them. How many of the Elder Races had that kind of introspection?

The first step of redemption was admitting a problem existed, and Balder had. *Tiffany wouldn't let him do otherwise.* He as paying for the mistakes he'd made. *Can I say the same for myself?* She frowned and turned her back on him as she retreated to the fireplace to restart the fire.

She built the base with kindling and newspaper as she considered her own mistakes. *I was right to refuse to take that man to Valhalla.* While her Shield Maiden sisters might have felt differently, she'd made the right choice. But perhaps the mistake existed in the way she'd defied Odin. She let that thought sift around her mind as she lit a match and ignited the paper.

Would Odin have allowed her to stay if she'd approached him a different way? She shook her head. No, he wouldn't have tolerated anyone defying his edicts. Her simple refusal represented challenge and no Viking worth his salt ever backed down from a challenge. The result would've been the same no matter which way she'd refused.

The flames caught the wood and warmed her face, but Svanhild's attention remained inward. What mistakes had she made during her time in the human world that she could fix now?

"What are you thinking about that makes your face turn that hard and cold, Svanhild?" Balder sat beside her and handed her a mug of hot tea.

She'd been so focused on her inner thoughts she hadn't heard the kettle or noticed the fire needed feeding. She blinked and shook her head as she added larger logs to the blackened maw of the fireplace.

"I was thinking about redemption."

He raised his eyebrows and nodded slowly. "I see. Whose? Mine?"

"In a way." She took the mug of tea and retreated to the couch once the fire had enough fuel. "I see you trying to change, to make amends for your previous life and actions. That's an admirable goal. I respect you for it."

"I think I hear a 'but' in there." He sat beside her and she realized he'd put on a shirt. *Damn, I missed everything.*

"No buts, just realizing I might need to take a hard look at my own existence and face the mistakes I've made."

Balder nodded. "What mistakes do you think you've made?"

She gritted her teeth. She hated admitting her faults, even to herself, but she'd started down this road and refused to quit. *No one likes a coward.*

"I think I've been too judgmental."

Silence stretched a beat before Balder barked a laugh. "A Valkyrie, too judgmental?"

She scowled. "There's no need to laugh."

"Right, sorry. Let me see if I can understand your perspective." He backpedaled and valiantly tried to lose his smile. "What makes you think you're too judgmental?"

The twinkle remained in his eyes, but he appeared to take her seriously so she shoved away her initial impulse to give up explaining.

"Valkyries are meant to judge the dying so we know where to take them. But since I've lived in the human world, I've learned there are many nuances to how people exist." She frowned and rubbed her mug with her fingers. "There are those who do heinous things, but realize their error and try to make amends."

"Like me."

"*Ja*, like you. But then there are others who outwardly look fine and upstanding, but inside they have a black heart or an empty soul." She rubbed the back of her neck, trying to ease the pressure on her muscles. "I have judged many by what group they belong to, by what name they carry or by the actions they've done, but not the whys behind them, or their intents, or even as individuals." She met his gaze with a grimace. "I should've treated you as an individual rather as member of a group. You're not like others of the Sword of God."

Balder nodded slowly. "No, I'm not anymore, but I was. I don't think your initial assessment of me was completely wrong, Svanhild. I was a full-fledged member of that cult and I carried out missions and actions in the name of their objectives." He took a deep breath and turned his gaze to the fire. "My past is ugly, no question about it. And I still have moments where I'm stuck there, listening to the voices in my head, and causing harm."

"But you're trying to be better. You're actively seeking to be different. I've been merely existing from one century to another. I don't think I've changed at all."

"No?" Balder raised his eyebrows. "You don't think so?" He leaned forward and captured her lips in a sweet, sultry kiss, and she let herself fall into the affection and comfort therein. When he pulled back, he smirked. "You just let a former Sword of God assassin and human man kiss you without gutting him. Still think you haven't changed?"

She opened her mouth to tell him off, but his words sunk in and she closed her lips. She had let Balder into her sanctuary and bed, and possibly her heart. *No, not that. Not yet.* But the denial rang false. She shoved it away and resolved to look at it later.

When she didn't answer, Balder dropped his chin and narrowed his eyes. "Two weeks ago, hell, two days ago, would you have let someone like me kiss you?"

She shook her head.

"So, what's altered between now and then?"

She almost told him, "Nothing," but that didn't ring

true, either. She frowned and tried to make her thoughts clear. "I met Bart, and Kate, and you."

"How has meeting me shifted your perspective?" Balder frowned thoughtfully.

"You're not…beyond hope."

He blinked. "I'm not?"

"No, and that's my point. You've seen your flaws and you're trying to mitigate them. It's admirable. I have ignored mine and—"

He pressed his fingers on her lips. "I don't think you've ignored your flaws, I think you never had to change them until you saw something different. Nothing challenged your view until you met me. But you're not wrong about the Sword of God. They are heinous people. And I was very much a part of them."

She frowned and tilted her head away from his hand. "But you're not, now, and you're trying to be better."

"I am, and I have been for several years. But the only significant changes have occurred in the last two days since I've come to Three Lakes." He shot a look outside. "Okay, one day, but still."

"You think my perspective altered yesterday?" She shook her head. "That doesn't seem to be enough time."

"I don't know if it's altered so much as you're willing to entertain new ideas and challenges to it."

He tipped his head back and drank his tea. She stared at the long column of his throat as he swallowed and let the pleasure of his beauty shiver through her. She wanted him to be right, that she was able to change, but she didn't think anything significant had happened.

"I guess time will tell if that's true or not." She wrapped her arms around herself. She'd never questioned her own view before, and it wasn't comfortable. What if she'd been wrong about everyone her whole life? *No, I was right about that dishonorable butcher.* But having spent time with Balder made her question other snap judgments she'd made.

Like that guy I met yesterday morning. But she'd seen the horrible things in his past the moment she dragged him from the water. Svanhild frowned. She'd seen the actions attributed to him, but he hadn't been present in images that flashed across her mind. Was she losing her abilities after all this time away from Asgard?

"That's a disagreeable expression. What are you thinking about?"

Svanhild blinked and rose from her seat by the fire. "I was thinking about...you leaving. You need to get the van back to Angelina, right?"

He rose as well and followed her as she returned to the kitchen. "I do, but the weather still looks rough. Do you mind if I stay a bit longer?"

"I...no, not at all. I don't know if Bart needs me to come into the Fix-It Cave, but I can call him." She bit her bottom lip, not sure how the ask her next question.

Balder tipped his head. "What, Svanhild?"

"I would like you to stay. I would like more of..." She gestured at the bedroom, not comfortable with asking for intimacy. Sex she could handle. Lovemaking was something else.

He stopped in front of her and held her arms making sure she met his gaze. "More of?"

They stood at equal height in bare feet and she liked that she could look him in his glacial blue eyes. Despite the color, he gazed at her with warmth she'd never seen.

"More touching, kissing..."

"More loving? Like this?" He bent his head and kissed the side of her neck, his beard and moustache tickling her skin.

"*Ja*, like that." She closed her eyes and let him run his hands under her loose hair to massage her head as he moved his kisses along her jaw. "Sweet glory, Balder. You must keep doing that."

He chuckled and pulled back. "Let's move this to the bedroom before it becomes too difficult to stand."

She allowed him to draw her back to the bedroom and couldn't help the smile curling her lips. She wanted more with Balder and she was supposed to be watching over him to make sure he was all right. *Oh, I'll make sure he's all right, and completely out of trouble.*

CHAPTER NINE

Balder smiled to himself as he drove the van back to the shelter. He'd had an incredible weekend with Svanhild and hadn't wanted to leave, but Angelina needed her van. *Yeah, that was finished on Friday night.* Fortunately, the weather had been awful until that morning, so he had a legitimate excuse to stay.

But the morning dawned clear, bright, and relatively warm. *Especially in Svanhild's arms.* He sighed as his cock marked its agreement by pushing against his fly. He'd lost track of how many times he made her orgasm, but he took deep satisfaction in bringing her pleasure. *It's better than all the times I completed a mission.*

Balder turned onto the main road and headed into town. His body complained with the unusual use it had sustained, but he counted it as good pain. *It just means I need more of that kind of exercise.* He laughed and the sound surprised him as much as the balmy temperatures outside.

He pulled into the driveway of the shelter and drove into the garage at the back. He kept a close eye on the yard in case some little people decided it would be a good time to run around and eased the van into its spot. As he got out, he checked the van for any damage from the storm and almost ran into a large Harley motorcycle with red and orange flame details. The bike looked freshly washed and well maintained, and he wondered whose it was.

He made sure he'd grabbed all his stuff from the van and headed into the shelter to hand over the keys to Angelina. She wasn't at her usual spot at the front desk, but a large bald man in a leather biker's vest and faded blue jeans leaned on a high stool in beside it, his expression calm and assessing.

Balder nodded to him, both curious and uneasy around the man. "Hello, is Angelina about?"

"Yeah, she had to go into the women's dorm for somethin'. Who are you?"

Balder pocketed the keys to give him time to assess the situation. He didn't know this man or what he was, but he could tell the biker wasn't human. Too much otherworldliness about him. *And in this town, that's not uncommon.* But he still had to watch his own back. He idly wondered where Tiffany was.

"I'm Balder, the handyman Angelina hired. Who are you?"

"Oh, right. Yeah, she mentioned that." He held out a big, beefy paw. "Name's Luke Everfall."

"Nice to meet you." Balder took the offered hand, but the moment they touched, he wished he hadn't.

Luke's appearance changed momentarily into a tall man with white blonde hair, short pointed horns, and glowing red eyes. Long claws appeared at the edges of his finger tips and a huge set of white bat's wings hung folded behind his back. Then the vision disappeared as if it never happened and back was the broad-shouldered stocky biker with a red bandana tied around his bald head.

"Yeah, good to meet you, too." The man's eyes grew thoughtful as he pulled his hand back. "Where you from, Balder?"

"Oh, here and there. I moved around a lot as a kid."
That wasn't strictly true as he really didn't know where the
Sword of God had kept the younger boys. "You?" Balder
leaned against the desk and hoped Angelina would be back
soon.

"Deep down south." Luke narrowed his eyes.
"Angelina mentioned you were once in that Sword of God
cult. That right?"

A deep well of guilt and regret yawned before him, but
Balder swallowed it back and nodded. "Yeah."

Luke whistled and shook his head. "Woo-wee, that
shit's tough. Them motherfuckers are crazy. Were you
crazy like them?"

"Yeah." Balder said it deadpan and Luke sat back as
his eyes narrowed.

"But you're better now, right? I mean, you wouldn't be
here in Angelina's place if you were still fucked up.
Right?"

I guess that's debatable. But he nodded, not wanting to
piss off the guy just in case he decided Balder was a threat
to Angelina. The momentary vision he'd had of the tall
man with red eyes made him think Luke might not be a
man to cross.

"Yeah, getting better all the time. Been a long haul."

"I hear that." Luke held out his fist, inviting Balder to
rap knuckles together. "I've been on my own road like that,
and I still ain't got that shit cleared up yet."

"It takes a while, that's for sure. Are you staying here,
too?" Balder stepped back enough to give him some space.
Luke's presence stretched larger than his appearance.

"Naw, well, kinda. Angelina's my woman." Luke
puffed his chest out and smirked. "I'm just on my way
through to a bike rally in Las Vegas, and thought I'd stop
by to see her."

"Las Vegas? That's a long drive from here."

"Yeah, but it's a helluva lot warmer down there than it

is up here." Luke shook his head. "I got no fuckin' clue why Angelina likes it here when it gets so damn cold I could end up with perpetual blue balls from it." He shrugged. "But she does, so I keep comin' back to see her."

"Oh, the things we do for love, yeah?" Balder laughed ruefully.

"Yeah, that's the truth. You got someone you love?"

For some reason, Luke's question didn't seem so offhand or flippant. His eyes were deep brown, but they seemed darker and wiser as well. *And what the hell do I say?* How did he feel about Svanhild? Could he call it love or was it too early for that?

Balder gave a one-shouldered shrug. "I've found someone who puts me in that frame of mind."

He expected Luke to smirk and make some sort of ribald remark, he only nodded. "Does this person like you back?"

"Yeah, I think so, but it's early yet."

A sad smile curled Luke's lips. "You're a lucky man, then. Everyone needs someone who loves them." He tilted his head. "You really were Sword of God?"

Balder gritted his teeth and nodded. "Yeah."

Luke returned the nod. "I met those people a time or two. They always claimed they were savin' folks in the name of God, but they had a funny way of doin' it. They left a wide wake of death as I recall."

Sorrow, guilt, and regret welled up inside Balder, destroying all the happy feelings he'd enjoyed that morning. "Yes, murderers and sociopaths, the lot of us."

"You include yourself in that?" Luke's eyebrows rose.

Balder took a deep breath. "Yes. At least the murderer part. I might have been brainwashed, but I did the actions and must deal with the consequences. I'm just grateful Angelina gave me a chance."

Luke grunted with what sounded like surprised approval. "Yeah, she's known for that. And she's pretty damn wise. She sees all sorts of things in people that others can't." But his eyes turned flat black as he lost his smile. "Just don't think to hurt her for any reason, Balder. Because I might not be here physically, but I do watch out for her, and I won't tolerate anyone hurting her."

The world blacked out until all Balder could see was Luke with his eyes glowing red. Bone-deep fear lanced through him and he swallowed hard. Luke wasn't remotely human. Balder didn't know the man's species, but he understood Luke had power beyond any other Elder Race being he'd met before.

"No, sir. I have no intention of hurting Angelina, or anyone else in this town." Did his voice just squeak?

"Good." The world returned to normal and Luke settled back on his stool. "Then we're cool. You met Kate Blackamber yet?"

Balder nodded quickly, trying to catch his breath and slow his heartbeat. *Who is this guy?*

"Good. I don't get to talk to her much on account of being gone all the time, but she's another good judge of character in this town." Luke scratched his jaw. "Have you met her husband?"

Balder shook his head.

"Oooh boy, he's a retired Navy SpecOps guy. If there's anyone you don't wanna piss off, it's him. He makes me look like a pansy-ass." Luke snorted with a smile. "I can hold my own, but Jayson Blackamber has a can of whoop-ass and you don't want him to open it on you."

Balder swallowed hard and nodded. How did he manage to find a town full of powerful beings all together, and most of them hated him? *Just lucky I guess.*

"Well, I gotta get going and put some things together before I get to work on Angelina's to-do list. It was good to meet you, Luke." Balder headed toward the hallway.

"Yeah, you too, Balder. Have a good one."

Balder snorted. *I will if I don't meet anymore super beings.*

****

Svanhild pulled the kettle off the stove and stirred her scrambled eggs as she let her eyes unfocus. The weekend she'd spent with Balder had been a revelation. Not only did she come to understand he was more man than his programming, but her own desires and needs had been met by his spectacular loving. She hadn't known she'd been missing that kind of touch and intimacy.

Until Balder, she hadn't needed it.

He'd made her feel things she hadn't known existed within herself. She'd found more acceptance and connection with him than she ever had with the other Shield Maidens. He knew who she was and what she could do, including kill him, and it never changed the way he interacted with her.

It certainly hadn't affected the way he loved her.

Despite his origins, he carried a strength and a warmth she'd not found in any other male in her long life. Bart came close, but she didn't want to have that kind of intimacy with the bear shifter. Balder had refinement in ways she'd never considered sexy. He'd also acquired an understanding of his own limits and handicaps that made her more willing to forgive them.

Watching him struggle to overcome his indoctrination gave her the courage to face her unquestioned beliefs. She could see someone's faults and past actions, but when she'd first seen Balder, she judged him as unworthy, not knowing the man sought atonement. There was no question that the Sword of God brought fanaticism to a whole new level, creating assassins for no other reason than fear and control. But no one had ever questioned whether or not a Sword of God assassin could be redeemed.

Or a Valkyrie, for that matter. She'd defied Odin because she'd seen the evil in the deeds the man had done. *But did I not look deep enough?* Balder was slowly teaching her there was more to a man than his past.

Svanhild dished up the eggs and set the pan aside just as her toast popped up. She smeared some butter on the bread and set her plate on the table. She'd eaten meals alone for centuries, and yet she missed Balder's company.

Freyja, a few nights with him and I turn into a lovestruck fool.

He'd stayed two with her while the last of the spring storms raged through Three Lakes and she'd learned a lot about him. *Ja, like his ability to give me multiple orgasms.* Since his break with the Sword of God, he'd started to see the Elder Races as people. He didn't like all of them and some he avoided with as much effort as he'd once taken to kill them, but he no longer blindly hated them.

Or me.

He also found he liked dark chocolate over milk or white, hated Brussels sprouts and cooked cauliflower, and preferred tulips to roses. She'd laughed at him for the ordinary revelations, but he'd been starting from scratch when he'd left the Sword of God. No one had ever allowed him to make his own choices. He'd done everything from sex to clothing shopping with someone else's choices or preferences.

One of the things he definitely liked with Svanhild was cunnilingus. He'd brought her to multiple orgasms over their weekend together, even enjoying sixty-nine a few times. She'd shown him the pleasure of a good cock-sucking, but he always returned to feast on her pussy until she could barely walk.

Not a bad thing in the long run.

Not bad at all. She found she wanted more. More sex, more intimacy, and more conversation with Balder. He had a unique way of looking at the world, often full of self-deprecating humor and intelligence. He'd laughed at some of her funny travel stories and she enjoyed the happy rumble. Crow's feet had developed around his eyes accompanied by deep lines around his mouth from the smiles and laughter.

He'd asked if she truly wanted to be his lover and she never hesitated. She'd rolled over and licked his penis until he hardened and she sucked him into release. She smiled and licked her lips now, remembering the sweet tanginess of his cum. She wanted no other man at the moment or in the foreseeable future.

He'd kissed her goodbye on Sunday morning and drove down her dripping driveway into the mist rising from the melting snow. She regretted going back to the world outside their weekend retreat, but he'd needed to return the van to Angelina and she had to get her mind back into her new life in Three Lakes. *As a mechanic.*

She finished her breakfast and took the dishes to the sink just as her cell pinged with a text from Bart. She grabbed her mug of tea and pulled out her phone to swipe the screen.

NEED YOU AT THE FIX-IT CAVE NOW. HURRY.

She set her tea aside, grabbed her jacket, and headed out the door at a run. The wet cold of the melting snow hit her face as she pounded toward the Cave in a hurry. Bart had never used capital letters in his texts so something must be truly worrying him to do so. Her breath plumed in the frozen air as she skidded around the corner to the garage and headed for the door.

"Bart!" She called his name as she threw herself inside. The heat of the shop slapped into her and she sighed with involuntary relief. She'd forgotten how cold the northern climes could be. "Bart, what's wrong?"

"Fire, in town. Get your ass in my truck. We're goin' to help."

"Glory be. Fire? Where?" She didn't argue just

followed him to his truck and climbed into the passenger side.

"Old apartment building near Harbor Lake. Sheriff Boulderson called asking for volunteers to get people out and situated until the fire department can get there." Bart floored the truck toward town, his jaw tight.

"Sweet Freyja." Svanhild swallowed hard. Fire in any structure was never good. "Where's the department located?"

"In Warbler Springs, twelve miles from Three Lakes. They service Three Lakes, Warbler Springs, and Last Mission."

She raised her eyebrows.

"All three towns are too small to support a full-time fire department, so we all chip in to support them and they have to care for all of us." Bart shrugged as he made the turn onto Main Street headed for Lake Superior. "Hopefully they'll get here before we lose too much. We have volunteers to help get people to safety and throw buckets on anything larger than a kitchen fire, but if the building goes up, we'll need a real crew."

She looked ahead out of the windshield and caught the smoke billowing above the buildings near the lake. "Holy Freyja, it's huge."

"Maybe." Bart's jaw tightened as he took in the smoke plume. "But it could be just the moisture reacting to the heat."

She hoped he was right, but he didn't sound very convinced of his own words. As they reached the intersection near the lake shore, they caught sight of the burning building. People scurried around the base as flames licked through the upper windows of a six storey brick apartment building overlooking the harbor. Bart pulled his truck over to the side of the road and they got out.

"Let's find the sheriff and see where he wants us."

Svanhild swallowed hard against the concern for the

people losing their homes to the flames. A bucket line had already started, adding water from the lake to the base of the building and the neighboring structures. Police cars blocked off the road on both sides to keep people away from the burning structure.

A huge man in a sheriff's uniform, standing damn near eight feet tall, directed people into moving water or helping others. He commanded respect by both his size and his demeanor, and Svanhild had the unreasoning urge to execute a quick bow before speaking to him. Bart, however, had no compunction of walking over to the sheriff and asking him where they were needed without protocols.

"Good of you to come, Bart. I need you to head back to those police cars there and keep out the lookie-lous as well as the press. I'm sure they'll be circling like vultures." The sheriff waved back the way they'd come. "The Warbler Springs Fire Department is on the way, ETA ten minutes, so I'll need you to allow them through, but keep the others back until the fire's out."

"Okay, Sheriff. Will do." Bart nodded. "This is Svanhild Bjørnsdottir. She's recently moved here and works with me."

"Nice to meet you, Ms. Bjørnsdottir. Would you help get any people coming out to the safe zone behind the bucket line? I'll send the paramedics there."

"Of course, my...er, Sheriff." She nodded, hoping her slip wouldn't be noticed. *Why do I want to treat him like royalty?*

He gave her an amused grin that pulled out wrinkles around his eyes and mouth, but only nodded. "Head on over there and help Iris Maple get folks blankets and water."

Svanhild nodded back and followed his directions to find a tall woman with pale blond hair wrapped in a braid around her head and a complexion like fine-grained wood.

She handed out supplies to folks, directing others to help them to the tents set up to keep the rain off.

"Iris Maple?" Svanhild dipped her head.

"Yes?"

"The sheriff directed me to come here to help."

"And you are?" The woman fixed deep brown eyes on Svanhild.

"Svanhild Bjørnsdottir. I work with Bart Fisher at the Fix-It Cave."

The pale blonde eyebrows went up. "I see. Welcome. Can you make sure everyone in the tents has enough blankets and water? There are more of both toward the back of the tents."

"Yes, ma'am." Svanhild dipped her head with a similar urge to bow. *What is it about these people who make me think they're royalty?*

"Good. If any of the people have injuries or burns, please send them to the tent closest to the lake. Angelina Burke is there doing triage."

"Yes, ma'am."

Svanhild went to work, helping those she could and arranging for anyone new to get what they needed. Her attention focused on helping others and she tried to ignore her Valkyrie senses judging those she met. *Especially because I don't know their full stories.* The fire department arrived a few minutes later and started working on the building as well as facilitating any rescue efforts. The paramedics pushed through to the tents as the bucket brigade backed off in favor of the professionals.

Just before the firefighters took over, Svanhild caught sight of a familiar red thatch of hair exiting the building ahead of a cloud of smoke.

Sweet Freyja, is that Balder?

CHAPTER TEN

Clashing emotions crashed over her. Worry, excitement, arousal, desire, fear, and surprise bounced inside her head. Her new lover carried a charcoal-smudged little girl in his arms, his expression exhausted. Svanhild hurried to meet him as he trudged toward the tent. The little girl wiped sooty hands across her cheeks, leaving dark smudges, but she kept her lips tightly closed as Balder held her against his body.

"Sweet Goddess, Balder, are you all right?" Svanhild fought a combination of excitement at his presence and gut-wrenching concern over his well-being as she walked with him.

"Yeah, just tired and smoky. It's hot in there." He brought the girl to the triage tent and set her down on a stretcher. "You just rest and let the paramedics look you over, okay? They'll fix you right up." The little girl nodded with wide, frightened eyes.

"What about you?" Svanhild took him aside and sat him down on an empty deck chair. "Any burns or wounds?" She knew she was mother-henning him, but the idea of him burning to death froze her guts solid. She looked him over critically, but while his jacket looked singed, he didn't appear to have any injuries.

"No, I'm fine. Tiffany made sure to guide me through the worst of it." Balder opened a bottle of water and sucked down the entire thing in one long drink.

The ghost materialized behind him, her expression uncharacteristically concerned, but whether it was for Balder or the little girl, Svanhild didn't know.

"*Tusen takk*, Tiffany." She nodded her head and the ghost managed to blush and smile.

"You're welcome." Then she said something to Balder Svanhild couldn't hear, but the man stiffened and shot her a frown over his shoulder.

Balder mumbled something that sounded like, "Give me a minute," and the ghost nodded before wandering off.

"Everything all right with her?" Svanhild handed him a blanket.

"Yes, fine. She wanted to talk to me about you, especially since I spent the weekend with you."

"Why? Was she worried I'd run you through?" She leaned close and whispered in his ear. "As I recall, you were the one to use your "sword" on me."

His eyes widened in surprise and a smirk curled his lips. "Yes, ma'am, as per your request." He chuckled. "No, she wasn't sure she should leave me with you as you had to deal with me all during the weekend." He managed to blush under the soot. "I didn't tell her how we spent our time."

Svanhild raised her eyebrows and nodded slowly. "Ah, I see. I would've expected her to be pleased with some time off from driving you. Didn't she stay with the *Morukai*?"

"Yes, I think so, but she's never been away from me for so long." He shook his head, watching the ghost ogle the firefighters as they went to work on the building. "She has seemed better, though. Less angry, but I don't think that's my doing. Or rather, not just me."

Svanhild nodded. "You are better, too, Balder. But why in *helvete* would you go into that building while it was on fire? Are you insane?"

He grimaced as he took another water bottle from her. "I couldn't stay out when I heard someone calling. The fire department wasn't here yet and no one else was willing to go look." He shrugged. "Someone had to do it and Tiffany guided me so I could get in and out safely."

"I'm glad she helped, but try not to do the heroics yourself next time. I'm not built for that kind of terror."

Balder blinked. "You were worried about me?"

"*Ja*." She didn't want to admit how worried. "I've got to get back to helping the others, but I'll check on you in a little bit. Are you going to be okay here?" It seemed odd to ask him such tender questions, but she couldn't stop herself.

"Yes, I'll be fine." He met her gaze. "Thanks, Svanhild."

"*Ja*, just take care of yourself. Drink lots of water. Smoke is hell on the throat." She patted him on the shoulder, wishing she could sweep him into her arms and hold him safe, but she moved off to check on the survivors of the fire.

She'd just checked on the little girl who Balder had brought into the tents when a woman came running in from behind the police barricade. She yelled a name, crying hysterically.

"Where is she? Where's my Tina?" She hurried through the tents, scanning the beds until she found the little girl. "Oh, Tina. Oh my God. Are you all right? Is she all right? Oh, thank God!"

"Ma'am, your daughter's had some smoke inhalation and exhaustion, but she's going to be fine. We'll want to take her to the medical center in Newberry to be sure everything checks out." The paramedic gave her a reassuring smile.

"Newberry? Oh dear. All right. It's going to be fine, Tina. I'm here now." She stroked her daughter's hair. "Did

you rescue her? Did you get my baby out of that building?"
She turned to the paramedic.

"No, ma'am. It was that man over there. He brought
your daughter out before the firefighters could get here."

Balder had shrunk in on himself as the woman turned
to look for who the paramedic indicated. His hand
tightened on his water bottle.

"Oh my God! Thank you so much, sir." She hurried
over to him and Svanhild hovered to the side in case he
needed backup. "Thank you for saving my little girl."
She'd started to cry again as she grasped his arm. "I don't
know what I would've done if she died. Thank you for
bringing her out and saving her."

"You're welcome, ma'am. I'm just glad I could help."
He tried to smile.

"Thank you." She threw her arms around him.

He shot Svanhild a bewildered look over the woman's
shoulder as he closed his arms around her, and Svanhild
covered her laugh with a cough behind one hand. *Guess
he's not used to getting much gratitude.* Eventually the
woman let go and went back to her child, but Balder kept a
wary eye on her until she and the little girl rode away in an
ambulance.

"Are you all right?" Svanhild handed Balder another
bottle of water.

"Yeah, I'm fine. I'm just going to rest here for a bit.
Let Angelina know I'm here if she needs me."

"Will do. Just get some rest, *ja*?"

Svanhild continued volunteering until everyone had
been checked and cared for, but she kept an eye on Balder.
She worried about his lungs and if he had any burns, but he
didn't seem to be suffering more than anyone else. Tiffany
returned periodically as if checking in with him, but would
fade from sight again if anyone got close.

Eventually, the wounded were sent either to Newberry
Medical Center or the Three Lakes Medical Clinic for

consultation with the local doctors. They took extra time with Balder at Angelina's insistence, but he was deemed well enough to return home. Angelina told him to take a couple days to rest. He didn't want to, but she gave a stern mother's look and he subsided.

The firefighters kept after the blaze until everything was sopping wet and smelled of watered down charcoal. The Newberry TV station had brought a film crew to get footage of the fire and its heroes, but the police kept them behind the barricades.

"How are you feeling?" Svanhild stopped beside the cot on which Balder sat. "Is your throat better?"

"Yes, thank you." He nodded and shot a look at the building. "It looks like they got the fire out, but all those folks are going to be out of a home until it's repaired."

Svanhild nodded. "Where will they go?"

"Probably to the shelter or the Inn. I think I heard the owners say they'd give up the rooms until people could move back into their apartments."

"That's very kind of them." She hadn't known many who'd be so generous. "Does that mean more work for you?"

"Maybe, but we're equipped to put people up for a while. We'll have to see." He slowly rose to his feet, grunting a little as he stretched his body. "I think I'm going to head back to the shelter."

"Do you need any help or a ride? I'm sure I can ask Bart for the keys to his truck." Although she wasn't certain the bear shifter would let her drive his baby.

"That's all right. Angelina's here and she can give me a ride. If not, I could use the walk to loosen my muscles."

He looked tired and she had the sudden urge to hug him, but the openness of the place made her uneasy. "Okay. I'm glad you're all right, Balder." She reached out to touch his arm, but pulled back immediately, not sure how to show her relief. Tapping into the emotions felt foreign and uncomfortable.

"Me too."

He gave her a warm smile and it melted some of the ice off her heart. *How in Fenrir's name does he do that to me?* She shrugged, glancing at the sunny sky. Something about the light eased some of the intensity of the morning's drama. The storms had blown themselves out, leaving everyone with a sense of hope. The fire effort had taken most of the morning and all the shadows of the vehicles and trees pointed east.

"*Ja*, well, I should probably find out of Iris needs any help cleaning up."

"Oh, yeah, that's a good thought. But..." He paused, assessing her as he bit his bottom lip. "You have to eat, right? How about we meet at the Ironwood Café for a late lunch after I get cleaned up?"

"Oh, um…" She'd never been so hesitant in all her life, but she was out of her depth here. *Did he just ask me on a date?* "Let me ask Bart if I can get the time off."

"Oh, right. I'd forgotten your hours are more regular than mine. Forget I asked. We'll do it some other time." He turned away to gather up his ragged coat, his expression closed.

"What about dinner?" She had no idea where the blurted question came from, but she didn't want him to think she'd rejected his offer.

"Dinner?"

"As you said, you have to eat, right?" She winked as his face cracked into a smile. "How about we do dinner at the Ironwood Café tonight? I think Bart has a loaner car I can use to get into town."

"Yeah, I'd like that. Seven thirty?"

"Seven thirty sounds good." She let her smile loose, but paused before she headed out of the tents to look for Bart. "One more thing, Balder."

"And that is?"

"Can you ask Tiffany to stay behind tonight? Three's a crowd." She nodded and headed out, satisfied with the look of hope on his face as she walked away.

****

Balder shivered with excitement as Svanhild sauntered away into the mob of firefighters and cops. The big bear shifter met her for a moment to talk then they melted into the crowd and disappeared. Balder missed her immediately, but reined in his remarkably smitten heart.

Who the hell have I become? He used to know himself as a stone-cold killer, an assassin of high marks and notable kills. After he'd killed Tiffany and her family, he became a lost and babbling derelict. A man with no people, no goals, and no way forward. But less than a week in Three Lakes, Michigan, and he'd become a smitten idiot mooning over a Valkyrie. How was that possible?

Tiffany's return to his side brought him out of his thoughts and he offered her a wan smile.

:Balder, are you feeling okay? You just smiled at me.: She tilted her head and raised her eyebrows.

He nodded as Angelina stopped by his side. "You're looking better. Why don't you go home and rest? I can help here until everything's cleared up."

"Are you sure? I'm happy to help."

"No, no, you've done enough. You just head on back to the shelter and get some rest. And mind the media." She pointed at the press still held on the other side of the police. "They don't get much chance to do anything up here in Three Lakes, if you get my meaning."

The Elder Races don't want to be publicized. Because of the Sword of God and other fanatics like them.

"So this is a rare opportunity for them."

"Yep, and they'll take advantage for the sake of some sparkly airtime." Angelina nodded to him. "Take your coat off and wear my hat." She handed him her baseball cap with the Minnesota Vikings emblem. "I'll bring your coat home as soon as I'm done. Try to look like a tourist. I don't think they got a good look at you, so you might be able to slip past."

"Why would they want to talk to me?" He shrugged out of his long wool coat and handed it to her.

"Are you kidding? You rescued a little girl before the firefighters could get here. They'll be all over that like white on rice."

"Oh. Right." He didn't think of himself as much of a hero, but he couldn't let a child burn to death.

Even an Elder Races child.

He shot a guilty look at Tiffany, who shook her head. He didn't know if the little girl had been completely human, but it didn't matter to him anymore. The Sword of God thought humans were different than the Elder Races, and they were. But he'd seen enough ugliness in the humans to balance out the ugliness purported by the Sword of God elders. The only difference lay in the strength and abilities of the different species, and all were capable of killing.

I certainly proved that more than once.

"So take care of yourself and I'll see you back at the shelter." She frowned as she looked at his wool coat. "Good glory, Balder, is this the only coat you have?"

"Yes, ma'am."

"It's full of holes and now it has burns." She shook her head. "We'll get you a new one or something a little less tattered." She paused and chagrin slid across her expression. "I'm sorry. This is yours. I shouldn't take it from you. But would you be agreeable to me getting you a new-to-you coat? One that's in better shape?"

Balder took his time fitting her baseball cap to his head as he considered. He'd worn the coat since he left the Sword of God, but only because it was the only thing in the gear he had on him.

"Yes, ma'am." He nodded before taking a breath. "I'd like a new coat. Something that can stand up to the weather."

"I think I have just the thing. Do you have any objection to leather?"

"No, ma'am. Leather works just fine in the rain and snow." He found his smile. "Thank you."

"You're welcome, Balder. Here." She pulled off her sweatshirt and handed it to him. "Wear this until you get to the shelter. It'll keep you warm."

He took the sweatshirt, but didn't put it on. It smelled like sweet cinnamon rolls and he didn't want to soil it with the smoky scent in his clothes. He tied it around his waist and nodded.

"Thank you. Uh, Ms. Burke?"

"You know you can call me Angelina, right?"

"Uh, yes, yes, ma'am. Would it be okay to go out tonight? Ms. Bjørnsdottir invited me for dinner and I'd hate to disappoint her." He wasn't used to asking for permission, but he wanted to stay in Angelina's good graces.

"The Valkyrie who works with Bart Fisher at the Fix-It Cave?" She graced him with a brilliant smile. "You have a date with her? That's wonderful, Balder. It's good to see you connecting with someone. You go ahead, but don't overdo anything." She winked.

"Yes, ma'am. No, ma'am. Thank you, ma'am."

"Good glory, Balder. Did you just say 'ma'am' three times? Angelina works just fine."

"Yes, ma'am." His cheeks heated as she laughed.

"Good, I'll see you at home." She waved as she walked away.

Home. The word had many meanings, but he'd never had one of his own before. At least, not that he could remember.

:You're really going on a date tonight?: Tiffany's expression held concern.

He nodded and got up, moving out of the tents so no one would give him odd looks for talking to himself. She drifted after him, surprise edging out some of the worry.

"Svanhild invited me to dinner tonight and I didn't turn her down." He headed for the police barricades, keeping his head down but moving with purpose.

:Why not?: Tiffany sounded bewildered.

"Because she asked and I like her." It was stronger than that, but he wasn't ready to discuss it with Tiffany. The emotions were too new and fragile. "It would be rude to decline."

:That's never stopped you before.: Tiffany sifted herself until she floated in front of him, making him stop. *:You really like the Valkyrie, don't you?:*

It sounded like disbelief mixed with hurt. They passed the police barricades and the gaggle of chattering press before he said anything more. He didn't need them to pick up on his half of the conversation. He kept his head down except for one moment when the sheriff asked if he needed a ride. Balder shook his head and waved before the giant man turned back to deal with the press.

"Yes, I like Svanhild." More than he'd liked anyone before.

:But she's a Valkyrie, one of the Elder Races.: Tiffany shook her head, the corners of her mouth turning down. *:Why her, Balder?:*

The real question she asked was why not herself. The answer was neither pleasant nor satisfying. Tiffany had been a job, a mark, to get him in position to kill her and her family. He'd been deep in his programming and not focused on real commitment or a relationship. But with her help, he'd begun to heal from the horrific path he'd been on and Svanhild captured his interest. Not as an assassin, but as a man. Tiffany had always been too young for him, but it hadn't mattered when his only goal was her death.

Balder met Tiffany's sad gaze and grimaced. "Because she's a woman and it's time."

:*I really was only a job to you, wasn't I?:*

"Yes." No point in sugar-coating it. He'd been a bastard and it would take him decades to make up for it. "I'm sorry, Tiffany. I have no excuse. To be fair, I'm only ready now because of you. You've helped me more than I can tell you."

:*But not through love. Through haunting and determination, but not from love.:*

"No."

She nodded, her expression going stoic, and they turned onto Main Street. Balder understood she wanted him to tell her he'd loved her in his way, but that would be a harmful lie and he was done with lying. She deserved better, particularly from him.

He wished he could give her some words of comfort, but he didn't have them. Of all the things the Sword of God had trained him to do with regards to seduction and manipulation, they'd never taught him about compassion. So he walked on silently, knowing she hurt and aching to help, but not having the tools to do so.

"I'm sorry I'm not who you thought I was. I'm just as disappointed as you."

:*Hardly. I thought I had a future with you, but you only gave me a twilight existence.:*

"That was your choice…" He shook his head to clear it of anger. "But I'm glad you did."

:*You are?:* Surprise filled her voice and her expression.

"Yes. Without your determination and efforts, I wouldn't have changed." He stopped and looked her dead-on. *Funny choice of words when speaking to a ghost.* "Thank you."

She blinked owlishly at him, astonishment threading through her wispy lines. :*You've never thanked me before.:*

"I was too stupid and self-absorbed. You've saved me more times than I've done anything good for anyone." He wished he could take her hands and squeeze them, but he'd lost the opportunity years ago. "Thank you for saving me, for dragging me out of the chaos of the Sword of God's psychosis. I'm sorry for the hurt I caused. I know I can't fix it, but I'm grateful for your help."

Tiffany didn't say anything for a few moments, gaping at him as if he'd grown a second head. *Maybe I have.*

:Why are you saying this now?:

"I don't know. I think it's because of the fire and the little girl, and her mother." He shook his head as he resumed walking. "I've never helped anyone before. And I've never taken the time to recognize when someone helped me. You've helped me since the first moment, even when I didn't deserve it. I should've thanked you long ago."

They walked in silence and Balder hoped Tiffany knew he meant every word. She'd done so much for him and he'd taken advantage of her every step of the way. Sorrow and guilt swelled up the back of his throat. *I've been selfish my whole life.* Until today when he'd saved a little girl from the fire. *But I don't owe her, I owe Tiffany.*

"Was coming here to Three Lakes the right thing to do, Tiffany?"

The ghost shot him a look of surprise as they wove between other pedestrians on the sidewalk. *:What do you mean?:*

"I mean, I know I'm benefiting from being here, but are you? Did we come to the right place to help you?"

She frowned. *:What help do you think I'm looking for?:*

He gave a one-shouldered shrug as they crossed the street to the shelter. "I thought we could find a way to release you from this life as a ghost. So you can move on to the next place."

Tiffany scowled. *:The next place? You're just hoping to get rid of me, and that's not happening anytime soon.:*

"No, Tiffany, that's not what I meant—"

She ignored him as she sifted through the shelter doors in front of him, her head high and her expression thundrous. He followed her, trying to figure out a way to explain what he was feeling. *What the hell? She should know, right? She's connected to—*

His strides faltered. The foyer stood filled with people talking about the fire. The children jabbered loudly about the firefighters and the trucks with lights, while the adults spoke about the tragedy and how folks were lucky to get out in time. But when they caught sight of Balder, they cheered and swarmed around him until he was forced to stop.

"Well done, Mr. Templar!"

"So glad you were there. Did you get hurt at all?"

"It's amazing you saved that little girl."

"Uh..."

The voices blended into a monstrous cacophony while the people surrounded him and patted him on the back. Some even came close enough to get a hug. While he liked the gratitude, the invasion of his space made panic rise in his chest. He tried to smile, to shake the hands of those who reached out, but his teeth gritted behind his frozen lips and his heart thundered in his chest. Even Tiffany's voice faded before the raucous gratitude and joy, and black started to crowd the edges of his sight. *Must make it to the room. Must lie down before I fall.*

Hands patted him, voices chatters, children brushed up against his legs, but Balder kept his gaze fixed on the hallway to his apartment. If he fell into that dark, cold place, he had no idea what the training would make him do. The others wouldn't understand and someone could get hurt. *Please, Goddess, don't let me hurt anyone.*

A shrill whistle rose above the chaos and folks turned

to look at Angelina as she stood in the entrance with her hands on her hips.

"You all going to let him get some rest or mob him? He just ran into a burning building and saved a little girl. He just might be a little tired. Why don't you let him get to his room so he can rest, yeah?"

The sounds settled a little, but the fog continued to crowd his mind and sight. He stumbled, lurching to one side, and grabbed for anything to keep him upright.

People made sounds of dismay and reached for him again, but panic surged along with the voices of his programming, and he shied away from them.

:Balder, listen to me. You need to focus or you will hurt someone. Listen to me.:

Tiffany, help me, please.

She nodded as she sifted through him, pushing back the fog with the fierce cold of her essence. *:You don't want to hurt anyone. You made me promise I wouldn't let you hurt anyone ever again. Do you remember?:*

He nodded, trying to keep his gaze fixed on the doorway he knew stood ahead of him down the hall. *Must make it to the door. Must get inside.* He kept the mantra up as he groped blindly for the wall. If nothing else, it would hold him up until he made it safely away from people.

Tiffany stuck with him, herding him closer to his apartment door. Her cold presence kept him grounded and focused despite the panic welling in his chest. When he reached his door, his hands shook so badly he dropped his keys twice before he could shove the one he needed into the lock. It rattled like a ghost come to haunt, but he managed to turn it and damn near fell into the room, releasing them to clatter to the floor. He had to use his feet to close it again and lay there, trying to calm his breathing and racing heart.

Too many people.

:Now do you see why you aren't ready to get rid of me

yet, Balder?.:

"That's not what I meant, Tiffany, but yes, I do see why I need you. And despite what you think, I am grateful." Tears leaked out of his eyes, sliding down the sides of his head.

Eventually, he rolled over onto his stomach and crawled toward the couch under the painting of Lucifer. He rested his forehead on the seat cushions and closed his eyes. *We all need a second chance.* But even if he deserved his, how could he make it when he couldn't face adoring crowds?

"I'm so fucked up."

:Yes, you are.: Despite Tiffany's agreement, she didn't sound derisive. *:But you're making progress and getting better.:*

"*That* was better?"

He felt rather than saw her nod. *:There's a new voice in your head, a strong one starting to take control. It kept you focused on a goal to get to safety without hurting anyone. It wasn't there before Three Lakes.:*

He rolled his head to the side and focused his gaze on her hazy shape in the chair near the window. The sunshine outside gave her a golden glow that brought out the color in her eyes and hair. She met his gaze with a pensive stare. Before, Tiffany had been a target. Now he saw her for who she'd been. A beautiful, friendly, generous young woman just coming into her own. He'd robbed her of so much.

"I'm really sorry, Tiffany. I don't have enough words to express the depth of my regret for what I did."

She nodded. *:I know, but I accept your apology from where you are right now.:*

"You really think I'm getting better?"

:Yes. I can tell. You don't have nearly as many episodes with your programming, and I don't have to step in as much.: She shrugged and rubbed her arms. *:I'd like to say I did a good thing bringing you here to meet the*

Morukai, *that she's really helped you.:* Tiffany raised her gaze and met his straight on. *:But you haven't spent very much time with Kate, whereas you've spent a lot of time with...:*

"Svanhild."

:Yes, Svanhild, the Valkyrie. I think she's good for you. I'm only sorry I wasn't better for you.:

He stood and dropped himself into the couch, thinking carefully before he responded.

"You were great for me, Tiffany. Without you, I wouldn't have been ready to face the *Morukai* or anyone here in this town, much less meet Svanhild." He swallowed hard and clenched his jaw before he plowed on. "I needed you so much. You made a huge sacrifice for me and there isn't enough thanks in this world to encompass what you've done for me."

:Sacrifice?:

Balder nodded, rubbing his knees with his sweaty palms. "Yes, you sacrificed going to your eternal rest to make sure I changed. You gave up your peace for my rehabilitation. That's what I meant when I asked if the *Morukai* was helping you. I want you to be free of this responsibility. It's a huge sacrifice."

She shook her head. *:It didn't feel like a sacrifice. It felt like a necessity. I hated you and what you'd done. I needed to hurt you, to make you feel the pain and fear I did in those last few moments. It was my job to give you retribution.:*

"You've done a good job." He snorted ruefully. "The episodes with drugs and alcohol were particularly harrowing."

:Harrowing. Good word.: Tiffany laughed and he realized he'd missed it. She'd had a bright and melodic laugh, a lot like a meadow lark. Another thing he'd taken from her.

"I know I can't say sorry enough, but I am very sorry.

Thank you for all your efforts."

:It seems strange to say 'you're welcome' for retribution, but that's the right response.:

He snorted as he rose, stretching out the muscles that tightened with his panic. "No one ever said our connection was typical. But I am grateful for your help and do want the best for you in the long run."

She gave him a sad smile. *:Thank you, Balder.:*

There didn't seem to be anything else to say so he gestured to the bedroom. "I'm going to take a shower."

She nodded and turned to look out the window as he headed into his room. He wondered if she really saw the world outside, or something far more esoteric and spiritual. Shaking his head, he retreated into the bathroom to start his shower. He'd taken so much more than her life, and he'd never be able to make it up to her.

Balder turned on the water and stripped, looking at his body for the first time in years. He looked older than he remembered. Hair covered his chest, belly, balls, and legs, but instead of being only red, a few silver hairs glinted in the overhead light. Lines creased his face around his eyes and mouth, and white scars crisscrossed his back from his pain training.

The muscles on his belly had lost their definition with their youth, but his chest and arms retained their strength. He hadn't gained a lot of fat, remaining lean, but he'd lost the gauntness that had hovered around after he first left the Sword of God. *At least I no longer look like death warmed over.*

He snorted at his own sarcasm and stepped under the warm spray, allowing the water to rinse his thoughts as well as his body. He closed his eyes and threw his head back to wet his hair, trying to release his tension. The scent of smoke filled the hot air and he groaned. He'd have to scrub everything to get the soot out of his pores and clothes.

But he'd saved a little girl and done something to help rather than hurt. He hadn't worried about the child's species while navigating the smoky hallways of the apartment building. He hadn't focused on the voices or the hate, he'd simply followed Tiffany's directions to find the girl.

Balder groaned at the memories of hot, heavy air assailed his lungs and made him cough. He remembered the blistering heat radiating off the walls as he pulled the girl from her closet and returned to the apartment hallway. Tiffany had guided him down a different staircase than he'd come up and it had been cooler there with less smoke. But the outer door had been rusted shut and he'd had to return to the first floor to make his way out of the lobby. Stepping into the smoky sunlight had been like finding salvation.

He panted under the spray as the water washed away the smells and soot. Both he and the girl had survived. They were safe and he had a date.

His mind's eye filled with the image of Svanhild helping people in the tents. Her glorious hair had been gathered into a long braid down her back and still managed to shine in the dim light of the cloudy day.

Brilliant and beautiful.

He remembered the smile she gave him when she agreed to have dinner with him. It had been a combination of anticipatory and sultry, and reminded him of their weekend together. He remembered her body, sleek, toned, and so flexible, and his cock rose in appreciation. *Oh yeah.* He grabbed the soap and lathered his hands up before grabbing his shaft. He closed his eyes again and stroked, letting the hot water relax his shoulders and back as he imagined Svanhild's mouth wrapped around him.

He moaned and stroked harder, allowing the pleasure to overtake the stresses of the fire and the people's gratitude. Pleasure built from the pressure of his palm slicked by the soap and he pushed the sharp memories away. Instead, he focused on the soft sounds Svanhild made when making love with him.

"Oh, God, yes, Svanhild. Suck my cock." The whispered words sounded loud in the shower stall, but he hoped the hiss of the water covered them as his release shot from his cock accompanied by a delighted groan.

He leaned against the cold tile wall and let his tension swirl away with the hot water. He'd rarely taken any self-pleasure while in the Sword of God, the prevailing doctrine ascribing sin to the activity. But he didn't feel any ugliness while touching himself with Svanhild in his mind.

He cleaned up after, his thoughts settled and ready to face the rest of the day, but unease eeled its way through his chest. *What if I get mobbed again tonight on our date?* He couldn't face another grateful mob without someone to keep him in check. What if he had an episode with the voices? He didn't want her to see him like that.

Balder took his time drying off and combing out his hair, sifting through the ways he could explain. He'd have to talk to Svanhild about their dinner date, but he didn't know what to say. He met his gaze in the mirror and scowled, pushing the hair out of his face.

He hadn't cut it in a while and it fell in long waves over his left eye. He looked at himself critically, trying to remember some of the expressions to seduce women. He lowered his lids and gave himself a half-smile, dipping his head in a quick nod. Was that sexy? He frowned. He raised his chin, narrowed his eyes, and crossed his arms over his chest. He shook his head. He had no idea what women found sexy in a man, but he wanted to be attractive to Svanhild.

Except it wouldn't matter if he couldn't go out with her in a public place. He sighed and finished drying his body before heading back into the bedroom to dress. He'd have to ask Angelina to use the shelter phone to call the

Fix-It Cave.

And say what? Sorry, I can't come because I might kill someone?

He groaned and rubbed his face with his hands. There had to be a solution. Maybe they could have dinner at her place. Except he didn't have a vehicle and it was a fairly long walk. *We could have dinner here at the shelter.* Yeah, with forty other people sitting shoulder to shoulder in the cafeteria. *Not exactly a date.*

He still hadn't come up with an idea by the time he'd dressed. He gathered up Angelina's sweatshirt and hat, and opened the door to his apartment to scan the hallway. Most of the people had gone on with their day, leaving the entrance he could see empty. Quiet murmurs of people somewhere in the building filtered down to where he stood, but the crowd had dispersed.

He headed for the front desk, hoping Angelina would be in her usual spot. He needed to return her things and ask about getting a new coat. He paused and peeked around the corner, but the foyer had emptied out. He listened for anyone speaking to Angelina, but relative silence greeted his ears. He sighed and continued his way into the lobby, careful to keep both the doors and the front desk in view.

Angelina looked up from her book with a smile. "Hey Balder. How are you feeling?"

"Better, thank you. I've come to return your hat and sweatshirt." He handed over the items. "Thank you for their use. Did you happen to find a coat that would fit me?"

"Oh glory!" She smacked her forehead. "Yes, sorry. I totally spaced it with all the cleanup. I got everything put away and sat down to read." She shook her head. "My mind is drifty today. What size do you usually wear? We've had a couple of men's coats donated recently."

Balder grimaced as he followed her back behind the desk into her storage room. "I don't remember. I just wore what I had and I haven't gotten new clothes in a while, so I don't really know."

"We should consider more than the jacket, then." She eyed him critically as they stopped in front of some bins full of adult clothing. "I think you'd wear large or extra-large given your shoulders. How did your clothes make out after the fire?"

"Not great. I left them on the floor. I'll need to find a laundromat to get them cleaned."

"We can wash them here. We have laundry machines, but you'll need something to wear in the meantime." She rummaged through the bins. "Here's a nice button-down shirt and...this soft V-necked sweater."

She handed him the white and ginger-orange plaid cotton shirt, and a rust-colored fine wool sweater. He fingered the different fabrics with surprise. Both were high quality and in decent condition.

"Do you need pants?" She eyed his faded blue jeans.

"My jeans are in good condition, but these are the only other pair I have."

She frowned and went back to the bins. "What size? You look tall. Of course, everyone is tall compared to me. What's your inseam? Thirty-two, thirty-four?"

"Uh, I think it's thirty-two, with a thirty waist."

By the time they were done looking though the bins of clothes, he had two more pairs of jeans, a pair of casual slacks, and three more button down shirts.

"And let's not forget this." Angelina handed him a butter-soft black leather jacket. "I've been saving this for someone special and I think you're just the guy. Try it on."

He set the clothes down on the desk and shrugged into the coat. It slid over his shoulders and settled around him as if it had been made for his frame. He ran his hands over the leather and shivered in delight.

"This is beautiful, Angelina. Are you sure you want to give it to me?"

"Oh, yeah, definitely. It fits perfectly, and it's lined so

it'll keep you warm in the winter." She beamed at him. "Now you're all set."

"All set?"

"With enough clothes to make it through a week, or at least a few days."

"Oh, right." He nodded and studied the jacket. He could probably wear it for his date tonight. *Oh, shit, I still need to call Svanhild and tell her about my problem.* "Would it be possible to use the phone? I need to call Ms. Bjørnsdottir and I don't have a cell phone." He gave her an apologetic grimace.

"One of the old holdouts, huh?" Angelina chuckled and waved at the phone. "Sure. You have to dial nine first to get an outside line. Here's the number to the Fix-It Cave." She slid a list on a well-worn laminated paper across the desk.

"Thank you." He read the number, picked up the handset, and held his finger down on the hang-up button as he considered what he'd have to say.

He stood there so long Angelina raised her eyebrows and tipped her head. "Problem?"

"I'm just figuring out what to tell her." He'd never not known before, but times and circumstances had changed. And he genuinely liked Svanhild, enough to wish for their date to go well.

"I guess it depends on what you're calling about."

Balder felt the heat rise in his face. "We have a date tonight."

She raised her eyebrows. "A date, date? That's wonderful." When he shook his head, she frowned. "What's wrong?"

He sighed and replaced the handset on the cradle. "You saw what happened when I came back to the shelter. I was overwhelmed and if it hadn't been..." He paused and chose his words carefully. "If it hadn't been for you, I might have lashed out and hurt someone. I don't want the same reaction in a public place with Svanhild. What if I hurt her? Or one of the waitstaff?"

Angelina snorted. "I don't think you have to worry about Svanhild. She could kick your ass six ways from breakfast. But I can see your concern with the other people there, and I'm sure you don't want to make a bad impression on your date."

"No, I'd rather she saw me in the best light possible." *And not have to kill me after I hurt someone.* He didn't want to mention the ghost. On the other hand, Angelina seemed to be fully aware of the Elder Races in the town. Maybe she could handle Tiffany's existence.

Before he could open his mouth to broach the subject, Angelina said, "And I suppose it would cramp your style of your ghostly friend came with you, right?"

Balder blinked. "My ghostly friend?"

"Yes, the woman who came in with you. She seems to keep you grounded when things go sideways." Angelina waved at the hallway. "I noticed she used her energy to bring you back to yourself when the people here mobbed you. Very effective and very costly to her. She must care a lot about you to do that."

He wanted to scoff and admit Tiffany only did it to pay him back for all the wrongs he'd committed, but stopped before he said something stupid. He understood the sacrifice of her eternal rest for his rehabilitation, but he hadn't realized how much of herself she used to bring him out of the programming.

"I think she does in her own way. We didn't start out like that."

"Because you're former Sword of God?"

How did this woman know everything about him? The archivist saw him as a threat from previous experience with Sword of God, and made sure everyone knew it. And Balder didn't blame him.

"Yes." He nodded. "The indoctrination of their

members is extensive and rigorous. And it still has a grip on me, especially when I'm overwhelmed by people like earlier. What if the same thing happens when I'm out with Svanhild? She might be fine, but I don't want to hurt anyone else, or embarrass her."

Angelina nodded. "Where are you planning to go for dinner?"

"The Ironwood Café because it's close and I don't have a vehicle."

"Oh, that's a great place to eat." She smiled and reached for the phone. "Let me call Iris Maple and let her know you're coming. I'm sure she can set up a secluded table so you and Svanhild can have a nice dinner without the mob finding you." She widened her smile to a grin. "We can act like you're our local celebrity. Which, come to think of it, you are after saving the little girl from the fire." Angelina winked. "Let me make some phone calls. Goodness, I feel like your press secretary."

Balder gaped at her as she picked up the handset and pressed the buttons in sequence. She winked as she held it to her ear.

"Hi, Iris? It's Angelina. Yeah, great. Hey, Svanhild Bjørnsdottir invited Balder out for dinner tonight at your place, but he was mobbed with well-wishers as soon as he got back here to the shelter." She paused and laughed. "Yep, our own celebrity now...Yeah, we'll have to keep the paparazzi at bay. So do you think you could find a rather secluded place so they can eat in peace?" She nodded and smiled at him. "Thanks, Iris...Yeah, he didn't mean to be so famous...I know, I'll tell him...Thanks. Seven-thirty?...Okay. Bye."

Angelina hung up the phone and smiled. "All set. You'll have a secluded place at the cafe around seven-thirty tonight. And Iris says she's very impressed with your efforts to save folks at the fire. She says you were very helpful."

Balder shrugged one shoulder and dipped his head. "Thank you, ma'am. I'm not trying to be a hero, just couldn't leave anyone behind if I could help."

"If you don't like the word 'hero', I won't use it, but doing something if you can help is the essence of heroism. Just sayin'." Angelina nodded with understanding. "So make sure you call Svanhild and let her know you'll see her at the Ironwood at seven-thirty and don't worry. You'll have the privacy you need to survive the night."

"My survival wasn't the concern." He grimaced and she nodded, handing him the phone and the Fix-It Cave's number. He punched the buttons and waited for someone to pick up, feeling relieved.

CHAPTER ELEVEN

Svanhild hung up the phone and tried to ignore Bart's inquisitive gaze. Unfortunately, the bear shifter wouldn't be put off.

"Did I hear you have a date tonight?"

"*Ja*, you did." She nodded, refusing to blush. *Why am I acting like a* tosk? "I meant to tell you about it."

"With that guy Balder?"

"*Ja.*"

Bart's grin widened. "Wow, you really like that guy, don't you?"

Her first impulse was to scoff and roll her eyes, but she couldn't deny she'd enjoyed every minute of the weekend she'd been with Balder. And she'd invited him to dinner tonight.

"*Ja*, I do. He's not as bad as I first thought." She shrugged to hide her discomfort. She hated eating crow. *Damn feathers get stuck in my teeth.* "He saved a little girl today."

"That was him comin' out of the burning building?" Bart whistled. "Damn, I didn't think he had that kind of heroism in him."

"*Ja*, me either." She certainly hadn't seen it in him

when she first spotted him on the road to Kate's house.

"Guess he's more than just a crazy fanatic." Bart nodded as he picked up a random part he kept on the desk to tinker with. "I had a feeling about him when he came with Angelina's van. I didn't like what I saw when he got to Kate's, but he was much better by the time he showed up that evening."

"You saw more than I did." Svanhild shrugged and rubbed her neck. "So I was wondering if I'd be able to take the loaner car into town tonight for the date? I got the starter fixed on my bike, but there's a lot more wrong with her than I thought."

Bart nodded, his eyes narrowed. "Yeah, you can take the loaner tonight. Just make sure it's got a full tank of gas when you bring it back."

"I can do that. Thanks, Bart."

"Yeah, you're welcome." He nodded again. "Come with me a minute. I got an idea about somethin'."

He set the random part aside and ambled into the garage portion of the Fix-It Cave. They'd left the bay doors open to let in the fresh, warm breeze along with the sunshine, and a general sense of well-being settled over her shoulders. She followed him to the back of the garage where a large lump sat covered in a canvas tarp. He grasped the tarp and yanked it off, exposing a forest-green VW Bug from the last century.

"Wow, what's this, Bart?" Svanhild gazed at the old car.

"This is a 1965 VW Bug with all the original upholstery, paint, and chrome." He wore a proud-papa expression. "I found her at an estate sale and just had to pick her up."

"For yourself?" Svanhild snorted. "Will you fit inside?"

Bart narrowed his eyes. "Are you callin' me fat?"

"No, just big. Those European models were smaller

than the current versions." She nodded at the roof. "I think even my head would be brushing the ceiling."

Bart smirked and winked. "That may be for the original versions of this car, but this little humdinger was owned by someone who knew a little magic. The interior fits the owner so if you're big or tall, it makes room."

"Really?" She grasped the handle to pull open the driver's door and it came off in her hand. "Uh, Bart, is this part of your anti-theft mechanism?"

He laughed. "Could be. No, I think she's just old and worn out. But what I was gonna suggest is if you wanna work on her and fix her up, I'll sell her to you for a reasonable price."

Svanhild blinked. "Sell her to me? What would I do with a car? I have my bike I'm working on."

Bart leveled a stoic stare at her for several heartbeats. "I dunno. Somethin' about it just made me think you might want a working set of wheels for date nights."

"Working?" She snorted. "I don't count this as working."

He laughed. "Yeah, maybe not yet, but I think you should consider it. If you do the work, I'll sell her to you cheap. Just keep it in mind." He threw the canvas back over the forest green vehicle.

"*Ja*, I will." Not likely. She wasn't planning to stay in this town…She frowned. That didn't feel right. She'd always stayed in places for short terms, but after meeting Kate, Bart, and Balder, she hadn't had the itch to move on.

"So what time's your date?" Bart sauntered back to the office and grabbed his fidget toy as he settled into his arm chair.

"Seven-thirty."

"Nice." He sat back and nodded. "It's five thirty now. Why doncha take off around six tonight? That way you'll have plenty of time to get ready."

"That's an hour and a half. I don't need that much

time." Svanhild raised an eyebrow. "Do you need such time to get ready for nights out?"

Bart snorted. "I don't do 'nights out', but I'm smart enough to try to get the grease and dirt out from under my fingernails if I did. I'm not sure 'eau de oil pan' is a marketed scent."

Svanhild inspected her nails and grimaced. "Oh, right. I'd best take care of that."

"Yeah. So you take the loaner at six and I'll see you back here tomorrow." Bart smirked as he handed her the keys to the loaner. "And have a good time with Balder."

"*Ja, ja*, I will." She snorted as she left the office to finish up on her current project. She'd be ready way before her date, but she'd find something to do. Her gaze slid back to the large lump under the tarp. *Nah, I don't need a car.*

She shook her head and got back to work. She replaced the spark plugs and refilled the oil reservoir when a horrible thought occurred to her. *Sweet Freyja, what am I going to wear?* Guess she would need that hour and a half to get ready after all.

****

Balder took a deep breath before he grabbed the door handle for the Ironwood Café and pulled it open. Conversations swarmed over him as he stepped inside. He tugged the hat lower over his eyes and looked for Iris as he waited in the front. Several people sat at the tables and booths around the café, enjoying a late dinner, but no one paid much attention to him.

Thank God.

He stepped out of the doorway to allow others to get past while he searched for Svanhild. It hadn't turned seven thirty yet, but he didn't want to miss her if she'd arrived early.

He studied the décor. It had been designed like the

bedroom scene from a children's book he remembered from his childhood. Vines hung from the rafters with flowering trees as 'supports'. Palm fronds waved gently in the breeze created when the doors opened. The scents ranged from temperate forest to savory bistro, and he had the sensation of standing in an outdoor garden.

The breeze ruffled the foliage, creating a gentle rustle that settled his mind better than any meditation or interaction with the divine. The sounds allowed him to forget the other people in the café and enjoy the movement in the evening rays of the setting sun.

"Balder? Are you ready for dinner?" Iris Maple stood in front of him with her pale blond hair pulled into a bun with a stick shoved through it.

"Oh, yes, of course, ma'am." He bobbed his head and squared his shoulders.

"Good. Let me take you back to the grotto." She gestured him to follow her through the people and tables toward the back of the café. "You look very nice tonight."

"Thank you, ma'am." He'd taken Angelina's advice and worn the orange and white plaid shirt under the rust-colored sweater and the leather jacket. "You can give the credit to Ms. Angelina."

"She made a good choice."

Iris took him through a rough-hewn doorway into a room with intimate tables set apart to encourage the sensation of being alone. A fountain of recycled water splashed happily in the corner of the room covered in ferns, moss, water lilies, and cattails. She led him to a table screened by the fountain, adding an extra layer of anonymity.

"Would this work for you, Balder?" Iris stood back.

"Yes, thank you, ma'am." He nodded as he found a chair. "This is very nice."

"I'll bring Svanhild back as soon as she arrives." Iris nodded and sauntered away with the regality of a queen.

She wasn't human, of that he was sure, but he didn't recognize her energy from any of the Elder Races he'd met in his life.

This seems to be a common theme lately.

Balder settled into his chair and picked up the menu to scan the contents, but he couldn't read the offerings. His mind kept drifting to the novelty of going on an actual dinner date with someone because he wanted to be there. How would he speak to her? What would he say?

Probably anything other than 'have you killed anyone today' would work.

He could use some of the lines he'd been taught in the Sword of God, but none of them sounded like him. In fact, all sounded rehearsed and canned, like they came out of a badly written joke book. At least he hadn't been tongue-tied when he called her on the phone.

He still hadn't come up with any answers by the time Svanhild strode into the grotto, but he forgot his worries the moment he saw her. *Oh my God.* Her golden blonde hair had been swept up in an elegant chignon with equal tendrils falling on either side of her face. She wore a blue silk blouse over her leather pants and her leather jacket over her shoulders that slid past her curving hips. His cock reminded him of the pleasure in gripping those curves as it shuttled in and out of her hot folds, and he swallowed hard.

He belatedly remembered to get to his feet when she reached the table, hoping his jacket would hide his hard-on. She smiled and her eyes lit up with pleasure.

"Good evening, Balder. You look handsome."

"Thank you." He cleared his throat. "So do you. Look beautiful, I mean." He tried to smile, but feared it came out lopsided.

"*Tusen takk.* Did you get some new clothes? The color suits you."

"Yeah. Angelina found some for me so I could dress nice." He shrugged. "And the fire ruined my old ones, so I didn't have much else."

"They look good and the jacket is handsome." Svanhild settled herself into her chair. "I'm so glad we could do this tonight. Have you ordered yet?"

"No, I haven't been here long. And I wanted to wait for you."

"That was kindly done, *takk*. Do you know what's good here?" She opened the menu and he forgot her question as she shrugged out of her jacket.

Her full breasts pushed against the silk of her shirt and outlined her nipples. His mouth watered with the memory of suckling her breasts and more blood headed south. He squirmed into his chair and tried to remember what she'd said. *She asked a question, right?*

"I don't know. I've never eaten here, but I was considering the spaghetti carbonara."

Svanhild nodded and perused the menu a little more before setting it down and fixing her gaze on him. She frowned. *God, she can't see my hard-on, can she?*

"Are you all right? Everything okay after the fire?"

"I—" He wondered if his near-breakdown showed on his face. "I'm better now. The fire was more exciting than I expected."

"Because of the rescue?" She sipped her glass of water.

"No, because of the result of it." He straightened his shoulders and the silverware on the table. "People called me a hero."

She raised her eyebrows. "Not something you want to hear?"

How could he explain to someone who regularly brought heroes to Valhalla?

"No, I don't deserve the description." He turned his attention to the menu again, looking for comfort in the delicious-sounding meals.

"I think you're being too hard on yourself, Balder."

He frowned. "I'm former"—his voice dropped to a whisper—"Sword of God. It's not something to be proud of. In this town that's as good as a guilty verdict, and I've certainly earned their animosity. For the majority of my life my goal was to hurt people. That's not a hero, no matter which way you look at it."

He shook his head and pushed the disgust back. "I'm not a hero. I just finally woke up to being human. Ironic considering that is my species. But while humans can be heroes, I shouldn't be numbered among them."

She opened her mouth to say something, but the server came by to offer them drinks and take their order. They made their choices and soon the only sounds in the room were the few other diners, and the fountain. He wished he could be the person everyone claimed he was, but he knew his past and the things he'd done were unforgiveable. He couldn't change them. He could only work toward being better than he'd been. But that didn't include heroism.

"I still think you're selling yourself short." Svanhild gave him a pointed look.

"You of all people here know that's not true. You can see my past actions like they're written down. You'd never take me to Valhalla."

"You're right, but that's because I can't."

"Because I'm not worthy."

"No, because I'm no longer a true Valkyrie. Odin banished me, remember?"

Balder nodded slowly. "I remember."

"Right, so because I defied him, I was exiled to this world, but I lost none of my skills." She shrugged as she picked up her water glass and studied the bubbles in the liquid. "While I know heroes better than most, I'm starting to understand I might not see everything I need to know to make that decision about their worthiness."

Balder blinked. "Are you doubting your abilities?"

"No, not doubting, but I think I made snap judgments

based on what I could see at the moment rather than what the warrior had become." She met his gaze. "When I first saw you, I saw only the horrible acts you'd committed in the past."

"There are a lot of them."

She nodded. "*Ja*, but I didn't see all the work you and Tiffany had done since leaving the cult. You've changed a lot, even since you met Kate and started working for Angelina. You're not the same man who arrived in Three Lakes."

Balder tried to think of something he could say to her assessment, but the waiter returned with their meals. *I can't have changed that much.* He watched the server lay out the dishes and thanked her before she left, trying to find a response that didn't sound narcissistic or stupid.

"Not the same man, I'll grant you, but not worthy of the title of hero."

"I don't think any of us get to make that determination. Others usually give us those titles, whether we like it or not. Anyone who calls themselves hero is wishing." Svanhild shrugged. "But I couldn't take you to the Warrior's Rest even if I wanted to."

"Fortunately, you won't have to make that choice, should I die here." Which was a real possibility if he pissed off the wrong resident.

"Maybe when you arrived, but not now, Balder. Your actions today showed that more than anything else." She gave him a sad smile. "But I'd really hate for you to leave that way."

He raised his eyebrows. "So you no longer want to kill me?" He was only half-joking.

"No, at least not with the blood and gore variety. But *le petit mort* would be fine with me." She flashed him a saucy grin and his cock filled the space in his jeans.

Oh, yes, please. Except he had to be at work in the morning and didn't have a car. They could try it in his apartment, but Tiffany would be there and Angelina had rules about sex at the shelter.

"I don't know…"

"You're not interested?" Svanhild's expression shuttered and she sat back to eat a little.

"Oh no, I'm very interested, but I have no vehicle and Angelina has rules about sex at the shelter. And Tiffany is at my place." He grimaced. "Three's a crowd."

She chewed thoughtfully for a few moments. "I suppose we could go to my place and I can run you back into town later tonight."

So this is what it's like when that little devil sits on your shoulder in the cartoons.

He wanted to be with her, give her pleasure, but he didn't want to upset Angelina by being late to work so soon after his short sabbatical with Svanhild the previous weekend. He went back and forth as they continued to eat, but he kept coming back to Angelina and having a place to stay.

"Maybe we should give it a few days. I don't want to get in trouble with Angelina. Maintenance happens at all hours and I should be around to deal with it." He dipped his head in supplication. "Can I take a rain check?"

She tilted her head, her eyes narrowed. "Afraid to be alone with me now, Sword?"

"That would be 'Blade', and no ma'am. I just don't want to make you drive all over hell-and-gone just to truck my butt around." He snorted to show he teased.

"Keep telling yourself that." She grinned and he suddenly wished he'd taken her up on her offer. Sharing levity with someone happened too rarely for him.

They finished their dinner and Balder insisted on paying the check. "I invited you out after all."

"That was for lunch, and I invited you for dinner, so why should I let you?"

He opened his mouth, but paused to think it through.

"Tell you what, let me get dinner and you can treat me for the next meal."

Svanhild raised an eyebrow. "Very well. But don't go all chivalrous and forget."

"No, ma'am."

Iris gave them both a warm smile with a little wink for Balder when they came to the front. He wasn't sure what she meant, but he smiled back and thanked her for the quiet place to eat.

"You're welcome. Anytime you need it, there's a spot to eat. Especially for our local celebrity."

Balder grimaced. "I'm not someone to celebrate."

"I think the folks of Three Lakes have made their own decision about that, but I'm sure it'll die down in a day or so." Iris shot him a look of gentle rebuke. "You have a good night and we'll see you again soon."

He shoved his wallet back into his pocket and zipped up his new leather coat as they headed for the door. A few people looked up and smiled or whispered to their companions while pointing at him, but no one made a move to talk to him.

Sweet mercy, no fanfare please. He gritted his teeth and hoped they'd make it to her car without being accosted. He'd enjoyed his evening and he didn't want it to end on a sour note. Svanhild shot him a look of concern before she took his hand, and his breath evened out as her calm settled over him. He hadn't even known he'd started to panic.

"Thank you for dinner, Balder. I enjoyed it." Svanhild squeezed his hand, an oddly feminine action for such a tough woman. "Can I give you a ride home?"

"No, it's just up the street. And you're welcome. I'm sorry we couldn't make a longer night of it." He paused as he took in the other people around them on the sidewalk. "I should really consider getting a vehicle of some sort so I can get around town on my own."

"Can you drive?"

He laughed. "Yeah, just about anything with four, three, or two wheels."

"Not a unicycle?"

"I never quite mastered that one. Why, do you have a need for a one-wheeled pedaler?" He grinned as she laughed and realized she didn't do it nearly enough. *Me either, truth be told.*

"No, that paints an image I hadn't considered, nor want to." She shook her head. "Bart has an old 1965 VW Bug he thought to refurbish. He got it an estate sale and liked its bones. I don't know who bought it first, but he said it has magical energy in it. It needs some upgrades like new upholstery and paint and a fresh dashboard, but he offered to sell it to me cheap if I work on fixing it."

"I thought you had a motorcycle. What would you need a car for?"

"I do have a motorcycle, but she's not fixed yet and we might be having a lot more of these dates." She shrugged with a little smile. "At least I hope so, and I suspect Bart's loaner won't always be available." She tilted her head. "Or I could fix the old girl up for you so you could buy it."

Balder grinned. "Are you trying to sell me the Love Bug?"

She laughed. "I hadn't thought about that, but perhaps I am. It would definitely give us more loving time."

"I'll ask Bart his thoughts on the car the next time I'm at the Fix-It Cave. In the meantime—"

Balder had been keeping a weather-eye on the other people on the sidewalk, but the sound of someone saying, "There he is" made him stop and tense just as a woman with a tape recorder hustled up to them, followed by a man holding a digital SLR camera with a large lens on it. "Excuse me, sir, but aren't you the hero who saved the little girl from the Windward Apartments fire earlier this morning?"

"Uhh…"

The camera shutter clicked like a rapid fire machine gun barrage as she shoved the tape recorder up to his nose. "What can you tell us about the fire? What was it like in there? How did you find the girl? What made you think to go into a burning building to look for her?"

Balder took a step back as panic loosened his leash on the voices a little. The cold calculation of his assassin's training settled over him and he inwardly scrabbled for purchase before it swallowed him whole. Before he could do more than take a breath, Svanhild stepped in front of him with her head up and her expression set in an implacable warrior's mask as she literally stared the woman down.

"Who are you?"

"Uhh…" The reporter took her own step back and swallowed hard before she squared her shoulders. "Madeline McHenry, Upper Peninsula News. And you are?"

"Not interested in your questions or your intrusion." Svanhild crossed her arms over her chest and stood her ground while the man clicked pictures.

"The public deserves to know about its heroes." Madeline raised her chin.

"The public doesn't deserve to know anything, though they like to think so. Not all people see themselves as heroes just because the media says so." Svanhild didn't budge. "Begone, troll."

The man behind the camera gasped in astonishment as the reporter's jaw dropped. Balder suspected no one had ever called Ms. McHenry a troll before. *At least not to her face.* The smaller woman tried to bluster and gather the courage to take Svanhild on, but the Valkyrie grasped the woman's shirt at the front of her breastbone and lifted her off her feet.

Ms. McHenry squeaked in terrified surprise and the cameraman's eyebrows went up as Svanhild brought her down nose-to-nose.

"You're dangerously close to losing more than just your story, *drit*-monger. I think now would be a good time to return whence you came. Am I clear?"

The reported nodded like a bobble-head and Svanhild dropped her on her feet. She skittered away with a hesitant look back while the cameraman nodded with respect and hightailed it after her. Svanhild waited until they'd climbed into their news van before she turned around.

"Are you well, Balder?" Real concern filtered into her expression.

"I am…" It was true. He'd felt remarkably protected by his Valkyrie lover, a place he'd rarely been. "I'm very well, thank you." He tugged on his forelock in respect.

"Perhaps you should spend some time at my place tonight." She tossed her head toward the news van. "I'm not convinced they will leave you be if you head home and you'll never get any peace if they follow you to the shelter."

He snorted. "That's a very convenient excuse."

"And no less true for it." She grinned, unrepentant.

He liked her determination to get him alone. "All right, Svanhild. Let's go to your place, but I'll need a ride back tonight so Angelina doesn't worry."

"Fair enough." She nodded, but her eyes gleamed with victory.

They headed off to the car she'd borrowed and he laughed with surprised admiration. He'd never, in all his years of job-related seduction, thought he'd enjoy being with one of the Elder Races, but Svanhild ignited his pleasure and ramped it higher the more time he spent with her. He took a moment to really look at her. Despite the only the lights on the street and the moon, her golden hair glowed with a softness not even found in shampoo commercials.

She unlocked the small fuel-efficient late-model Chevy

and they climbed in. It had the "new car smell" courtesy of the little paper car silhouette hanging from the rear-view mirror, but the vehicle was clean and well-maintained.

"New car smell?" Balder raised his eyebrows.

Svanhild smirked. "Yeah. Bart says it gives people a feeling of confidence that he can fix their cars to perfection. He says humans discount their noses far too much, but he knows how to make them satisfied to leave their cars with him."

Balder laughed. "I'll have to remember that. He's right about humans and their noses."

"Oh, I don't know. Some humans use them well. Like for roses, or coffee, or fresh bread. I've seen a lot of people drift into coffee shops with fresh bread cooling, just following their noses." She grinned as they turned onto the road to the Fix-It Cave. "And perfume. The French nailed it with that."

"Do you like perfume?" He couldn't imagine a Valkyrie being attracted to scented oils.

"I don't choose to wear it. It lets your enemies know where you are, particularly demons." She shook her head. "And most are too strong for my nose or too sweet-smelling. But I do like roses and fresh bread. Cookies, too."

"Cookies?"

She didn't answer as they pulled into her driveway and parked. They got out just as her phone pinged with some sort of message. He had the oddest sensation of displacement as the battle-hardened Valkyrie pulled out a smart phone and typed something across the glass.

"Oh *helvete*." Her shoulders slumped.

"What's wrong?"

"I have to make cookies for the bake sale this coming weekend." She sounded horrified. "What do I know about making cookies?"

Balder swallowed his laugh as she shot him a panicked look. "You've never made cookies before? I thought you liked them."

"*Ja*, to eat, not to bake. When would I have time for cookies? I was too busy delivering the dead to Valhalla." She snorted and scowled.

He thought it wise not to mention her long stint in the human world.

"Is this for the shelter's bake sale on Memorial Day Weekend?"

Svanhild nodded.

"I'll help you. I know a great recipe from a lovely Norwegian woman I met a few years ago. She made the best baked goods. I asked her to show me how to do it in case I had kids one day."

Svanhild raised an eyebrow and he blushed.

"Yeah, it was a ruse at the time, but the recipe was fairly simple and so good, it was worth it." He shrugged, hoping she'd let it go. "Let's go in and get started. We have to let the butter warm up anyway. Do you have brown sugar, eggs, flour, and dark chocolate?"

"I…" She gaped at him a few moments. "I don't know. I think I have butter and sugar."

"Maybe you should ask Bart. I'm sure he'd have the ingredients, or could bring them. Or we could go out to Gemini's store and pick some up." This was the strangest conversation he'd ever had on a date, and he'd been on some weird dates in his profession. "Come on. Let's go to the store and I'll show you how to make cookies."

CHAPTER TWELVE

Svanhild still couldn't believe she'd gone shopping while on a date with Balder, but they'd found the ingredients for the recipe he had in mind at Gemini's store. The faerie teased them about being domestic, but Balder laughed it off and Svanhild couldn't help but smile.

Now they stood in her meager kitchen while she chopped dark chocolate into chunks.

"Therese called these *Deilig* Cookies."

"*Deilig*? As in 'delicious'?"

"Yep. And believe me, they live up to their name." He braced the big bowl they'd found in the cupboards against his hip as he whipped the butter and sugars together.

She had no idea why they needed two different kinds of sugar, but he'd insisted. He added three eggs, one at a time, to the batter, beating it senseless. She enjoyed watching his muscles flex while mixing. His coppery red hair fell over his eyes and he smudged some flour across his cheek as he brushed it aside.

"All right. Let's add the flour."

"Dump it all in?"

"No, Therese said it was better to do a little at a time because it made it easier to mix completely."

His muscles really strained then. She finished chopping the chocolate and just stood back to watch him flex. *Holy Freyja, he's sexy when he bakes.* She'd be happy to just sit and watch him, but he shot her a raised eyebrow and she checked the chocolate.

"I think the chocolate is done."

"Good…"

When she looked back at him, his eyes had narrowed and a half-smile curled his lips.

"Do you want it now?"

He took a breath to answer, but thought better of whatever he'd been about to say. "Yes, please. Add it to the bowl, then we'll drop it on the cookie sheets."

She scraped the chocolate into the bowl and waited for him to start stirring. When he hesitated, she raised her eyebrows. "Problem?"

"Yeah, I think you should stir it in. These are supposed to be your cookies, after all."

"Oh, *ja,* that's right." She took the bowl and the wooden spoon from him, and paused, trying to decide the easiest way to stir the thick batter.

"Put the bowl on the counter and brace it with your body. Here, like this." Balder stood behind her and wrapped his arms around her waist as he reached for the bowl. She tried not to shiver with his chest pressed to her back. "Brace the bowl with your hip, take the spoon in your fist…" He had her grip the spoon as if holding a sword. "And stir like you're making stew."

They worked the batter together for a while until it became obvious he enjoyed their closeness as much as she. A hard ridge rubbed against her backside and he paused to drop light kisses on the back of her neck. Her nipples hardened under her shirt and her pussy clenched with the memory of his talented lips on it.

"Balder?" Was that her voice sounding so breathy?

"Hmm?" He laid another kiss on her shoulder.

"I think the dough is done."

He paused to look over her shoulder. "Hmm, yes it does look ready." He didn't move.

"Should we put it on the cookie sheets?"

"Is the oven hot enough?" Why the hell did that sound so suggestive?

She cleared her throat. "I think so."

"Mmm, good." He stepped to the side, his jeans swollen at the crotch, and picked up a big soup spoon out of the drawer. "Therese said to scoop out a mounded tablespoon's worth and put it on the sheets. She usually made them big enough that only nine would fit on each sheet, about two inches apart."

He showed her what he meant and she grabbed her own spoon, filling a second cookie sheet. They still had a little dough left when they'd finished, but instead of fitting another cookie on the sheet, he set the bowl aside.

"I can't quite remember how long they're supposed to bake, so let's set it for twelve minutes and check on them." Balder opened the oven and they slid the sheets in.

"What should we do while we wait?"

Balder tipped his head as he washed his hands in the sink. "I think I might have an idea or two."

He took the bowl and grabbed her hand to tug her over to the table. "Sit for a moment, my lady."

She snorted at the title and sat in the chair, wondering where the courtliness came from.

"Good. If I've learned anything from Therese and other bakers, the one who prepares the dough gets to eat a little of it before it's made into cookies." He grinned as he set the bowl on the table. "Since I didn't eat any before we baked, I think now is a good time to make up for that."

Balder reached into the bowl and scooped out a little dough. His grin turned sultry as he reached for her face. "May I?"

Svanhild blinked. "May you what?"

"Do this." He stuck the dough to the end of her nose. She almost jerked out of his hands, but he followed up with licking the dough off in a sensual caress. She gasped just before he dropped to her lips to brand her with a kiss.

She moaned as the lust and pleasure rose through her with his lips on hers. He tasted of the cookie dough he'd stuck on her nose and of hot man. She wanted more. She opened her mouth and tilted her head as he grasped her shoulders to deepen the kiss.

"Mmm. So sweet, Svanhild." He grinned at her as she snorted.

"I don't think I've ever been referred to as 'sweet.'"

Balder tipped his head as he pushed a tendril of hair behind her ear. "Maybe I need to test the theory more. I won't be able to say with accuracy unless I try."

"You really think you'll find me 'sweet'?"

"Not until I know for sure." He winked and leaned in for another kiss, but the timer on the oven went off and he sat back. "Saved by the bell. Let's check the cookies, then I'll conduct my sweetness experiment."

She laughed and helped him pull out the pans from the oven. The cookies looked like heaven on a plate, each about four inches across. Despite the overwhelmingly sexy man in the kitchen, her mouth watered for gooey chocolate and dough. She eyed him for a moment. What would it be like to have gooey chocolate and Balder? She didn't know a mischievous smile had curled her lips until he raised his eyebrows at her.

"What are you thinking, Svanhild?"

Her smiled broadened. "I think we should test one of the cookies. You know, just to see if it's as good as you say." She raised her chin. "And I think we should test it on you."

"On me?"

"Oh, yes. On you, Balder." She took him by the hand, grabbed the bowl with the leftover dough, and headed for the bedroom. "Too bad they're too hot yet. We'll have to do it later. But I have plans for this dough."

"I'm sure they'll cool fast—"

"Then we'll enjoy them at that time. But for now, I want to enjoy you." She set the bowl on the bed and reached for his belt. "Let's get you out of those confining pants."

He allowed her to unbuckle the belt and pull down the zipper of his jeans. She licked her lips in anticipation of touching him. He moaned as she reached into his boxers and pulled out his hardening cock.

"Oh, I think this needs some extra sweetness." She shoved his jeans off his hips and reached for the bowl. "Have you heard women are big fans of chocolate?"

"I have heard that rumor, yes." He grinned down at her as she smeared dough over his cock. "Oh holy saints, that's cold!"

Svanhild laughed. "I'm sorry, but I promise to warm you up." And she licked the cookie dough.

The sweet, tasty mixture combined with his tangy pre-cum on her tongue and she damn near swooned. *Goddess, he should be bottled for sale in a delicacies shop.* The combination of flavors enticed her to suck harder. Fortunately, Balder didn't seem to mind as she went to work.

She rimmed his glans and licked the slit, savoring his pre-cum with the sweetness of the melting chocolate. The weight of his balls in her hands added to the delicious tautness of his shaft and she reveled in the sensations. She rubbed her tongue over the edges of the head until he stiffened more. *He's close.* She sealed her lips around him and increased the suction.

But he groaned and pulled his cock out of her mouth, scooting back as he held her shoulders.

She looked up at him with reproach. "But I wanted cookies 'n cream."

Balder laughed. "That may be, my sexy Valkyrie, but I'd like to enact the Ride of the Valkyries. Fair trade?"

His play on words made her grin. "Well, when you put it like that…"

He shimmied out of his jeans and boxers as she unbuttoned her silk shirt and threw it off her shoulders. His gaze latched onto her breasts and his cock flexed in appreciation. *Oh, he likes that.* She dropped the shirt and slid her hands over her hips to unbutton her jeans as slowly as possible, teasing him.

"Holy God." He swallowed hard and watched her every movement.

Svanhild loved teasing and tantalizing him. Sex before Balder had been pleasurable, but he made it fun, like a game where they both won. She slid the jeans off her hips and turned around to present him with her ass as she bent over to take them off her feet. Balder growled and scrambled off the bed. He knelt behind her before she could turn and grasped her hips before he kissed the small of her back.

Tingling pleasure zipped up her spine as he added his tongue to the top edge of her cleft. He massaged her hips before sliding his hand down to her groin and tangling his fingers in her curls. She shivered as his fingers dipped between her netherlips to expose her clit. Sweet ecstasy zinged through her, weakening her knees. She whimpered as he rubbed her nub with firm strokes and she stiffened her legs before she dropped to the floor.

"Oh, *hjertet mit,* you're so wet for me already."

"I blame your cock and the cookie dough."

He snorted with amusement. "Let me take care of both those problems."

He stepped back and rose, turning her in his arms. His cock showed his approval of her taut nipples and wet pussy as he pulled her close for a hot, deep kiss. She fell into the sensation of his clever tongue sliding over hers. *Holy*

Freyja, I want him to do this to me forever.

The thought was so astonishing she almost froze, but his kiss pulled her back into his erotic efforts and she let it go. He tugged her to the bed and pushed her onto it, following her until he crouched over her. His cock hung below his body, the tip dripping with his arousal and her mouth watered with the urge to suck on it again. She wriggled in hopes of enticing him to rub the hard length against her aching nether lips, but he ignored her. When he wouldn't move from the attention he gave to her breasts, she reached for his shaft, tugging him closer.

"You're a minx, *kjære*." He rocked his hips so his cock slid along her slit and she whimpered. "That's it. Feel me wet with your cream, *hjertet mit*."

Until Balder, she'd never considered speaking during sex as erotic, but his soft, gravelly voice turned her on. It sparked her pleasure even more than the sensations of his cock on her netherlips.

"Let me wet you for real, *kjekken*. Fill me with your shaft."

"Sweet heaven above." Balder appeared to enjoy her speaking to him as much as she did because he thrust in hard, filling her completely.

They both moaned and she held him tight to her body, her hands clasping his hips between her legs.

"Don't move."

"What?" He raised his head to look down at her.

"Not just yet. Just let me savor your presence inside me."

She savored more than just his cock. She enjoyed the heat and weight of his body over her. She reveled in his lovemaking, but she'd started to see him as more than a physical outlet for her lust. He had smart responses to their discussions. He saw both sides to the question of humans and Elder Races. And deep down, below the training and the horrible things he'd been programmed to do, he was kind and compassionate. Her Valkyrie senses had already started to pick up on his qualities shining through the tarnish.

"Let me love you, Svanhild. Let me show you pleasure." Balder moved, sliding his cock out of her slick pussy, only to reverse and thrust back in. "Oh God, you're so hot and tight, *hjertet mit*."

My heart. He kept saying that. She wasn't sure he even knew he'd spoken the endearments, but his continued motions built up her arousal too much for her to care if he'd done it intentionally. He rocked his hips, steadily building desire and need. He never looked away from her as he moved, his expression intense and watchful.

Her orgasm came upon her so fast she didn't have time to do more than throw her head back and clamp down on his cock. She wailed her delight, sailing beyond the heavens, beyond the stars where Valhalla resided, and let go of her earthly worries.

When she settled back down into her body, Balder brushed the sides of her face with his fingers, the long forelock of ginger hair falling over them. It was soft and smelled of him mixed with some sort of masculine scented shampoo. *I love his hair*. That wasn't all she loved about him.

Love. The word wasn't in her vocabulary, at least not when it came to men. But Balder wasn't an ordinary man to her. *Not anymore*. In just a few days, he'd become something more, something precious and valuable to be defended and held. Not a possession, but definitely a treasure. *I need him...to make me laugh, to make me feel*.

He smiled down at her. "You look somewhat satisfied, *kjære*. Perhapø I haven't done enough, yes?"

"Not done enough?" She blinked up at him. What more could he do? She was already happy and boneless. And she didn't mind staying that way.

****

Balder grinned at Svanhild's relaxed confusion. He'd pleasured her well, but he wasn't done yet. "No, *hjertet mit,* not nearly enough. Come ride me. Ride me like a true Valkyrie."

Her eyes flashed with lusty pleasure and she rolled over with him until she sat astride his stiff shaft. She squeezed her inner muscles around him and he swore he saw stars. Every time they came together like this, he fell deeper under her spell, and his heart opened more and more. He wanted her, but not just for sex. He wanted time with her to share meals and make cookies, to talk of inconsequential things, to revel in her company even with they didn't speak.

I'm in love with her.

He gasped in surprise, and his eyes widened. Fortunately, Svanhild had closed hers and rode him hard and fast, unaware that something momentous had happened.

Maybe not for her. What would a Valkyrie want with an ex-Sword of God assassin? He wasn't worthy of her heart or her love. He made a decent lover, a fuck-buddy as he'd heard them called, but not someone worth a deeper connection. He was too tainted and damaged. *Oh, God, I'm not good enough.*

"Oh, yes, Svanhild. Ride me hard. Ride me."

He thrust his hips up, making her moan as she sat him with each undulation. He shoved the aching sorrow away from him and strove to give her another powerful orgasm to match the one building inside him.

He refused to let the disappointment of his realization mar the beauty of watching Svanhild take her pleasure from his body. Her breasts bounced in erotic motion and he gripped her hips to keep them steady. He wanted her to sail into the cosmos, behind reach of anger, sorrow, and hatred.

He wished his past could be cleansed with his release, as if she could purify him from the hurts he'd caused.

Take me, my love. Take all of me and use your light to scrub away the ugly.

He wanted to say the words aloud, but all that came out as he reached his peak was an ecstatic groan. His release swamped his mind and shot him away from his body, into nothing but bliss. He wished he could stay there forever, in the place of such peace and love, but he knew it wouldn't last long and he'd have to face himself once more.

But for now, he'd revel in her beauty and pleasure, and count it as enough.

CHAPTER THIRTEEN

"Make sure the table cloths are in the van, Balder. And the chairs. I have the money box." Angelina lifted the metal ammo can she used for the bake sale donations.

"Yes, ma'am. I got the chairs. I'll check on the table cloths."

Five a.m. came earlier than he remembered and he stifled a yawn as he looked through the milk crates holding the supplies for the bake sale. *Of course, I don't usually spend the evening in the arms of my lover.* Svanhild had brought him back to the shelter a little after midnight and Tiffany had given him an indignant glare, but said nothing. He'd wondered if she questioned the method of his positive changes, but was too tired to analyze the idea and let it go for another time.

In the early morning silence before the town work up, the question returned to the forefront of his mind. Did Tiffany resent his efforts and progress toward healing after all the hurts he'd caused? Guilt still rode his soul and he'd never forget what he'd done to her family and others, but he wanted to move on. And Svanhild was helping him do that.

Maybe Tiffany wants me to stay miserable. Maybe I

should...

The thought seemed so ugly he gagged and had to take a few deep breaths. Surely the Goddess and the *Morukai* hadn't wished him to be miserable forever. Repentant, yes, but not slogging through guilt, fear, depression, and despair every waking moment. He shook his head as he found the table cloths and the chairs Angelina had asked about. Change had already started within him and he wanted it to continue.

"Table cloths and chairs accounted for." He nodded to Angelina as she appeared beside him, Tiffany hovering in the background. "Anything else we need before we go?"

"Nope. The cookies and the other baked goodies are all loaded up. Looks like we're ready." She rattled the keys. "Climb in the front. Let's get this show on the road."

Balder settled himself in the passenger seat as Angelina started up the van and they headed toward the lake. He smothered a yawn and she handed him a Thermos of hot liquid.

"Coffee. There are two mugs in the crates in the back. Best thing humans ever came up with." She gave him sleepy grin. "Coffee makes the sun rise as far as I'm concerned."

Balder laughed as they stopped in front of their marked spot on the road along Harbor Lake, the small body of water attached to Superior. The road would be closed for three days for the holiday weekend and tourists, locals, and nearby townsfolk would be roaming around enjoying the vendors. Angelina told him she made three quarters of her yearly budget on this one weekend.

He looked forward to the event. Usually he hated being around people, the crowds pressing on him and the voices in his head screaming to kill everyone who wasn't strictly human. But something about this town and these people made him curious to see how they relaxed. And he wanted to relax with them. *Now, if I can just tune out the voices enough to do so.* It would be a challenge, but he liked the people and the town of Three Lakes enough to try.

He helped Angelina unload and set up her stand while Tiffany drifted around them. She murmured directions every now and again, and soon they had the table and chairs set out. Angelina erected two café umbrellas to keep the cookies from melting in the sun or stay dry in the rain.

"Michigan can be so temperamental, even in the summer." Angelina shook out a table cloth with bright multi-colored hand prints all over it. "But I've done this a few years now so I've got it covered."

Balder shot a look at the sky. The sunshine from the day before returned and it looked as if they'd have another clear day. They set out the baked goods in companionable silence while others bustled around them setting up their own tables and kiosks. He saw the Gitchegumee Inn had set up across from a candle-making kiosk. A few tables down he saw the Library with shelves of books and even a set of chairs for folks to listen to storytime. The medical clinic and the sheriff's office had their own spaces, and he saw the Warbler Springs Fire Department had set up a table with rubber boots for donations.

Tiffany's gaze seemed stuck on the firefighters standing around their table.

"You can go and visit if you like, Tiffany." Balder chuckled. "No harm in looking."

Tiffany gave him one of her rare smiles, but shook her head. *:I'm afraid they'll see me.:*

He frowned as he set out trays of cookies Angelina handed him. "Why would they see you?"

:Because some of them are Elder Races.:

He shrugged one shoulder. "They'll only see you if you let them. The Elder Races can't see ghosts any more than humans can."

:I'm not a voyeur.: Tiffany managed to blush enough to show on her pale cheeks.

"You're not?" Balder raised an eyebrow as he stacked the empty milk crates behind the chairs. "Could've fooled me."

Tiffany stuck her tongue out at him and he laughed, making Angelina throw him an amused smile. It felt good to tease Tiffany. He remembered the times before her death when they'd had fun. Not 'good, clean fun', but fun. Now it seemed more pure and real.

"You go on ahead and ogle them, Tiffany. I'm sure they're used it." Angelina nodded before she bent down to grab another plate of cookies.

Balder and Tiffany both paused. He'd forgotten Angelina could see her.

:She can see me?: Tiffany swallowed hard as her eyes grew wide.

"You can really see her, Angelina?" Balder fingered the little hand-written signs for the cookie plates.

"Not always, but I can feel her around you and I know when you're talking to her. And if she's half as interested in men as she was when she was alive, I'd say she should go look at the hot firefighters." Angelina winked. "I would be if I was her. What kind of a person wouldn't go look? Anyone who appreciates the male form, no matter the species, would enjoy those firefighters. Don't worry, Tiffany. I'll keep Balder in line while you go observe them."

Tiffany blinked, blushed, and disappeared.

Balder laughed again and didn't begrudge her the freedom to look. Hell, he'd looked at women for years, both on and off assignment. *If I stopped looking, I'd be dead.* Of course, it amused him that Tiffany was dead and still looked. *Good to know.*

With the tables and umbrellas set up, the cookies displayed with their pretty little signs, Balder and Angelina settled into the chairs. She handed him a steaming mug of coffee and they enjoyed the sounds and smells of the morning. He sat back and let himself relax a little, an unusual aspect after having been hyper-vigilant for all of his adult life. He never stopped listening and watching, but his shoulders loosened and he breathed a little easier.

"How are you and Svanhild getting along?" Angelina smiled at him over her mug.

He said nothing for a long time, unused to the idea of sharing his personal feelings with anyone other than Tiffany. Angelina seemed content to wait on him, her hands cradling the hot coffee as she sat in her chair, bundled up against the early summer chill. He didn't want to tell anyone how he felt, not until he understood the emotions floating through him. He thought of deflecting her with questions about Luke, but rejected the idea. *It's none of my business.* Angelina understood him better than most people and he figured he owed her a little description.

"I don't know."

"You don't know?" Angelina raised her eyebrows. "That's not a good sign."

"No, no, that's not what I meant." He squeezed his mug and stared at the contents, hoping the swirls of hot liquid and steam would help him sort out his thoughts. "We get along well. Considering our backgrounds, you could say we're getting along famously."

Angelina snorted. "Especially in bed, I'm guessing."

Heat bloomed across his cheeks and he couldn't meet her eyes. "Yes."

"But?" She prompted him with a touch on his shoulder and he met her gaze.

"There is always one of those, isn't there?"

She nodded. "More often than not."

"But I'm feeling emotions I've never experienced before." He frowned, trying to put into words things almost too nebulous to mention. "I like her, it's true, but I want more…I think. I want her smiles, her joy, I want to do things that bring her more of both. And I want to defend her." He snorted and shook his head. "As if I could defend a Valkyrie."

Angelina tilted her head with a thoughtful grimace. "Actually, warriors sometimes need the biggest defenders. Especially of their hearts and homes. They're used to being the ones who fight, but when it comes to their inner fortifications..." She shrugged. "You're a fighter. I'm sure you know this."

"I have the skills, it's true. But that's not who I am now." He rubbed his bottom lip. "I don't think I want to be a fighter anymore."

"Oh, that's good." She sighed theatrically. "I don't want to find another handyman."

He laughed at her wink, but she sobered and sipped her coffee. He sensed she would say more and held his peace.

"Don't give up on your heart, Balder." She gave him a sad smile. "It's wiser than you know and sometimes it asks for odd things, but they're not bad, and they definitely help you grow into a better person. Maybe even a different kind of fighter. Have you told Svanhild how you feel?"

He shook his head. "Not in clear words, no. I, uh. I just came to the realization last night."

Angelina nodded. "It's okay to savor it. It's your treasure after all. But don't wait too long to tell her. It might help her understand herself and you."

He grimaced. "That's more frightening than facing off with a dragon."

She laughed. "Yes. The dragon can kill you, but love can scar your soul." She gave him another sad smile, the corners of her mouth pulling down, and he wondered who'd scarred hers. *Maybe it's Luke.* "But the good news is scars provide character and strength in tough times. And help you see you can survive and work things out because you've done it before."

He nodded, still wondering if she talked about him or herself.

They would've said more, but the festival had gotten underway and some early shoppers stopped by the table to buy cookies and donate to the shelter. At first, he hung back and let Angelina do the talking as he watched people approach. But eventually, he put on his public façade and hocked delicious desserts. His undercover role-playing mask fit like a well-worn glove over him and he used it to the best of his ability. He just hoped he could take it back off again when it was time.

Later in the morning, Kate Blackamber arrived dragging a wagon piled high with cookies. A tall, long-haired werewolf stood behind her, his gaze on Balder. Balder's smile froze and panic worked its way up from his gut. *Sweet mercy, that must be Jayson Blackamber.* Balder remembered what Luke had said about Jayson's can of whoop-ass. Did he know what Balder had done to Tiffany's family? The voices in his head rose in pitch and urgency and he forced himself to stand back.

He's not the enemy. He tried to scream louder than the programming and clenched his fists to keep from moving. *Stay still. Stay safe.*

A touch on his shoulder made him open his eyes—when had he closed them?—and Angelina gave him a concerned frown.

"Are you all right, Balder?"

The voices quieted and the silence in his head became deafening. "Uh, yes, yes, thank you. Angelina." He tried to find his smile. "That sure looks like a lot of cookies." He switched his gaze to Kate's. "What all did you bring?"

The tall werewolf stared at him a few moments before Kate snorted. "What didn't I bring?" She grinned. "Seven layer cookies, chocolate chip kiss cookies, thumb print cookies, shortbread without nuts, cookie-cutter sugar cookies, lemon bars, coconut macaroons, and peanut butter cookies."

"She's been baking for like three days straight. I've

never smelled so much chocolate and sugar in my life." The man shook his head and held out his hand, palm down. "Hi, I'm Jayson, Kate's husband."

Balder cleared his throat. "Yes, hi. Balder Templar. Nice to meet you."

The *Morukai* had married a werewolf? *I thought he was just a Navy SpecOps guy.* Balder tried to think of why that seemed strange to him, but nothing logical came to mind. The town was full of the Elder Races mixed with humans, but everyone took it in stride. *Or doesn't know.* But it didn't seem to matter. If he'd learned nothing from Tiffany, he at least understood the monsters weren't always non-human. *Like me. I'm the monster here.*

"Thank you so much, Kate. Your cookies are magical and they always sell so well." Angelina beamed, patting Balder's shoulder. "Balder, help me arrange them so folks can see them. Once people find out they're from Kate, they'll go fast."

He nodded and took the plates Jayson handed to him. The Alpha werewolf shot him an enigmatic smile and helped him rearrange them on the table. He shifted closer to Balder while the women talked and seemed to be waiting for him to speak. Tiffany reappeared on the other side of the table, her gaze glued to Jayson.

:That's the Alpha.: Her voice sounded reverent in Balder's head.

He nodded and moved aside a plate of jelly-filled cookies to make room for the lemon bars.

:Why is he here? Does he know who you are and what you've done?:

Balder shrugged and hoped to God Jayson didn't know his past. Given that he'd married the *Morukai*, Balder suspected the man knew everything.

"How are you fitting in to our town, Mr. Templar?" Jayson gave him a friendly smile, but his eyes remained wary.

"I don't know if I fit in yet, but I like it here. It's not like anywhere else I've ever been."

Jayson snorted ruefully. "Ain't that the truth? It's a great little town, though. Good community."

"I see that." Balder nodded.

They continued to work silently a few moments while Tiffany stared and the other women gabbed about events going on during the weekend.

"You do know there's a higher than usual population of Elder Races, right?" Jayson's comment was conversational, but Balder suspected it wasn't casual.

"Yes, sir, I do."

"And I understand from Kate that you're former Sword of God?"

An edge appeared in his voice and Balder tensed. He had no illusions about Jayson's abilities. While he didn't know what the man did for a living now, he remembered Luke's warning about his skillset. *Aw hell.* Add that to a werewolf's strength and speed, and he'd be dead meat. *I don't want to fight.* Hell, he didn't want to die, but he'd defend himself. *If I can.* He just didn't want to damage the relationship he had with the residents of this town.

"Yes, that's right."

"Why are you here, then?" Jayson didn't pull any punches. *Probably not physically, either.*

"Redemption." Balder meant the word to the depths of his soul. He'd done horrible things, and he took responsibility for them. Now he wanted to help his community and atone for his actions. *And stay here with Svanhild.* The thought sent shock through his system, but he didn't have time to think about it at the moment.

"That could take awhile."

"Yes, sir. I have a lot to make up for." He raised his gaze and met Jayson's head-on. "I can't change the past. I can only work on being better from now on."

Jayson measured him with his gaze, his expression

thoughtful. After several heartbeats, he nodded and smiled, clapping Balder on the shoulder.

"That's the best answer I could ever expect, Mr. Templar. I'm glad to hear it. Any progress?"

"Some, sir. I still have a long way to go."

Jayson nodded again. "Yeah, but you're making the effort. That's half the battle right there." He shot a look at his wife before sobering. "I've met Sword of God before, when they sent someone here to kill Kate."

Balder's gut sank and his shoulders slumped. "I'm very sorry, sir. They aren't good people and they don't understand…well, much of anything."

"No, they don't. I stopped him, but they still sent another assassin to kill our librarian, Mr. MacGregor. His wife got that one. Do you see where I'm going with this?"

"Yes, I think so, sir. If it's all the same to you, I'd rather not be the next dead guy on your list. I don't want to kill anyone ever again, but I will defend myself." He shot a look at the women before returning his gaze to the Alpha werewolf. "Angelina is helping me regain control after all the programming and so is my friend Svanhild."

"That's the Valkyrie, right?"

"Yes, sir." Balder straightened some of the plates as he gathered his thoughts. "I can't guarantee I won't make mistakes, but I'm trying hard not to give into those old patterns. I don't want to die, but I don't want to hurt anyone either." He swallowed hard. "I'm hoping my friends will be able to stop me if I lose control."

Jayson nodded slowly, inhaling the way Balder remembered Tiffany's father did when he searched out lies.

"If they don't, we will, Mr. Templar. I appreciate your awareness and efforts, but I'm still going to keep an eye on you. We have some very clear memories of the Sword of God and they aren't pretty."

"I understand, sir." What else could he say? They had every reason to hate him and who they perceived him to be.

He couldn't argue. He'd be wary and skeptical, too.

"You're not scaring him, are you, Jayson?" Kate's voice cut through the tension and Balder sighed as his shoulders relaxed.

"No, just getting an understanding between us."

Kate swung her gaze back and forth between them, her eyes narrowed. "Oh, glory, you're not doing the old-fashioned pissing contest, are you? I couldn't stand that when I was single."

"Now, now, you have to leave us some of our male illusions. Sometimes we have to strut around all puffed up and beat our chests. It's a guy thing." Jayson gave her an unrepentant grin and winked.

After a few moments, she smiled and shook her head. More of Balder's concerns melted.

"A guy thing. Nice. Just don't hurt each other, okay? I have this sneaking suspicion you're both going to need each other as time goes by."

"Oh, really? Is that a proclamation or just an observation?" Jayson grasped his wife and pulled her close, kissing the side of her head.

"What fun would it be if I told you?" She grinned at his groan. "I'm glad to see you doing so much better, Balder. Keep up the good work. Now, I want to go visit with those sexy firefighters."

"Firefighters? I thought you preferred Navy SEALs." Jayson sounded indignant, but he grinned.

"Oh, you know you're my all-time favorite, especially for all the times you saved the world. But let's go give some love to the local home-grown heroes." She took Jayson's arm and dragged him toward the firefighters' table while Angelina laughed.

"Firefighters get all the love at these festivals." She sighed dramatically, but merriment danced in her eyes. "But quite a few of them come to my table to donate to the shelter just to get the goodies."

Balder nodded. "I can see why. After all the cookies Kate brought, there's a lot to choose from."

"Oh, you if think this is a lot, just wait. She'll bring more tomorrow and the next day, too." Angelina grinned. "We're set for cookies."

"Svanhild has some to bring as well, but she has to work today."

Angelina raised her eyebrows. "Really? That's terrific."

Balder nodded. "I helped her make them." He refrained from mentioning what accompanied the cookie baking process.

"Oh-ho, you have unexpected talents."

He laughed. "Some, but don't compare me to Kate. She wins."

Angelina snorted. "No one does cookies like Kate."

He had to agree, although he was more than happy to make more cookies with Svanhild. *Among other things.* He hoped she'd be able to stop by.

CHAPTER FOURTEEN

The festival celebrating Memorial Day went by in a blur, but Balder couldn't remember a time he enjoyed more. Just as Angelina predicted, Kate Blackamber brought cookies each day, and they sold so fast they couldn't keep them on the table. Svanhild had to work the first two days, but she came by in the evenings to help pack up and spend some time with Balder. He enjoyed her visits and wanted to spend more time with her, but random maintenance issues cropped up at the shelter. By the time he fixed them, he fell into bed, asleep before he hit the pillow.

Angelina ribbed him a little for the looks he shared with Svanhild, and he couldn't help but grin. He enjoyed the feeling of having Svanhild in his life and bed, but worried how Tiffany would take it. She hadn't reacted much at all. She'd only cocked her head, given him a half smile, and disappeared to ogle the firefighters again.

An emergency maintenance issue got Balder out of bed early the last day and he didn't arrive at the bake sale table until after lunch time. Angelina was helping some people from out of town who chatted with her about the shelter and its mission. Balder nodded to her, but stayed out of the way. Something about the people made him hesitant to draw attention to himself. He'd met many such folks from all walks of life during his time in the Sword of God. He was worse than all of them, but he still kept his distance.

He turned his attention to the table and anyone else coming to investigate the goodies. The day had warmed up and a mellow breeze blew in from Harbor Lake. A small boy stood to the side, fooling with a plastic model airplane. Balder recognized him as the boy he met in the library just a week before. He shot a look at the crowd, wondering where the vampire was.

The boy tossed his airplane a few times, but for some reason it wouldn't sail far. After the third time, Balder came around the table and crouched to pick up the latest crash, holding the plane out to the boy.

"Looks like the tail fins are causing drag. You might need a stabilizing strut."

The boy took the plane and stared at Balder, his expression wary and grave. Though he looked to be only five or six years old, he had an otherworldliness in his silver-gray eyes that spoke of more time and experience.

"Who are you?" The question came out with reserve, and his body tensed as if poised to run.

"My name's Balder. I work at the shelter with Ms. Angelina." He held out his hand to shake it. "I think I met you a few days ago at the library, right?"

The boy considered him a long time and Balder's heart ached. He'd tried not to hurt children, but he'd done so inadvertently while assassinating their parents. While he didn't recognize this dark-haired boy from his past, more than likely someone from the Sword of God had hurt him.

"Nice to meet you." He didn't sound very pleased to meet Balder, nor did he take the offered hand, but he had manners. "Are you a bad man like my Papa says?"

The way he asked confirmed Balder's suspicions. *Yeah, when one came to kill his father*. Balder thought hard before he answered. His first reaction was to deny it, but he couldn't deny his past.

"I used to be." Balder nodded. "But I stopped doing that and my friends Kate Blackamber and Ms. Angelina are helping me get better."

The boy nodded. "You don't seem like the other bad man I knew. He tried to kill Papa Drake."

Balder's heart sank. "I've heard. I'm sorry."

"Are you here to kill someone?" The boy clutched the plane to his chest and stared at Balder hard, his shoulders tight.

"No, I'm not. I came here to ask the *Morukai* for help so I don't have to live like that anymore."

"Is she going to help you?"

Balder nodded. "Yes, she is. She thinks I can get better."

"My mama and Papa Drake don't like the bad men." The boy tilted his head and narrowed his eyes. "I don't like them, either. But you're different."

"Really? How am I different?" Maybe there was hope for him if this little boy could see improvement.

"You smell like…" He frowned as he searched for the right description. "Like fireplace smoke and cookies."

A smile curled Balder's lips before he could stop it. "I have been helping Ms. Angelina at the bake sale table. Maybe that's why I smell like cookies."

The boy shot a look at the table, shrugged then held out the plane. "Can you fix it?"

Balder took the plane and examined it a little closer. "Looks like we need to make new tail fins for it. A strut won't be enough. Come over to the table. I think we have some paper plates we can use to make new fins."

The boy followed him as he returned to the table and picked up the pen Angelina used for writing up receipts for the donations. "Let's use these old paper plates and trace out a new set of fins. We can probably use two plates to be strong enough for the tail. What do you think…?"

He waited for the boy to supply his name. "Tom. And I think that might work."

"All right. Let's pull out the tail fins and trace them on the plate. Do you want to do that?" Balder held out the pen. "I'll hold the fins down and you trace them."

"Okay." Tom picked up the pen and traced around the shape of the plastic fins. His little tongue stuck out of the side of his mouth as he concentrated. "There. Done."

"Good." Balder lifted the fins away. "Now we need to find a pair of scissors and some tape so the plates stay together." He turned to look over his shoulder. "Ms. Angelina, do you have some scissors?"

"I have a pair of scissors." The vendor at the next table held up a pair. "You may use them if you're careful."

"Thank you." Tom took them with a grave nod. "Here, Balder."

"Thanks. Let's try to cut them now." Balder cut along the lines drawn on the plate. He pulled out the shape and handed it to Tom. "Will that fit?"

They held it up to the tail fins and made a few adjustments before using some tape to keep the plate pieces together. With the fins reinforced, they slid it into the slot where the old ones sat and Balder handed Tom the plane.

"Shall we try it?"

Tom bit his lip. "Okay." He turned his head to scan for a place to toss the plane. "Where?"

"There's an open spot behind the chairs here. That way it won't get stepped on when it lands." Balder gestured to the space between the road and the berm above the beach. "Try it there."

Tom hesitated, looking around for something. Evidently he found it and nodded before he strode behind the table. He didn't go far, keeping whatever he'd been searching for in sight, but he stopped, pulled his hand back, and threw the plane. It did an immediate nose-dive.

"Hmm, I think the flaps need to be adjusted." Balder

picked up the plane and fiddled with the new fins until they tilted up a little. "Try it now."

Tom threw the plane again. This time it sailed up before stalling and spiraling to the ground. Balder adjusted the fins a bit more and on the third try, the plane flew straight and true. Everyone cheered and Tom grinned as he ran back with his toy.

"Looks like it works pretty well now." Balder smiled, his heart warming more than he thought it would.

"It does. Thank you, Balder."

"You're welcome." He patted the boy on his shoulder. "I'm happy I can help."

A snarl was the only warning he had before a juggernaut hit him like Thor's hammer. The voices in his head rose in a furious crescendo and his fighting skills took over as they hit the sand of the berm. Balder twisted into a roll, using the momentum to throw the creature off him. Flashing red eyes and fangs hit his awareness after he'd tossed the being from him, and he spun into a fighting stance, pushing all other sounds away as he focused.

His attacker moved with lightning swiftness and came at him again, but Balder was ready. Again he used his assailant's energy and momentum against him, this time swinging him into the berm, away from people. The voices screamed in his head, ordering him to kill what came after him. He gritted his teeth and pushed them back. Even if he wanted to kill, he had no weapons. All he could do is stay alive.

And that might be a challenge against a vampire.

He recognized the man who rolled to his feet dressed like a scholar with a pair of khaki shorts and a light button-down short-sleeved shirt. But though he wore glasses and his silver hair lay styled against his skull, his glowing red eyes and elongated canines marked him as something more than human. *Tom's father from the library.*

He came at Balder again and hit him with enough force

to knock him down. Balder got his knees up between them, but the fury of the vampire gave him extra strength, and Balder could only hold him off.

"You touched my son." The snarl was barely coherent. "I will kill you and scatter your body where only the dryads can find your bits."

Balder didn't doubt it, but with the vampire's hands around his throat cutting off the air, he didn't have the voice to protest his innocence. He gritted his teeth and tore at the vampire's hands, his vision going gray. *Must stay conscious. Must stay alive. He had to.* The Goddess had tasked him with helping Svanhild to heal and find redemption. He had to stay alive for her.

And I love her.

He hadn't had the chance to tell her and that meant more than even the Goddess's charge.

Tears leaked from his eyes as he held on, but before he lost all sense of time and place, a great golden glow appeared behind the vampire and a brilliant feminine hand gripped his shoulder. The vampire snarled, but the hand tugged at him with insistence and eventually he released Balder's throat.

Blessed, sweet air filled his chest and he gasped as the darkness retreated from his vision. *Thank you, Goddess.* He lay in the sand, his eyes closed, and just breathed. In the past he would've been on his feet and in a defensive stance immediately, but he couldn't dredge up the energy. If he was meant to die on the shores of Harbor Lake on Memorial Day weekend, so be it.

Voices from the crowd penetrated the adrenaline pounding in his skull. Tom's higher pitched complaints slid between the strident voices of the adults. Balder remained still, catching his breath and regrouping. *I don't want to fight.* He didn't particularly want to die, either, but interest in fighting against the residents of his new adoptive town had deserted him.

I want to stay here. With Svanhild and Angelina and the Morukai.

He'd found home. His past would always haunt him and he accepted the wariness from the other residents of town. The Sword of God had harmed these people and his previous membership made him suspect. He was determined prove his innocence, but he would defend himself if attacked. *Just not kill if I can avoid it.*

He thought back over the fight he'd survived, glad he'd made no aggressive moves, even when the vampire came for him. *Maybe I am finally starting to heal.* The voices had screamed at him, but he'd kept his focus on evasion and defense rather than killing.

Good thing, because he didn't want to kill Tom's dad.

Balder sucked in a deep breath and opened his eyes. The wide bowl of the blue sky greeted him, bathed in the brilliant sunshine of a Warbler Peninsula afternoon. He'd asked Angelina why they called it the Warbler Peninsula and she'd showed him a satellite map of northern Michigan. A spit of land stuck into Lake Superior with the distinct shape of the little bird's head. Three Lakes sat between three smaller lakes on the back of the head of the warbler. He couldn't think of a better place to be.

"Hey, Balder, are you all right?" Jayson appeared beside him, offering him a hand.

"Yes, thank you. Just trying to collect my thoughts."

"Well, let's get you upright at least. The women are worried about you lying there in the sand." Jayson grinned and hauled Balder to his feet.

He brushed himself off and took his time getting used to being vertical. He didn't really want to face the community just yet. They'd blame him for the altercation. He'd heard it all before. If he hadn't been in town, the vampire wouldn't have attacked him. Goddess, he didn't want to move on.

"Better?" Jayson brushed off his back.

"Yes, thanks."

"Good. Come back over to the table so the doc can check you out."

Balder shook his head. "I'm all right. I don't need a doctor."

Jayson snorted. "The bruising on your throat suggests otherwise."

Balder rubbed his neck as they returned to the table and the anxious faces waiting there, including Tom's.

"Are you okay, Balder?" The little boy clutched his plane again.

"I will be, Tom." He tried to smile even as his voice came out as a painful croak.

"Let's have a look at you." The doctor was a Hispanic woman with Peruvian features and her expression remained professionally impassive. "Do you make a habit of fighting, Mr. Templar?"

"No, ma'am. Not for a long time." Balder held still while the doctor checked his throat.

"He wasn't fighting, Mama. Papa Drake attacked him." Tom tugged earnestly on the doctor's shirt. "Honest. Balder wasn't doing anything. He helped me fix my plane." The boy held up the toy as evidence. "See? He helped me make the flaps."

"Is this true?" The doctor met Balder's gaze and he suspected he teetered on the edge of life and death. She might appear small, but like Tom, she had a powerful otherworldliness disguised by her outward appearance.

"Yes, ma'am." He swallowed painfully and hoped there wasn't any permanent damage to his throat.

"He really did help, Mama. I know he used to be with the bad men, but he's different. He smells different. Can't you tell? Please don't be mad at him." Tom bit his bottom lip and sent his mother a hopeful look.

"You're former Sword of God?" Her murmur barely reached his ears, but he heard it.

"Yes, ma'am."

Her mouth tightened as she probed his neck. "You know how we feel about the members of that cult?"

"Yes, ma'am." And if he hadn't before, he certainly knew now. He grimaced as she hit a particularly tender spot.

"Tom's entire family was murdered by those monsters, so if he says you're different, that's high praise." She tilted her head to get a better look at his neck. "You have multiple contusions all around your throat. It'll be tender for several days, but it should heal completely. However, if the swelling gets bad, come to the clinic to have it treated. I can prescribe a painkiller if you like."

"No, thank you, ma'am. I'll just take over-the-counter pain relief."

"All right." She hesitated a moment, considering him with narrowed eyes. "On behalf of my husband, I'm sorry. He had reason to attack you, but that doesn't make it right."

Balder nodded. "Yes, ma'am. As I told Mr. Blackamber, I'm not here to hurt anyone, but I will defend myself. I know my past makes me suspect, but I'm here to heal, not kill."

"The *Morukai* and her mate know about you?"

"Yes, ma'am. She was my first stop when I arrived."

The doctor nodded. "All right. If you need anything else, stop by the clinic, but I suspect the swelling will go down in a few hours."

"Yes, ma'am. Thank you."

"Come along, Tom. Let's go find your father." She took the boy by the hand to lead him away.

"Bye, Balder. Feel better, okay?"

Balder smiled. "I will. Thanks, Tom."

He nodded and followed his mother into the crowd. Balder rubbed his throat and found a chair to sit in, trying to ignore the pain. *Not as bad as it could've been.* Angelina appeared beside him and held out a steaming to-go cup.

"Here, this is Myriam's best medicinal tea. It should help your throat."

"Thank you. Who's Myriam?" He sipped the hot liquid and his throat immediately felt better.

"She owns the Silk Road Tea House and I've found her brews are magic." Angelina winked. "She has a table right across from the firefighters this year. Lucky duck, she gets to look at man candy all day."

Balder chuckled, but immediately took another sip as his throat screamed in protest. The tea soothed his raw flesh and the everyday conversation settled his anxiety. Angelina didn't seem angry with him. *Odd.*

"Are we still okay, Angelina?"

She raised her eyebrows. "What do you mean?"

"The fight with..." He trailed off and scanned the crowd. No one stood near the table. "The vampire. I don't mean to cause trouble. But if you'd like me to pack my things and leave, I understand."

"Oh, no, Balder, I don't want you to go. I know you're trying to overcome your past and heal." She shook her head. "There will always be people who judge you by it. Most of the Elder Races in this town know who you are and where you've come from. You can be as kind as possible, and people will still see what they want to see." She nodded after the doctor and Tom. "Give Drake some time. He has vivid memories of the last assassin he encountered. He's going to react first and ask questions later. Especially when it comes to Tom."

Balder nodded. "Because he's Drake's son."

"Adopted son, but yes."

Balder sipped the tea as Angelina moved to deal with someone wanting to make a donation. Would it always be that way here? Would he always be considered a risk? Balder recognized of all the towns he could've settled in, this one would be the hardest for him.

But I like it here. I want to stay. And Svanhild's here.

Not that she had to stay, but he didn't want to be without her. And he liked Three Lakes with it's *Morukai* and the Elder Races. He didn't want to move on.

He stayed quiet for a short time, letting the people and time pass without much acknowledgement until someone crouched beside his chair. He made an effort to return to the present and met the storm-gray gaze of the woman he loved. Worry tightened the skin around her eyes and her brow wrinkled with her frown. Still, she was the most beautiful woman he'd ever seen. *I have to tell her I love her.* Svanhild took in his face and injuries with intense scrutiny until she returned to his gaze.

"Are you all right, Balder?" She grasped his arm in a firm grip.

He shrugged one shoulder. "I will be. Bruises, minor damage only."

She grimaced. "Your voice sounds terrible. Who did this to you?"

"Vampire." He shrugged again. "Thought I was hurting his son."

She raised her eyebrows. "Were you?"

He shook his head. "No, helping him fix a toy."

"It's true." Angelina said over her shoulder as she put away the cash she'd received. "Balder helped Tom Cantora fix his airplane and his father Drake took exception because of Balder's past."

"No one stopped him?"

Angelina snorted. "No one saw it coming until it was too late. Balder held his own, though. Drake will be feeling it for a while."

"Not as much as I will, I suspect." Balder shook his head. "And he'll heal faster, too."

"Keep drinking the tea. It'll help." Angelina nodded. "The festival goes for only two more hours. Why don't you take him home, Svanhild? I can manage and some of my staff will be joining me to help clean up. Take him to his apartment and make him rest."

"I don't need to rest." His voice came out as a painful croak and Svanhild snorted.

"You're not convincing me. Let's go back to your place and get you settled. We can stop at the Ironwood to pick up some soup. That should be easy to swallow with your sore throat."

Balder wanted to protest, but the women were decided. He allowed them to bustle him into the loaner car and Angelina sent them off with strict instructions to drink and rest. Svanhild bought more tea from the Silk Road Tea House table and some soup from the Ironwood Café before she took him home to the shelter.

She parked the car on the side road and helped him to his apartment. He kept sipping until he got inside his room and closed the door. Tiffany materialized in the sitting room, perched on the arm of the couch.

Exhaustion hit him all at once and he swayed into a wall.

"Whoa! Okay, time for you to get some sleep, Balder." Svanhild shoved her shoulder under his armpit and draped his arm across it. "Let's get you into bed. I think you need to rest more than food."

He wanted to protest that he was fine and didn't need to be coddled like a child, but he could barely keep his eyes open and his throat hurt. His legs felt like lead weights as she helped him into his room and deposited him in the bed.

"Boots off then belt." Svanhild sounded amused, but he didn't have the energy to check.

She pulled his shoes off, followed by his belt and jeans. He lay there like a sack of herring as she dragged the covers back and shoved his feet under them. The last thought he had before he succumbed to his exhaustion was the plaintive wish to have her in bed next to him.

CHAPTER FIFTEEN

Svanhild rubbed her hands over her face as she regarded Balder's snoring body under the covers. Vivid purple and black bruises decorated his throat like a hideous Victorian cravat, and she couldn't believe he could still speak. Anger still burned in her gut and had since the moment she received Angelina's call. Balder hadn't done anything to provoke the attack, but the vampire in question, Drake MacGregor, had no love for Sword of God members and trusted none of them.

She couldn't blame him, but it didn't stop her fury. Or her concern.

She wanted Balder to be safe and find the solace he looked for. She understood his need for redemption, but she also understood the town might never wholly trust him. The Sword of God members were excellent at infiltrating a community only to turn on them after they'd gained trust and favor. Tiffany's presence remained a terrific example of their expertise. *And none of the people here know for sure if he'll turn on them or not.*

That wasn't completely true. Svanhild suspected Kate Blackamber knew, and so did Angelina or they wouldn't have let him stay. The question in her mind was, did she know Balder meant what he said about seeking redemption or was it her love for him blinding her?

Faen, I am in love with him.

She dropped into a chair beside the bed and gaped at his sleeping face. When had she fallen in love with Balder? She tried to think back to the moment her feelings changed, but she couldn't pinpoint a time. It had developed over time like the fog rolling in off the fjords, stealthy and quiet until it filled her being.

I should tell him.

She waited on him to wake, but after three hours, she admitted she should leave him to find sustenance and let him rest. Tiffany watched her go with her own concern written on her ghostly features. Svanhild had no words of comfort, so she let herself out into the hallway with no more than a nod to the ghost.

"How's he doing?"

"Sweet Freyja's shield! You startled the *drit* out of me." Svanhild widened her eyes at Angelina.

"Sorry." The older woman didn't smile. "Has there been any improvement?"

Svanhild followed Angelina into the lobby and waited for her to resume her usual spot at the front desk. The woman had lines around her eyes and mouth Svanhild hadn't noticed before and her brows dropped in concern.

"Sleeping. Been that way since I got him in the room."

Angelina's expression cleared. "Oh good. Myriam's tea is doing its job, then."

"The tea?"

"Yeah. It's infused with healing herbs, Stevia, and a little magic to give them extra oomph in both healing and sleep. He should be out for a while." Angelina smiled and it made her look at least a decade younger. "How are you holding up?"

Svanhild opened her mouth to give a flippant non-answer, but stopped and seriously considered the question.

"I'm well, but concerned."

"Concerned? Here, pull up a chair. It's usually pretty quiet here this time of day on Sundays." Angelina waved at the empty foyer.

"*Ja*, but it's Monday."

"Of a holiday weekend. That translates to Sunday with regard to traffic. Grab a chair."

Svanhild didn't see any reason to argue and dragged one of the stools from the payphone station over to the desk. She settled onto it and rubbed her eyes as her own fatigue dropped onto her shoulders.

"Why are you concerned?" Angelina pushed a plate of leftover cookies from the bake sale across the desk.

"I'm worried about Balder being in Three Lakes. The community is full of…" She hesitated and scanned the room for human ears. Satisfied they were alone she turned back to Angelina. "Elder Races here. Elder Races who know of and have experienced the Sword of God cult. Drake MacGregor won't be the last to distrust Balder, and I suspect he won't be the only one to respond with violence."

"Yes, it's a volatile situation, for certain."

"It is. Balder's past of infiltrating a community only to turn on them makes it harder."

"True, it does." Angelina nodded. "But Balder himself has acted honorably and when confronted with this attack, only defended himself. He didn't go on the offensive and try to kill Drake."

"You know that and I know that, but how many others saw it? How many others trust he wasn't playing another mind game?" Svanhild shook her head. "I don't want him to get hurt, but he's not a child and doesn't need to be smothered in cotton wool." She sighed and rubbed her face again. "Holy Freyja, I just want him to be safe. It preys on my mind to think he'll always be fighting for his place here."

Angelina rested her hand on Svanhild's arm. "You

really love him, don't you?"

Emotion swamped her heart and tears started in her eyes. "Goddess help me, *ja*, I do. I don't understand it, I didn't look for it, but he's captured my heart. Am I stupid? Am I blind? Have I lost myself to someone who's only here to hurt others?"

"Whoa, whoa, whoa. Let's back up a bit here." Angelina smiled to break up the tension, but her eyes held compassion. "Let me give you a little something to ease your mind. Balder truly is here to find redemption and rehabilitation. Never doubt that. I read it in him when he first stepped through my doors. And I wouldn't have let him in here otherwise."

Svanhild released her breath in a relieved sob, tears sliding down her cheeks. "Thank the Goddess."

Angelina nodded. "And Kate wouldn't have let him on her property, much less in her house without his earnest commitment to healing and recuperation. Do you know she has a ghost herself?"

Svanhild shook her head. "No, I didn't sense or see it."

"She does. The first Sword of God assassin who came here to kill her." Angelina pointed to the desk to indicate location. "Jayson caught him and mortally wounded him before he could do anything, but upon his death the Goddess gave him a job. To redeem his soul, he was required to protect Kate's home and family from all threats, including those from his own cult." She shrugged. "So if Balder had any threat to Kate or this town in his heart, Kate's ghost wouldn't have let him on the premises. I don't know what all the ghost can do, but I suspect he's pretty powerful."

"I met Balder on the porch, so he made it onto Kate's property." Svanhild shook her head. "And promptly collapsed. Maybe the ghost had a hand in that."

"Possibly, but did Kate bring him inside and nurse him back to consciousness?"

Svanhild nodded. "Yes."

"She wouldn't have done that if he was a real threat to her well-being." Angelina sighed and grimaced. "Balder has a tough row to hoe here, but only time and his continued actions to help people will convince those who don't know his heart. It will take Drake and Dr. Aliandra a long time to trust him. But I think Tom sees Balder for his true self and Tom's pretty wise for being less than a hundred years old."

"Less than...What is he?" Svanhild blinked.

"Oh, you didn't know? Tom's a dragon like his mother, Dr. Aliandra." Angelina grinned. "He's pretty special, though. I think he has healer abilities."

Svanhild had met a few dragons on her travels, but always in passing. She'd never lived anywhere with such beings as residents. "So she's the dragon who killed the last Sword of God assassin?"

"Yep, to save both her mate and her son."

"Wow. I bet she has no love for Balder, either."

Angelina shook her head. "Probably not, but she treated him today, and listened to what her son said about him. I heard Tom say Balder smelled like cookies and 'fireplace smoke.' Fire and hearth are very important to dragons. They associate both with home, protection, and comfort. If Tom said he smelled like fireplace smoke, it could be he sees Balder as one of the good ones, one of the protectors rather than destroyers."

Svanhild mulled that over for a few moments. The *Morukai* had asked her to help Balder return to the community. She suspected it meant protecting him in name and person, and standing with him when the shit hit the fan. *I might be dodging more shit than I thought.*

But she'd seen a person like herself when she'd met his gaze that first day. Lonely, desperate for connection, and resigned to never finding it. He needed her and she couldn't let him down. Helvete, *I can't let the* Morukai *down.*

"I'm glad Tom can see him clearly, and that he has your support, and Kate's." She sighed and rubbed her lips with her hand as she made a decision. "I have a feeling something's coming. I don't know what it is, but my gut is screaming that there's something in the wind. He's going to need everyone's help to face it, too, but there are plenty of people here who'd like to see the end of him."

Angelina nodded, her smile gone. "Yeah, I have that feeling, too. I'll keep my eyes open around here and I'll mention it to Kate when I see her, but I suspect she knows. In the meantime, you might want to spend more time with Balder whenever you can. I'm sure he'd tell you he doesn't need a bodyguard, but I also think he's never been the prey before. He's always been the hunter."

Svanhild shook her head. "So have I, to be honest."

"But you've also been a protector. You know better what he's up against." Angelina tilted her head, her lips curling into a smile. "And I think it might give you more time with him. Just a thought."

Svanhild raised one eyebrow, but she couldn't hold back the laugh. "Are you trying to matchmake me and Balder, Angelina?"

The shelter owner snorted. "As if I have to do that. You're already well on your way. I'm just giving you the excuse to be with him more often."

Svanhild laughed again. "I won't turn it down." She patted the desk and got to her feet. "I'm going to get something to eat at home and I'll be back in a little bit to check on him. Would it be okay if I stayed here tonight to keep an eye on him? I'm concerned his throat might swell so much he'll stop breathing."

"That's fine with me, but I do have one request."

"What's that?"

"No sex tonight, please. I try to keep this rule here at the shelter because of the shared living conditions. And it's not fair if he gets preferential treatment."

Svanhild fought against her instant embarrassment and firmed her voice. "No sex. I don't think he's in any condition for it, anyway, but your rules are sound."

"Good. I'll see you when you get back, then." Angelina smiled and waved.

"See you."

Svanhild replaced the stool at the payphone and headed out the door into the warm afternoon. The sun had found clouds to dance with, but the shade was hot and muggy without wind. She sighed and strode to her car, sniffing the air. Something sat just out of reach of her senses, teasing her with foreboding. Her gut said something was coming, but she couldn't get a clear picture of it yet.

She opened the car and rolled all the windows down. *Thank Freyja for the electric windows.* The heat sat like a heavy blanket over her, but she turned the ignition and pulled into traffic before pointing the car toward home. She'd need something to eat and something to sleep in while she watched over Balder. Though she'd rarely had the opportunity to play nursemaid, she truly didn't mind this chance. And as Angelina had pointed out, it gave her the extra time to be with Balder.

She couldn't begrudge that.

CHAPTER SIXTEEN

Balder woke with a start, his heart hammering in his chest as he clawed at his throat. He gasped as he realized nothing tightened against his windpipe. *Just a dream.* He lay on his bed and breathed, taking stock of his body. His throat remained tight, but without much pain. Memories of the librarian vampire's attack slowly faded into the background and his heartbeat slowed.

Silence enveloped him and it took him a few minutes to realize he was alone. *Where the hell am I?* He scanned the room around him, finding the comforting décor of his apartment in the shelter. But no ghost or Valkyrie. The window showed no light and his room sat in darkness. He listened hard, but if anyone talked outside his door, they did so quietly.

He reached up and touched his neck, checking for damage. While the muscles twinged with tenderness, swallowing didn't hurt at all, and nothing felt swollen. He slowly sat up and swung his feet to the floor as his body reminded him he'd been resting a long time. He staggered to the bathroom and relieved himself before daring to look in the mirror.

He wore a pair of handprints around his neck in

mottled yellow and brown, and matching dark circles filled the spaces under his eyes. *Holy shit, I look like death warmed over.* He grimaced and shot a look at the living room, hoping Tiffany couldn't hear him. But she didn't seem to be in the apartment at all.

That's weird.

Balder turned off the bathroom light and ambled into the living room to determine what time it was. The glowing blue numbers of the stove clock showed it was just after three in the morning. He found a teapot full of Myriam's tea and a note from Angelina to keep drinking it. He swallowed experimentally and found his throat no longer hurt. *Guess the tea works.*

Beside the note sat a little black rectangle with a smooth surface. He picked it up with a frown and turned it over. Glass reflected in the blue light from the stove and he realized he held a cell phone.

Did Svanhild leave hers here? It would certainly make him easier to reach. He set the phone down and realized an envelope sat on the counter beside it. He reached over to turn on the overhead kitchen light and opened the paper flap to pull out the note inside.

Just wanted you to have a phone of your own so I no longer have to be your press secretary. This will give you a chance to spend more time with Svanhild and I'll be able to contact you if the shelter needs repairs. Welcome to the twenty-first century. Angelina.

He snorted with her sardonic humor. He'd had a cell phone when in the Sword of God, but had left it and all his possessions when he escaped. This phone looked more sophisticated than the one he'd owned before, but he'd use it to keep in contact with Angelina. And Svanhild.

He ambled back to bed with a cup of Myriam's tea and thought about the Valkyrie. She'd been his first thought when death threatened. He didn't want to leave her. He'd never tried to live for anyone before, but Svanhild made him want to be alive.

The problem was he wanted to stay in Three Lakes, and if Drake MacGregor was any indication, Balder had a lot to do to earn his place. He had a few supporters like Kate and Angelina, but opposition wouldn't be absent. Balder sighed. The first thing he needed to do was talk to the archivist. He didn't expect it to be easy between them, but at least they could call a truce.

The second question was whether Svanhild would stay. She'd given the impression that she only planned on being in town for a short time. Him, too, but since meeting her and Angelina, his intentions had changed. Had hers?

Can I convince her to stay?

He didn't know enough about her future plans to devise a strategy to change them. And he suspected his usual tactics of manipulation, so well-honed in the Sword of God, wouldn't work.

Plus I don't want to use them. No, he wanted to convince her to stay with him because she liked him. He hoped that to be the case. She certainly liked the sex. *Me, too.*

Just the thought of her moaning made his cock rise with interest, but when he shifted to stroke it, pain shot up his side and reminded him of his brush with the vampire. He groaned and settled himself back in the bed, sipping a little more of the tea.

He needed thoughts, not action tonight. He closed his eyes and focused on what he wanted. He wanted Svanhild and he wanted to stay in Three Lakes. He also wanted to help Tiffany get to where she needed to be. *Preferably not haunting me anymore.*

Hopefully, the *Morukai* would help with the last request. He'd brought Tiffany to Three Lakes, but he had no idea what more he could do. *Maybe there's a ceremony to let Tiffany rest or something.* He'd ask Kate when he got the chance, not because he wanted to be free of Tiffany, but because he wanted her to be free of him.

She deserves it.

With a plan of action to one of his three major problems, Balder let his mind drift. He needed to find a way to convince Svanhild to stay. But exhaustion claimed him again before a plan became clear.

****

It took longer than Balder liked to heal from the altercation with Drake MacGregor, but he had to give the man points for deadly ability. He still hadn't worked out a plan to parlay with the archivist, but he didn't want to face him until he was at full strength. Having a steady income and Myriam's tea helped with the healing, but he resolved to take his time.

Balder also hadn't figured out how to broach the subject of staying in Three Lakes with Svanhild, though he'd seen her far more often. It just never seemed to be the right time to bring it up. And really, what right did he have to ask her to stay? He was still ruminating over the best way to make his feelings clear at the Silk Road Tea House two weeks after the attack. Despite selling only varieties of tea, it seemed to be the local watering hole for all of Three Lakes. Everyone came to either share a pot, grab a single cup in her ornate crystal and silver glasses, or drown their sorrows in her special *Anorah* tea. No one quite knew what was in it, but it definitely made the problems seem far away while sipping.

Balder made sure to keep his wits about him, but he enjoyed some potent peppermint one evening as he puzzled over the best way to approach Svanhild. Myriam had thrown her doors and windows open to allow the cool winds off the lake to meander through the building. The scents of the lake and forest brought as much peace as the tea.

Balder closed his eyes and took a deep breath. Peppermint and steam filled his nose, and he savored it as he focused on letting worries go. The Sword of God might have been a maniacal group bent on killing, but they also managed to teach their operatives how to find calm when the world appeared to be falling apart. It was the way he'd been able to save the little girl in the fire, and he used the techniques now to settle himself to think of a way to convince Svanhild to stay with him.

He hadn't come up with any clear answers when the air shifted with the scents of blood, moist soil, and the hint of dragon. A chill ran up Balder's back and his instincts screamed a warning, but he didn't turn. Drake MacGregor, vampire. His erstwhile assailant sauntered into the room and sat down at Balder's table, his eyes hard.

"Why are you here?"

What, no hello, I've missed you? Balder sipped his tea to keep himself warm as the old angers and assassin's tendencies rose in his chest. *I'm not going to bait him.* But he wouldn't take his shit, either.

"Drinking tea and enjoying the warm evening." Balder kept his voice level, but he suspected the vampire heard his sarcasm.

"That's not what I asked."

"Yes, it was, and I answered. Why are you here?"

Drake closed his mouth in a hard, flat line and his arms flexed as if he tightened his hands into fists below the edge of the table. Balder keep this own hands around his mug of tea and held his gaze on the vampire's body language.

"Why are you really in Three Lakes?" Drake's voice came out flat and angry.

Balder resisted the urge to needle him. "Redemption and healing."

Drake barked a short, humorless laugh. "There is no redemption for your kind."

"Like there's no redemption for yours?" Balder raised

his chin, but tightened his hands on his mug. He expected the voices to scream at him about sitting with a vampire, but they were barely a murmur in the back of his head. *Must be Myriam's tea.*

"What do you know about my kind? All you've done is killed people like me."

Drake's fury hissed across the space between them, but Balder forced himself to be still. He understood the vampire could kill him and no one would be able to stop him, but he was done accepting blame. If Drake killed him, he'd be free of the guilt, anger, and regret, and he was okay with that.

Balder shrugged with one shoulder as he nodded his head, conceding the point. "That's true. But vampires aren't exactly blameless. However, I'm not here to point fingers. I'm here to enjoy my tea, and I'm in Three Lakes to find redemption and healing. I'm pretty sure you can understand that no matter what species you are."

Silence descended again and Balder sipped his tea, staring Drake down. He was done apologizing. He knew what he had to work on and no one else could tell him his faults. He knew them well enough. Drake would have to come to terms with that, even if it meant Balder's death.

"You're former Sword of God. You'll always carry that stigma."

Balder nodded. "I know. Nothing I can do about the past. The only way to make up for any of it is to work in the present."

"You'll never make up for it." It sounded like a life sentence.

Balder shrugged again. "That may be, but any actions you take on that score will be yours alone. I came here to heal. The *Morukai* accepted my suit of contrition and redemption, and that's where we stand. I can't change the past, I can only do better now. As for your family, I know you're not..." He lowered his voice. "Human. And it doesn't matter to me anymore. I'm slowly learning to ignore the training I've sustained to see beyond it. I'm learning people are people, and there are good ones in every species, just as there are bad. We can choose which to be and how to respond. I'm done with killing. What will you choose, Mr. MacGregor?"

The man in front of him sat back in his chair, his eyes narrowed. Again, a long silence settled over them as Balder drank his tea. This time he let his gaze slide away from the vampire and out to the evening light on the gardens around the tea house. The soft scent of jasmine floated on the air and reminded him of one of his trips to Italy and a small hole-in-the-wall cafe in Siena. While he didn't look at Drake, he kept his attention on him because an angry vampire made a deadly opponent.

Would he allow himself to die? He didn't know, but he didn't want to fight anymore and he wanted to stay in Three Lakes. *With Svanhild. Shit.* He still hadn't figured out a way to convince her to stay.

"So you're staying?" Drake's voice held caution.

"Yes."

Drake nodded, his expression closed. "You know half of this community will never trust you."

Balder shrugged again. "That's a possibility and their choice. I can't change how others feel just like I can't change my past. All I can change is myself and my actions. I can't guarantee I won't make mistakes, but I am trying to be better than I was."

"Stay away from my family."

Balder sighed. "I won't seek them out, Mr. MacGregor, but I can't avoid them all the time. Especially because your wife is a doctor. But I can promise you I'm done with killing and I'm getting help with the indoctrination I sustained in the Sword of God. Beyond that, I can't promise anything."

"I'll be watching you, Mr. Templar." Drake stood.

"You know where to find me, Mr. MacGregor." Balder finished his tea. "Will I be able to come to the library to check out books, or is it off limits?"

Drake ground his teeth. "You may come to the library."

"Thanks." He met Drake's gaze and resisted the urge to goad him. "Anything else I can do for you?"

Drake shook his head, a frown creasing his brow. "I don't know what she sees in you."

Balder raised his eyebrows. "Who?"

"The Valkyrie."

Balder snorted. "That makes two of us, but I know what I see in her."

"And that is?"

"None of your business."

Drake coughed a sound suspiciously close to a laugh and nodded. "Yes, I suppose so. You'll be working with Angelina in the shelter?"

"That's my current plan. I like it there and her steadiness helps me find mine."

Drake nodded again. "She has that effect on people. I don't like you, Mr. Templar."

"Thanks for the heads-up, Mr. MacGregor. I think I've figured that out."

Drake cracked a smile. "Yes, I suppose you have."

"There is one advantage to having me stay in this town." Balder poured a second mug of tea from the pot on the table.

"And that is?"

"I'll recognize and know any Sword of God member long before anyone else will." Balder sat back in his chair. "No one knows them better than me."

"That's if we can trust you to tell us. What would keep you from letting them do their job on our town?" Drake sneered, showing off one long canine.

"Because I want to live here, too, and because it's a

psychotic cult."

"On that we both agree. But it doesn't mean you won't let them harm people."

Balder shook his head. "It also doesn't mean I will. I like it here. I like the people and the energy of Three Lakes, Mr. MacGregor. I don't want to leave and I want it to be safe. If another Sword of God assassin shows up, you can bet your ass I'll let people know about it."

"Do I have your word on that, Mr. Templar?"

Balder raised his eyebrows. "I thought my word means nothing to you."

"Touché, but we all must start somewhere."

"You have my promise that I'll warn you and the other town members if I see anyone I recognize as Sword of God." He held up his new cell phone. "I even have a new phone so I can text you."

"Sure. The number is 1-800-FUC-KOFF."

Balder laughed out loud and Drake cracked another smile. "I'll put that in my contacts."

"You do that." Drake rapped his knuckles against the table in parting. "Have a good night, Mr. Templar."

"Not 'eat shit and die'?"

Drake shrugged. "I wouldn't rule it out." He smirked and walked out of the tea house, and Balder laughed again. A vampire with a sense of humor. Thank goodness wonders never ceased.

Balder drank more tea and silently saluted Mr. MacGregor for his help. He finally realized what he could say to give Svanhild a reason to stay with him. He could recognize any Sword of God operative a mile away, and she'd be the first one he'd tell. The townsfolk might not trust him, but Svanhild did, and they trusted her.

Thank you, Mr. MacGregor. Balder smiled at the lengthening shadows outside. *I wonder if I should text him?* He laughed and finished his tea.

CHAPTER SEVENTEEN

Svanhild glanced down at her phone as it rang in her pocket. She'd just finished fixing William Lutrenin's car and she was so glad. The damn thing smelled like old fish and bait, and her nose couldn't take much more. She pulled the phone out and looked at the number, not recognizing it. Usually, she let it go to voicemail, but this time was curious.

"Hello?"

"Hello, Svanhild. This is Balder."

She blinked. "Balder? Where are you calling from?"

"Currently, I'm at Myriam's Silk Road Tea House."

"You're using their phone?" She glanced at hers to be sure, but it didn't look like the Silk Road Tea House's number.

"No. This is the new cell phone Angelina got for me. It makes calling very convenient."

Just wait till you see what it can do on the internet. She thought better than to tell him that. *Goddess knows he might start watching YouTube for the novelty.*

"I just bet it does. Congrats on your new phone. How are you feeling?"

"I'm better, thank you. Can we get together soon? I have something I want to talk to you about."

"Sure. When?"

"When do you get off work tonight?"

"Uh..." She glanced down at the phone again. "In about a half an hour. I can come pick you up in about an hour or so. Would that work for you?"

"That's okay. Why don't I meet you at your place in an hour? It'll take me that long to get what I want together and walk there.'

"Are you sure, Balder?" She closed the hood of the car and wiped her hands on a cloth as she hugged the phone between her shoulder and ear. "I don't mind coming to get you."

"I'm sure. I'll see you at your cabin in about an hour."

"All right. See you then."

The call ended and she held the phone in front of her, staring at it. *That was weird.* He'd sounded excited and pleased, as if he'd discovered something important. She shook her head and shoved the phone back into her pocket before cleaning up her tools. She liked to have everything in its place for when she returned to work in the morning.

I like it here.

She stopped and blinked a few times. It was true. She did like it in Three Lakes with Bart and Balder and the rest of the town. She liked coming to work in the Fix-It Cave every day, and sharing Bart's work load. She shot a look at her bike in the back of the garage. Pretty soon she'd have the iron maiden fixed and she could leave.

I don't want to leave. For the first time in centuries, she felt like she'd found a home. She snapped her toolbox closed and ran her hands over the lid. Home. The word had a different meaning now that she'd been in the mortal world for all this time. Originally it had meant Asgard with the Shield Maidens and the gods presiding over its shining shores. But now, it meant...

"Hey, Svanhild?" Bart's voice broke into her thoughts.

"*Ja*, Bart?"

"Could you come into the office when you're done? I wanna talk to you about somethin'."

Svanhild blinked. *Freyja's sword, do all the men in this town need to talk to me tonight?*

"*Ja*, I'm coming." She shut off the lights in the main garage bay and headed into the office where Bart sat in his cushy "computer" chair. It was actually an armchair, but he claimed the usual office chairs wouldn't hold his weight. "What's up, Bart?"

"Pull up a chair and have a seat. I wanna talk to you about somthin' important."

She snagged a stool with her foot and settled onto it. "What's going on?"

"Y'know how I asked you to help me out with the work load this spring?"

She snorted. "*Ja*, it was only a few weeks ago and I was there, remember?"

He rumbled a laugh. "Yeah, yeah, don't be a smartass. You might be a Valkyrie, but I can still pummel your butt."

"I'd like to see you try, Teddy Ruxpin." She grinned and he matched it.

"Don't tempt me." He snuffled, sounding like the bear he was. "Anyway, I was thinkin', we've done pretty well this summer and, well, I'd like to keep you on if you're of a mind to stay in Three Lakes."

Svanhild tilted her head. "You want me to stay? What about when business drops off in the winter? You won't need me then."

"Actually, that's not completely true." Bart shrugged his massive shoulders. "Bears get sleepy in the winter, but folks still have car troubles. It would be good to have someone who isn't so seasonally affected working here."

"What about your cabin? I won't have a place to stay if you need it for the winter."

221

Bart huffed and waved a huge hand. "Nah, I got my own place that's a little bigger. That little cabin is good for human-sized people, but not so much for bear-sized people, if you know what I mean."

She nodded, thinking over what he'd offered. It would be nice to stop roaming around and plant some roots. And she'd been accepted in the Three Lakes community among the Elder Races. She certainly liked Bart, Kate, Angelina, Gemini, and even the gruff Sheriff Boulderson, though she hadn't talked to him much.

Since Odin banished her more than half a millennium before, she hadn't stayed anywhere very long, wandering like a Romany person. But then no one ever offered her a place or more than casual friendship. Three Lakes had crept into her heart and warmed her more than she'd thought possible.

"I see you're hesitatin' so let me sweeten the deal a little."

Svanhild blinked at Bart's comment. "Sweeten the deal?"

"Yeah…" He rubbed the back of his neck with one hand and his cheeks turned pink. "I was thinkin' it'd be nice to have a partner."

Oh, sweet Freyja, he's not propositioning me, is he?

"A partner?" She couldn't help her eyes going wide. "Uh…"

"Yeah, in the Fix-It Cave. You know, give you stock or part-ownership in it." He noted her wide-eyed stare and narrowed his own gaze. "Whadya think I meant?"

"I, uh, well, I just thought…"

His own eyes widened and he threw his head back to bark a laugh. "You thought I was askin' you to be my mate, didn't you?" He laughed harder. "I like you, Svanhild, but you're really not my type. I like a woman who's round on butt, boobs, belly, thighs, and hips. You're a helluva woman, but too slender for me. Besides, I'm pretty sure you're in love with Balder."

Svanhild opened her mouth, but nothing came out. How did everyone seem to know it before her? Did Balder suspect? She didn't know, but she'd shifted her thinking. She'd definitely have to tell him.

"*Ja*, I am in love with Balder. It's a curious feeling."

"I thought so. No, what I meant was to give you half the stock in the Fix-It Cave. It'd give you a steady income, help you hone those mechanic's skills you got, and it'd help me a lot, especially in the winter when I get sleepy. Whadya say?"

Did she want to take him up on his offer? It would tie her to this place and keep her from moving on. *Moving on to what?* She'd been moving on for centuries with nothing to look for and nowhere to call home. But Bart was offering her a home. A permanent place she could always come back to should she need to travel. A base camp where she'd always be welcome, and a place where people had her back.

Svanhild nodded slowly. "*Ja*, Bart. I'd like that. Thank you for the opportunity."

"Yeah? You'll stay?" The delighted grin on Bart's face made him look positively boyish.

"*Ja*, it feels like a good place to make a home. Never had a place like that before and I think I'd like one. *Tusen takk.*" She stood and held her hand out to the bear shifter.

He rose and engulfed her in a huge bear hug. *Emphasis on bear.* Svanhild wrapped her arms around the big man and closed her eyes, resting against his massive chest. He smelled warm and comforting, like a big brother or comrade-in-arms, and he squeezed her tight enough to steal her breath before releasing her.

"Hot damn." He bobbed his head. "That's better than a big mug of honey mead. I'll get the papers written up for you to sign so we're all fair and square. We can even take 'em to the notary at the Lake Shore Bank in town. It's run by gargoyles so you know it's safe."

"I've never met a gargoyle." Svanhild shook her head.

"Just picture a winged demon with fangs, claws, a muscled tail, and a body built like a powerlifter all made of stone." Bart snorted. "Even the bear clans around here won't take them on. And if you want to call someone stoic, gargoyles are masters of stoicism."

Svanhild laughed. "So you've never made one laugh?"

"Heh, I'm not sure they know how to laugh. But they're good at keepin' stuff safe and orderly." He nodded. "I'm pleased you wanna be a partner in the Fix-It Cave. Real pleased."

"Thanks, Bart. I appreciate it." She nodded to the computer on the desk. "Do you need me to do any paperwork? I still have about twenty minutes left on my shift."

"Nah. You go ahead and head out. I'll close up tonight." He waved her out, satisfaction filling his face.

"All right. I'll see you in the morning, Bart."

"Yup. See you tomorrow."

She let herself out into the soft evening air, her own satisfaction simmering in her chest. She had a home, a place to be, where people needed and wanted her around. It had been so long, the feeling of it now was damn near euphoric. It resembled the battle excitement she used to experience when launching into the fray, and she laughed out loud as she strode through the trees toward her cabin. Balder wouldn't have arrived yet, but that gave her time to take a shower and tidy up her morning dishes.

She didn't know how Balder would react to her news, but she looked forward to telling him. Especially if it led to more pleasurable pursuits.

****

Balder purchased some homemade Turkish Delight

from Gemini's store on his way out to Svanhild's cabin. The soft evening air flowed around him like silken scarves, brushing against his skin with gentle touches. He took slow, deep breaths as he strode along, enjoying the evening noises and waving to a few cars passing on the road. He'd arranged a truce with a powerful vampire and found a way, hopefully, to convince Svanhild to stay in Three Lakes. Life was good.

Now all he had to do was figure out how to free Tiffany from her cursed existence and he'd be set. The breeze shifted direction and sent a chill running up his back as motion out of the corner of his eye caught his attention. Visceral and preternatural awareness had him tensing, but he kept moving. Hitting a moving target offered more of a challenge and a better chance of the target surviving.

He kept his gaze scanning the world around him as the sun dipped behind the trees. While not true dusk, the forest remained darker than the sky above and gave many places to hide those intent on threat. He watched the trees and the world around him, glad he'd brought a pocket knife at least.

Another flicker of motion darted through the dark trunks as he headed up the road toward Svanhild's cabin. *That looked like a wolf.* He didn't think Jayson Blackamber would tease him with a game of hide-n-seek, not after the vampire had attacked him. And if that wasn't Jayson, then who would it be? Despite his intent to stay away from his Sword of God skills, he felt himself settle into the cold awareness of his assassin's training.

Svanhild's cabin appeared up ahead with the lights on and he moved steadily toward it, catching flashes of something slipping through the trees around him. More than one something. He debated changing direction to keep her safe from whatever stalked him, but he didn't want to piss her off trying to protect her, and he was safer with her. He had no doubt a Valkyrie could take on just about anything in these woods.

He remembered Angelina mentioning Iris Maple was related to the Dryad's Garden of Three Lakes and likely had friends among the trees. He wondered if they were aware of the new wolf, but decided to give warning anyway.

"If anyone's listening, please give a message to Iris Maple that there's are wolves in the woods, and I don't think they are Jayson Blackamber." He muttered the words as he kept his strides even and swift.

The breeze kicked up and whispers rode along its force, making the trees rustle and rattle with flashing leaves and brittle needles. A ripple of energy fled through the trunks just as Balder reached Svanhild's front door. He rapped his knuckles against the wood, holding his breath as he listened for someone coming at his back.

The door opened and Svanhild smiled at him until she read his expression. Her eyes sharpened and looked beyond him as her shoulders tensed under her wet braid.

"Come inside, Balder."

"Thanks." He stepped across the threshold and the itching between his shoulder blades eased. "There's something out there stalking me."

"*Ja*, I feel it too. Did you see what it was?" She closed the door and threw the lock, though he suspected if the stalkers wanted in, they'd come in.

He shrugged one shoulder. "Looked like wolves to me."

"Wolves? In the woods around Three Lakes?" She frowned and headed for the kitchen. "Do you think Jayson Blackamber invited someone?"

"I guess it's possible. I'm not in the know about such things as the comings and goings of werewolves." He grimaced as he thought about Tiffany. "At least not anymore."

"You're sure they were werewolves?"

Balder thought back to the sense of being watched on

his walk. "Yeah, I'm sure."

"Tomorrow we should mention it to Kate or Jayson. In the meantime…"

She planted her feet, closed her eyes, and pounded her fist toward the floor as if she held a staff or spear. A loud crack hit the air and a flash of light shot out of the spot between her feet, expanding like a light ripple. After a few moments he heard some yelps, like a dog being beaten and Svanhild nodded sharply.

"There, now we should be left in peace for a while."

"What was that?" Balder raised his eyebrows.

"I don't have much magic left from my time as a practicing Valkyrie, but I still can set up a decent ward now and then." She grinned. "And if it singes their backsides a little…" She shrugged and he laughed.

"It's very good to have a Valkyrie on my side."

She raised her chin and smirked. "*Ja*, it is."

"Speaking of that, I wanted to talk to you about staying." He settled himself in one of her hardwood dining chairs.

"Staying?" A curious expression flitted across her face.

"Yeah, in Three Lakes." He met her gaze, screwing up his courage. "With me."

She nodded, but said nothing, and his heart sank a little as she wandered into the kitchen to grasp a teapot and two mugs. She brought them to the table and sat down before meeting his gaze.

"Very well. I'm willing to hear your suit." She poured the tea and waited for him to speak.

Balder took a deep breath. "When Mr. MacGregor attacked me at the festival, it became crystal clear to me that you're an important part of my life. I know that seems odd given my past, but you make me more human than I've ever been. You see me, not my training, not my previous actions, but the man who's trying to be better. I need that more than I can tell you."

She didn't say anything, but her expression remained open and thoughtful.

"So I wanted to ask if you'd be willing to stay in Three Lakes with me, to help me grow and improve, but also to help translate between me and the other Elder Races here in town."

Her brows lowered. "Translate between you?"

"Yeah." He nodded and tried to find the clarity he'd found after talking to Drake. "I have one unique skill I can offer the people of Three Lakes that no one else has. I can recognize the members of the Sword of God before anyone else. I know how they work, what kinds of appearances they take, even some of their faces. The only problem is my past inhibits my ability to be believed by most of the people here. They don't trust me because I was part of the Sword of God, which I can easily recognize. That's why I need you."

"You need me for what?"

"You know me and trust me to tell the truth. Hell, you can see me for who I am, beyond the stigma of my previous appointments." He grimaced and rubbed the table with his fingers. "And they trust you to tell the truth and root out evil. They'll believe a warning coming from you."

He raised his gaze to hers, waiting to see what she'd say. Her expression had slipped into stoicism and he wondered if he'd lost any chance at all.

"You need me…to make sure you're understood and your warnings are heard? That's it?"

"Yes." He wanted to tell her he loved her, but he didn't want to overwhelm her with all of his sentiment. Hell, he didn't even know if he was ready to show his heart to her yet.

But given her expression, it might not matter now.

****

Svanhild digested Balder's words and some of her pleasure at his visit evaporated. He wanted her to stay because she could make sure his messages clearly got through to the powers-that-be in town? Not what she'd been hoping for.

What, were you expecting a declaration of undying love?

Frankly, yes, she had, but her practical mind had finally caught up with her heart-in-the-clouds and reined it in. They were friends, or friends-with-benefits she'd heard it called, and he trusted her to help him with a legitimate issue. Like a friend would, or a comrade-in-arms. *In this, my heart doesn't matter.*

At least that was what she told herself when he looked at her so hopeful. She dredged up a smile from somewhere, but she feared it came out more of a grimace.

"Balder, I'll do my best to back you up when needed, but I suspect over time you'll become a part of this community and won't need my help." *Friendship. Focus on friendship.* "I'm honored you would think of me or that I have the regard from the people in this town, but I think we have bigger problems at the moment."

He frowned. "Which are?"

"The wolves in the woods. Jayson Blackamber needs to know about them and all the other Elder Races, particularly the *Morukai*, need to keep an eye on them." She nodded her head toward the door. "I don't know if you're the only one they're stalking, but I'm pretty sure there are protocols about this sort of thing."

There. She didn't sound hurt at all. *Woohoo for me.*

"I don't know what we can do about it." He shook his head. "I doubt they're gone."

"No, probably not. But I can give you a ride home where you'll be safe and head on over to the Blackamber house to fill them in."

"Now? But I just got here."

"I know, but I don't think we should wait. The sooner they know about this the sooner something can be done." She pushed her mug aside and rose, heading for the kitchen where she kept her keys. "Come on. I'll make sure you get back to the shelter safely and then talk to the Blackambers."

Balder rose more slowly. "You don't want me to stay?"

She refused to meet his gaze as she took the mugs back to the sink. "I don't think it's wise tonight." *I have to repair my wounded heart.* "You'll need to get back tomorrow while I'm at work and it's too far to walk when this threat is here." She ignored the possibility of her taking him back in the morning before work, but she didn't think she could handle being with him tonight.

"Are you all right, Svanhild?" He shot her a concerned look as she damn near shoved him out the door.

"*Ja*, I'm good. I'm just worried about this situation." She didn't mention the situation pertained to her heart. She kept her gaze on the trees, watching for anything moving. "I think it's safe to get in the car."

He went without fuss, but his shoulders had tightened with unease. She didn't know if it was from the wolves or her refusal to let him stay, but she didn't want to ask. They got in the car and she threw it into reverse while watching for anything in the trees. It gave her an excuse not to meet his concerned gaze.

"Are you sure you're okay?"

She nodded as they turned onto the main road. "*Ja*, just planning what I'm going to say to Kate and Jayson." The lies tasted bitter on her tongue. "Something feels off about this. Mr. MacGregor attacked you because he worried over his son and your previous life. But I didn't think there were more werewolves in Three Lakes. And even if there are, Jayson would've set them straight about you."

"You think these wolves came from an outside

source?" Balder rubbed his chin. "To be honest, I can't argue that. I've hurt too many people over the years. How they found me now after all the time I've been away from the Sword of God, I'm not sure—"

He looked at her with wide eyes as she turned the car onto Main Street. "The reporter after the fire."

Svanhild grimaced and nodded sharply. "That'd be my guess, too. Which means these wolves could be from anywhere. The problem is we're going to need the help of the others to protect you or stop them." She slowed as they approached the shelter. "Mention it to Angelina and let her know I'm on my way to talk to the Blackambers about it."

"Shouldn't I come with you since I was the one who saw them?"

She shook her head. "Not this time. Wolves hunt at the fringes of the herd. Kate's house is out of town and they might be tempted to attack if you are their intended target. You're safer in town at the shelter with Angelina. Until the *Morukai* knows about this, it's better to stay in town."

"Won't my presence endanger the others at the shelter? I can't see the town supporting that."

"No, the shelter won't be attacked because it's in the center of town and there are too many people around it." She hoped that was a logical reason because she needed him in Angelina's capable hands while she nursed her heart. "I'll text you as soon as I get done with the Blackambers." She stopped the car at the curb. "I promise."

He hesitated, his hand on the door handle. "Are you sure?"

"*Ja*, I'm sure. Stay safe here for now. I'll text you as soon as I'm done."

"Okay." He gave her a brief smile that didn't reach his eyes before he got out. "I'll talk to you soon."

"I won't leave until you're safely inside."

He nodded and closed the door, his brows pinched over his eyes. She wished she could erase the concern, but she didn't have the energy to spare. She was too busy shoring up the walls of her heart. He retreated into the shelter's doors and she waited until they'd closed before easing back into traffic.

She needed him safe for tonight so she could turn her attention to protecting him and healing. But despite her ability as a warrior, she didn't know how to fight the sorrow and disappointment of unrequited love. She'd never given away her heart of hearts, and the fear of his lack of regard cut deeper than Odin's banishment.

Sweet Freyja, how will I recover from this?

She shook her head and squared her shoulders as she headed toward Kate's house. It didn't matter at the moment. Her first job was to make sure the town, and Balder, was safe. *That's my story and I'm sticking to it.*

Too bad it didn't ring true.

CHAPTER EIGHTEEN

Balder finished tightening the screws on a light switch plate and shook his head. His gut churned with unease, but he shoved it back. Finished. He crossed the last item off the day's to-do list and stuffed his tools back into his tool bag. Too bad he couldn't shove away the last few weeks of his life.

Since the night he walked to Svanhild's house and asked her to be his liaison to the other Elder Races in Three Lakes, she'd retreated from him a little. They still shared meals and conversations, but she seemed distracted and reluctant to share intimacy. He understood something had gone wrong with their relationship, but he wasn't sure where he'd made a misstep. Despite her retreat, he'd found himself falling deeper and deeper in love with her, though he still didn't have the courage to tell her.

Hell, I don't even know how to tell her. And how would she react to a declaration of love from a former Sword of God operative?

Balder scrubbed his hands over his face and finished the job with a scarlet bandana Angelina had given him. He wished he could wipe away the uncertainty. Svanhild had told him she spoke with Kate and Jayson Blackamber, and neither of them knew about werewolves being in the area. However, they'd spread the word and have the community keep an eye out. He'd asked if he could do anything to help and she'd waved away his offer.

Balder frowned and stuffed the bandana into his back pocket as he headed toward the foyer of the shelter to check off his work for the day. When he'd asked Svanhild why she seemed so distant, she'd said her attention was on the wolf sightings and his protection. He didn't buy her explanation, but he didn't press her for more.

I should have. He didn't want to lose their connection, but he didn't have the confidence or certainty to tell her what his heart wanted.

Fortunately, work had taken up the time between their interactions since maintenance at the shelter happened at all hours. Angelina seemed to be offering him more than when he started, but it made sense as her confidence in his abilities increased. She usually gave him the evenings off when Svanhild finished for the day.

Matchmaker in the house.

Maybe, but he suspected Angelina knew about the wolves and made sure he had protection night and day. He'd seen some of the them in their human forms around town since the night they stalked him on the road, young men he didn't recognize who watched him with hostile eyes as he visited various businesses on errands. He mentioned them to Angelina and Svanhild, and their expressions grew grim.

Balder sighed and deposited his tool bag on the shelf in the room behind the front desk. His neck twinged and he hissed, slowing his movements as the muscles protested. He tilted his head to loosen up his neck and eased his arms back down to his sides.

Thanks to Myriam's tea and Svanhild's care, he'd healed fairly well. Better than expected. His voice had come back with a little extra rasp, but it had made

Svanhild's eyes flash with arousal despite her distance and he couldn't begrudge the change.

He rested a moment, taking stock of himself and his connection to Svanhild. Had she completely written him off? He'd started to think so until she'd invited him on a dinner date.

Tonight. This is it.

He'd have to screw up his courage and tell her how he felt. *Even if she laughs in my face or tries to let me down gently.* He had to let her know he'd fallen for her. It didn't matter that she belonged to an immortal race and he remained merely human. He'd tell her and let the chips fall where they would.

He took a deep breath and straightened his shoulders before digging out his phone to check the time. He still had a half an hour. Enough time to take a shower and get ready for his dinner date.

Hopefully the first of many more.

He crossed the last scheduled maintenance item off the day's list and turned to find Angelina at the front desk, working on a crossword puzzle like usual.

"All done?" She gave him a warm smile.

"Yep. The lights in the women's dorm room work now. We should consider getting LED bulbs in the track lighting. Would cost less in electricity."

She nodded slowly. "Hmm, might be a good idea. I'll definitely consider it. You off for the night?"

"Yes, ma'am. Svanhild has something special planned so I gotta grab a shower before she arrives."

"Oh?" Angelina's brows lifted and her smile widened. "I'm glad to hear it. You've seemed a little down in the mouth for the last week."

That's because I'm pretty sure I screwed up.

"Yeah, being stalked by werewolves does that to a person." He smirked to show he teased. "I'm going to shower. Send her to my room if she gets here before I'm done."

"I will." Angelina smiled.

Balder headed to his rooms and let himself inside. Despite his intention to stay in Three Lakes, it still felt like a temporary housing arrangement, as if he was only meant to be in the shelter for a short time. Tiffany appeared in the chair near the window and he smiled in greeting.

"Good afternoon, Tiffany. How are you?"

She tilted her head with a frown. *:You're different.:*

He raised his eyebrows. "I am?"

:Yes. More...settled and determined.: She frowned as if she didn't like that explanation. *:Those aren't the right words, but they encompass some of what I see. I think you're on your way to healing, Balder.:*

Despite that being his goal, sadness welled up in his chest. "What does that mean for you?"

She shook her head, her expression pensive. *:I don't know. Maybe it means I'll be able to move on. I just have no idea where I'll go.:*

His shoulders slumped. "Heaven?"

:I don't know. Maybe I'll ask Kate.: She frowned and bit her bottom lip. *:It just feels like I have something more to do, but I can tell you don't really need me anymore.:*

He gaped at her. He didn't need her anymore? He'd never been without her. Tiffany was as much a fixture in his life as his left arm. She'd calmed him and helped him focus through all the times of stress. *What will I do if she's not here?* But she'd given him the tools to find a solution, and he'd used them, thinking of what she'd do, in the times she wasn't with him and the programming had come back.

And I have Svanhild. At least he hoped he did. She too helped him remain in the present.

Balder sat down on the couch beside Tiffany and met her gaze. "I might not need you for the things you had to do for me, but I sure do like having you around. Don't leave on account of my healing, Tiffany. You're welcome in

Three Lakes just as much as I am. Hell, you're probably more welcome."

Her lips curled into an amused smile. *:That's changing. The people here are used to you and they know you're here to heal. Even Mr. MacGregor.:*

"Yeah, he and I came to a truce of sorts. I don't think we'll ever be friends, but at least he won't try to kill me every time he sees me."

:See? Healing. That's what this place is for.: Tiffany frowned and shook her head. *:I know I have more to do, I just can't see what it is yet.:*

"Maybe you have some healing of your own to do." He held his hands up when she shot him a sharp look. "It's a suggestion not an observation. The Goddess seems to throw stuff at us because we've ignored things." He smiled. "You taught me that. Whatever you decide, know that I'm grateful for your help and I like your company, Tiffany." He rose. "I'm going to take a shower before my date."

:With Svanhild tonight?:

"Yes. She didn't say what she had planned, but I'm going to try to be honest with her tonight."

Tiffany gazed at him a few moments and a sad smile curved her lips. *:You're in love with her, aren't you?:*

"Yes, ma'am." He nodded with his own smile. "I just have to tell her."

:Does she feel the same?:

He shook his head. "I don't know, but I'm not willing to let that stop me from telling her how I feel. I'll deal with whatever consequences come."

Her smile broadened. *:You have grown. That takes a lot of courage, Balder. I wish you luck.:*

"Thank you." He retreated into his bedroom to take his shower, hoping the Goddess heard Tiffany's benediction.

He showered and shaved, leaving a goatee Svanhild had once said she preferred, before he dressed in clean jeans and a light blue button-down short-sleeved shirt. The evening remained warm, but he sensed a weather change in the air, and tied an ox-blood red I ♥ Three Lakes sweatshirt around his waist. He'd bought a new pair of Doc Marten's shoes because Svanhild said they would support his feet best and they looked good with everything. He couldn't argue.

When he'd finished dressing, he found Tiffany had left the apartment. He hoped she found a purpose again now that her time with him appeared to be done, but he didn't want her to leave. He brushed his hair back from his face and considered cutting it. The sides had grown long.

He took a last look in his mirror and headed out to the lobby, locking his door behind him. He hoped he wouldn't be back tonight. If luck and the Goddess was with him, he'd be staying with Svanhild.

I just hope it goes as I'm planning.

He found Svanhild waiting for him at the front desk. His heart studdered at her glorious beauty and the urge to confess his love and attachment now that it was real swelled in his chest. He wanted more. More time, more intimacy, more reality. He'd acted the part of a lover many times in the Sword of God, but he didn't want to be false with Svanhild. Hopefully, this evening and the Solstice celebration would give him inspiration how to tell her his feelings.

"Ah, there you are, Balder." Angelina smiled. "We were just talking about you."

"No wonder my ears were burning." He grinned, his gaze focused on Svanhild.

She'd worn her hair up in a complex braid encircling her head and a light three-quarter sleeved linen shirt with a leather waist cincher corset. It made her breasts stand out and highlighted her hips. He loved her curves. She was strong without losing her femininity.

"Are you ready to go?" Svanhild's gaze sharpened as she took in his outfit as if assessing its practicality. "I like the boots."

"Thank you." He smiled. "I'm ready. Been looking forward to this all day."

Angelina grunted and grimaced. "Just be careful. It's the Solstice and while that can be a glorious time, it can also be a time of upheaval. The day feels…odd."

"Odd?" Balder grunted. "I'm sure it'll be fine, but I'll stick with Svanhild and keep an eye on things." His gut tightened at the unease in her voice. If Angelina thought something was up, he'd be careful.

"He won't be alone." Svanhild smiled, but it didn't quite reach her eyes. "I'll watch out for him." She gave a little nod and Angelina responded, but he didn't understand the reference.

"Have a good time tonight, no matter what, and don't feel like you have to hurry back. Shania and I can take care of things here. You just have a good time." She hesitated for a moment, biting her lip. "And watch your back. As I said, the day feels odd."

"We'll be careful. Thanks, Angelina." Svanhild nodded and fixed her gaze on Balder. "Ready?"

"Yes, ma'am."

He waved to Angelina as he followed Svanhild out of the shelter and took a deep breath. The scrutiny he'd felt for the last week continued and the back of his neck itched with it.

Svanhild shot Balder a look and took his hand, something so out of character it surprised him. But his heart swelled along with his cock. He loved that little display of affection and it broke some of his unease.

"So where are we going?" He squeezed her hand.

"Kate and Jayson are having a small intimate party on the beach on Bodi Lake and asked us to join them for their Solstice celebration." Svanhild pulled him toward the car she'd parked in front of the shelter. "I thought that would be a nice way to celebrate and do something a little more special than falling on each other like ravenous dogs."

"I don't know, I kinda like that about us." Balder grinned, but didn't argue. "I really wanted to apologize for whatever I said last week. I sense I said something wrong and I still don't know what it is."

She waved his words away. "It was nothing. I'm just focused on the threat to your life and getting the parts for my bike."

Balder raised his eyebrows as she released him to go to the driver's side. "Still haven't fixed it?"

"Not quite. I had to order a part and it'll take a few days to get here, but otherwise, she's finished."

His gut sank as he climbed in the passenger side. If she fixed the bike, would she climb on and ride away forever? He didn't want to entertain such thoughts so turned his attention to the drive out of town into the woods. The sun hadn't set yet, but the blue shadows between the trees took over the farther they drove from town. They even passed Kate's house on the way and Balder swore he saw a silvery-white shape standing among the trees at the far northern edge of her property.

The Sword of God ghost.

Soon they'd turned onto a Forest Service road and parked in the open area near the lake. A small lake house stood on the shore and extended out into the water. It almost appeared to be part of the natural surroundings, though he could discern where the water stopped and the building began. Several people already gathered on the beach beside the house, with a fire pit cracking in a nice cheery blaze.

He hesitated a moment, watching the people. Though he'd made inroads toward trust and friendship, he still had tense moments. Particularly around the Archivist and his family. They were major features in the community and he recognized their opinions of him reached many. *Hopefully, I've diffused some of that bomb last week.*

"Are you all right, Balder?" Svanhild shot him a look from across the car.

"Yeah, I think so. Just hoping I'm welcome rather than an intruder here tonight."

Svanhild nodded without a smile. "Kate and Jayson asked for you specifically and Sheriff Boulderson and his fiancée Gemini mentioned they'd like to see you."

"The sheriff is engaged to Gemini?"

She grinned at him. "*Ja*. I don't know the date, but it's supposed to be a fantastic party when it happens."

Balder shook his head, but he took a deep breath to settle his nerves. "They really wanted to see me?"

Svanhild nodded again.

"All right."

"Come on. I promise to hold your hand and stand with you if anyone gets testy." She winked as they headed over to the gathering of people.

He snorted, but followed along and tried to remember to keep his expression relaxed. *Just like when I infiltrated a new community.* Except this time the only thing he tried to hide was his fear.

Kate and Jayson smiled and handed him a plate full of homemade foods. Ben and Iris Maple nodded and asked him how he was feeling. Everyone had heard of Drake's attack at the Memorial Day festival. Balder made friendly conversation with the folks around him, but his shoulders itched. Something or someone watched him, he was sure of it. He tried to keep an eye on the trees around them, but he kept getting distracted by people and conversations.

"Hey, Balder, are you okay? You look stressed." Jayson took a swig from his red plastic cup.

Balder shook his head. "I don't know. Just tired I guess. Unsettled." He shrugged.

"Yeah—"

"Jayson." Kate waved at him from the deck of the house.

"Yeah?"

"Can you get more ice from the house? We're almost out."

"Yeah." Jayson grimaced and shook his head. "The wife calls and I come like a good dog." He winked and Balder laughed at his joke. He doubted the Alpha werewolf ever behaved like a well-trained dog.

Balder drifted closer to the fire, inhaling to see if any scents seemed out of place. While he didn't have the nose of a werewolf or vampire, he'd trained himself to catch unusual smells. Nothing beyond wet sand, humid forest, and burning wood came to his senses. He turned his head away from the fire and scanned the trees, his eyes adjusting to the darkness. Still nothing, but his gut told him someone watched him.

"Are you well, Balder?" Svanhild came up beside him holding her own red cup.

He gave a one-shoulder shrug. "I feel like someone's watching me." He shivered and rubbed the back of his neck with one hand. "It's been going on for a little over a week now. It's probably nothing, just my old habits refusing to die."

Svanhild nodded slowly and leaned forward to brush his ear with her lips. "I don't think you're wrong."

He blinked. "What am I not wrong about?"

"About someone watching you." She stood back and met his gaze somberly. "Jayson and Kate spread the word. We've all been on edge for the last week because of the wolves in the forest."

"Does Jayson know them?"

"No. Apparently they hadn't made the proper introductions to be in his territory."

Balder nodded. He figured it would be something like that. "Does the sheriff know?"

Svanhild nodded. "*Ja*. It's why we're having this Solstice get-together out here at Anja Freyasdottir's house.

If they show, we want to be here to have your back."

"So I'm the bait?" He scowled.

"In a way. We need to flush them out and deal with whatever brought them here."

"I suspect that's me." He sighed.

"Possibly, but according to Jayson, they've violated Pack rules and etiquette. They should've sought him out and asked permission to come into his territory to hunt."

Balder raised his eyebrows. "What if they didn't know he was here?"

Svanhild shrugged. "This isn't the eighteenth century. They could've asked around to other regional packs or *helvete,* made an effort to ask the other Elder Race residents. It's not like they can't smell the difference between humans and other species."

He nodded slowly. "So this party was both a way to make them show themselves and confront them for violating the rules."

"*Ja.* And I'll have your back no matter what." She cupped his jaw in a tender move at odds with the warrior he knew her to be. "You have my word."

"Svanhild—"

His declaration was cut off by a low menacing growl that made his hair rise on the back of his neck. Out of the flickering darkness came a pack of large wolves, larger than any he'd ever seen, including those repopulating Yellowstone National Park. He and Svanhild turned to face the threat, and his gut sank. He didn't want to do this here. He was done killing the Elder Races, but he refused to die. Especially now that he had a community to live for. And a woman he loved. It didn't matter that she wasn't strictly human. He loved her anyway. *And I stupidly haven't told her yet.*

The Alpha of the invading pack had a white coat, his blue eyes malevolent and intense. Balder dropped his drink and prepared himself for the possibility of battle. The last thing he wanted to do was prove he could kill the Elder Races, but he wouldn't go down without a fight.

The forest had grown still as the wolves approached and a strange ripple of energy skittered up Balder's spine. He kept the wolves in his peripherals as he swung his gaze around the clearing beyond the fire. Nothing looked different, but a subtle hum had filled the air like the forest watched and waited.

Svanhild stilled beside him, her own focus on the Alpha wolf. Goddess, Balder didn't want her to get hurt. She said she was a Valkyrie and he sensed her differences from the humans in town, but part of him still feared she could be killed by werewolves. And he had no doubt they faced a full pack.

"You should go back to the house, Svanhild. They're here for me." He took a deep breath to settle himself and stepped ahead of her. "And Jayson needs to know about this."

"You're right. He does and he will." She raised his chin and moved up beside him. "You wolves are intruding on a private party and are not welcome here. Begone from this place."

The Alpha snarled and bared his teeth, his gaze never leaving Balder.

"Have the decency to treat with me in human form, wolf, before I run you through." Svanhild's voice grew cold and powerful. Balder shivered.

The wolf finally moved his gaze to the Valkyrie and snorted with disdain. But he shifted shape into a white-blond man with blue eyes not unlike Tiffany's. He scowled, his chin lifted in the same disdain he'd offered in his wolf form.

"This is not your fight, woman. You should go back to the house like you were told. This is pack business and doesn't concern you." His lip curled.

More energy rippled through the air as Svanhild

became "more." Balder didn't know any other way to describe it. He'd never seen her assume her true form, but he'd felt the hint of it a few times. Now it swelled to press against him and the wolves. A few of the lesser packmembers shot looks at each other and their tails lowered a little. But the Alpha only sneered.

More fool you.

"Pack business, you say?" Svanhild shook her head. "I've spoken to the local Alpha, little wolf, and he knows nothing of you or your 'pack business.' Odd, don't you think?"

Anger pulled the new Alpha's lips down. "These are extenuating circumstances and the usual protocols don't apply."

Or don't apply to him. Balder's gut sank. This wolf hadn't done his homework, but didn't seem to care. That meant he didn't care who he killed to get to Balder. Fuck that. He wouldn't sacrifice Svanhild for his sins. He tried to move again, but she stepped in front of him. Other members of the community slowly gathered behind them, including Kate, Tiffany and Sheriff Boulderson. Balder wondered where Jayson was, but remembered he'd gone for ice.

"No, the usual protocols don't apply, but new ones do. You've stepped into a well-defended territory without permission, wolf. I suggest you retreat and regroup, before coming back with supplication to Mr. Blackamber and beg his forgiveness."

"This is my kill and my hunt. The kill is retribution of wrongs done to my pack. That"—he pointed at Balder— "has killed a whole family of wolves in my pack, and he must pay. His life is forfeit. Nothing stops me from getting what I want."

"Things are more complex than you think, wolf, and rules must be adhered to before you can kill with impunity."

Svanhild remained unmoved, but sorrow filled Balder's gut. So these were the other members of Tiffany's pack come to exact payment for their losses. He shot a look at Tiffany's familiar ghost who'd settled in behind Kate on the beach. *Goddess, I'm sorry, Tiffany.*

:I know, Balder.:

"Now get out of way, bitch, before you get hurt."

Aw hell...

Svanhild laughed, which only made the Alpha angrier, and before Balder could warn her, the man shifted into his wolf form and leapt at them.

****

Svanhild let go of her human disguise as soon as the wolf launched himself at her and pulled her sword *Forsvarer* free from her scabbard. *Come at me and we'll play your little game, hairball.* It'd been so long since she'd dressed in her full armor, but it felt good. Her helmet with the bear claws in spiked ring decorating it settled over her head. The string of her bow hung across her chest and she felt the weight of the quiver on her back. It brought her comfort to wear her gear and she grinned as she smacked the snarling wolf in the side with the flat of her blade, throwing off his charge.

The wolf yipped in surprise and fell into the sand of the beach before rolling to his feet. Svanhild blew a kiss at him as the battle rage rose in her, the blood of her ancestors igniting. Oh, she knew she might die in this fight. Werewolves were notoriously tough to kill, especially with their ability to heal quickly, but she'd fought them before and she had experience and patience. All she had to do was anger him so much he'd forget his common sense and skills.

Here, little puppy. She wiggled a finger in a "come-here" motion and he snarled.

For some reason the other wolves stayed back, but she suspected they either bided their time or kept Balder in their sights. She hoped he'd be able to hold them off until she took care of the Alpha. If he wouldn't be dissuaded by force, she'd kill him. *No one touches my man.*

The Alpha charged again, this time coming low. Svanhild danced aside and swung her sword down to meet the wolf's shoulder. The animal squealed in real pain and snapped at her, snagging the edge of her arm brace with his teeth. It jerked her off balance, but she dropped to one knee and brought the blade edge into his hind leg beneath the bushy tail.

The wolf squealed and tried to savage her arm above the brace, but Svanhild brought the pommel down hard on his head and he released her. She lurched to her feet and swung back to face him. The wolf shook his head and staggered, his hind leg bleeding from the tear in the flesh.

What are you going to do now, hairball? She scanned his body language, trying to figure out what he'd do before he did it.

In the back of her awareness, she caught figures moving at the edges of her sight. Human shaped images, though the energy signatures showed something else entirely. She recognized some of them. The *Morukai* stood off to the side next to Iris Maple, who had her arms crossed over her chest as a wheat-haired man with powerful shoulders stood behind her. Both had the energy of the forest in them and she suspected they represented the Dryad's Garden. No help for the wolves in the trees, then.

The energy of the wolf she fought had diminished with the blow to his head and the cut in his haunch. She'd given him a good concussion and he bled out from the leg wound. It wouldn't take much to kill him. While she had the right given his attack on her, she supposed it was pack business and she should give him an out so Jayson could deal with him.

She dredged her voice up from the center of her chest, trying to find coherency in the battle rage. "Do you yield, wolf? If you do so, I shall leave you to the tender mercies the local Alpha, and you'll have a chance to live."

Maybe. If Jayson isn't so angry he tears out your throat.

The wounded Alpha swayed, his eyes glazed over in pain and disorientation. But his snarl remained firmly etched into his muzzle. His gaze slid back and forth as if he couldn't focus, but then it sharpened on someone behind her and a menacing growl sounded across the space.

She didn't dare look away, but Balder's energy sizzled at her back, stronger than usual, but still human. *Not this time, fang-face.* She settled her mind into cold focus and waited, watching the Alpha's motions.

When the wolf howled and launched itself at her, she was ready. She responded with her own bear-like battle roar and swung her sword up from below, cleaving the wolf from belly to rib-juncture. The animal yelped and floundered, snapping as he dragged her blade down. She pulled it free, pivoted, and stabbed him through the heart from the side.

A keening wail filled the air around the lake as Svanhild twisted the blade in his body.

"Jeg frigjør deg fra din harme pine. Gå i vei og finn fred." *I release you from your angry torment. Be gone and find peace.* She yanked the sword free and wiped it on the white fur, leaving a crimson streak.

She stepped away from the carcass and positioned her body to keep it and the other wolves in view as she shot her gaze to Kate and the ghostly form of Tiffany behind her. Her breath came in gasps as the adrenaline started to settle and the battle rage waned. She waited to catch her breath before she faced the consequences of her actions. She'd killed a wolf in another Alpha's territory.

"I killed this intruding wolf in defense of the Three

Lakes community and of Balder Templar." She stopped herself from saying more about their relationship. She wouldn't share that with strangers. *Helvete, I don't even know what our relationship is.* Except that she loved him. "This wolf violated protocols by coming in without permission and he disturbed the peace with intent to do harm to a fellow resident." She shoved her sword into the scabbard. "Despite that, I accept responsibility for my actions and await the decision of the local Alpha and *Morukai.*"

One of the other wolves had shifted into his human form, his face contorted in rage. "You'll pay for that bitch!"

He took a few steps toward her and she whipped her bow over her shoulder, notching an arrow before he could blink.

"Make a move, fleabag, and I'll put an arrow in your throat."

CHAPTER NINETEEN

No one laughed. *Maybe because I'm deadly serious.*
She held her gaze on the man surrounded by the other
cowering wolves, but motion in the corners of her vision
told her Balder stood with Gemini, Anja, Iris and Ben. She
couldn't see the sheriff anymore, but Kate moved into her
sight near the trees. The pack sidled closer to the man who
must have been the beta before she killed his Alpha. He
snarled at her as he stopped, his hands fisting at his sides.

"You gonna hide behind women's skirts, boy? Not
much of a man if you do." The beta sneered and tipped his
head with an ugly smirk.

Svanhild resisted the urge to roll her eyes. *As if women
haven't ruled your ass forever there, big dog.*

Another snarl filled the clearing as a new werewolf
stalked, stiff-legged, up beside Kate. *That must be Jayson.*
His long canines gleamed in the light of the fire and the
other wolves backed up a step, their tails tucked tight to
their asses. *Oh yeah, have you met the local Alpha
werewolf yet?*

Kate patted Jayson's shoulders and braced her feet
shoulder-width apart before clapping her hands together.
She curled her thumbs as if snagging something before

pulling her palms apart. A bright square grew between her expanding hands, creating a shimmering space reminiscent of a piece of glass. Svanhild couldn't look over her shoulder without losing her mark while she held the bow, but the beta she aimed at gasped.

"Does your Alpha bitch let you talk to her that way, Tad?" A young woman's voice carried clearly to where they stood and light spilled from the shining space onto the ground.

"Tiffany!" Tad took a step forward, but Svanhild shifted the point of her arrow to fit neatly between his pectorals. At this range she'd blow right through his ribs into his heart. He growled and stopped again.

"Why did you come here, Tad?" Tiffany's voice had a hollow quality as if she spoke down a long tube.

"To avenge you and your family, Tiff. He took you from us." Tad stabbed a finger in Balder's direction. "Ricky said we had to come for him when we saw him on the news. They called him a hero." He spat on the ground. "Why should he walk free when he killed so many?"

"And now your vengeance has cost you another packmember. Your Alpha." Tiffany sounded disgusted. "That was stupid of Ricky. He should've known better. Go home to your Luna, Tad, and explain to her why you got her mate killed." She paused as if counting. "Why isn't she here? Did she send you all after Balder?"

Tad appeared to sink lower into his own shoulders. "No, Tiff, we don't have a Luna. Ricky never mated. He was too worried about avenging you."

"Oh, for the First Canid's sake." Svanhild could hear Tiffany's "facepalm" without seeing it. "And what has that gotten you? More death, more loss, and farther from the Goddess."

"What were we supposed to do?" Tad's chin came up in challenge. "He killed members of our pack. Your family and you. And made you a ghost—"

"And he's paid for it, believe me. I've made sure of it."
Tiffany snorted.

Svanhild felt Balder's sorrow and chagrin as well as
his agreement. Her own heart lifted at the thought. He'd
paid and regretted, and would continue to work toward
redemption. *He's a good man.* The thought made her
shoulders tighten, but she held her arrow steady.

Tiffany sighed wearily. "Kate, would you grant me one
more request?"

The *Morukai* tilted her head. "What would that be,
Tiffany?"

"Would you grant me the ability to go with them so I
can help them find a new Alpha or Luna?"

"Go with them?" Balder's voice sounded strange, like
a mixture of hope and dread.

"Yes, Balder. You don't need me anymore. You have
plenty of help right here in Three Lakes. You're strong
enough on your own now." Compassion filled Tiffany's
voice.

"How will you go with them if you're a ghost,
Tiffany?" Jayson had shifted into his human form beside
Kate, so he could face Tiffany, but his gaze never left the
rogue pack.

"I'll give up my form for her, Lady Kate."

Svanhild's aim remained steady and true, but her heart
stuttered in pain and fear. Balder would leave this world,
abandoning her here alone once more? *No, Balder, you
can't.* But she hadn't told him how much she loved him.
*Sweet Freyja, he doesn't know I love him and need him
with me.*

"Give up your form, Balder?" Kate shot him a look
over her shoulder. "As in give up your body?"

"Yes. She can have my physical form, the energy of
my body so she can do this work. As my final penance, I
offer up everything I have so she might help the pack I
harmed." He stepped into Svanhild's line of sight beside

Jayson, his expression resigned.

NOOOOOOOO!

The wail echoed through Svanhild's heart, but she blinked back the tears and held the notched arrow still. Screaming loss bounced around inside her like a spiked mace, ripping gaping holes in her soul. Losing Balder would be akin to losing the Sisterhood of Valkyries all over again.

Please, Freyja, don't take that from me, too. I need him. He's my heart and anchor. He's my home port. Please.

Kate's gaze shifted to Svanhild and her brows went up, but Svanhild kept her focus on Tad.

"No, Balder, you've done enough. That won't be necessary." Tiffany's declaration offered relief, followed by confusion. The fear burning in Svanhild's gut dampened down.

"I'll stay with Tad and the others to help them find a new Alpha and Luna. They need to return to the Goddess and they can't do that without me."

"You mean, haunt them instead of Balder?" Jayson snorted. "Sounds good to me. You kept him in line so well I figure you can do the same with Tad here. I don't see a problem with that and it gets them out of my territory. Kate?"

"You know this means you'll have to find another *Morukai* to release you from your ghost life with them, Tiffany." Kate's voice held caution and warning. "Once you choose to haunt another and go with them, I can't do anything unless you all come back here."

A collective growl rumbled through the gathered Elder Races. *Guess no one wants to see these dogs again.*

"I know. I'll help them and find a new *Morukai* where we end up."

"Are you sure, Tiffany?" Balder's voice held genuine concern and Svanhild's arms threatened to shake.

"I'm sure. This is what I'm meant to do. I'm a teacher, a leader, even if my methods are kinda unorthodox."

"Yeah. Just a little." Balder gave a painful laugh. "Take care of yourself and your pack, Tiffany. I truly am sorry for the hurt I caused."

Tiffany snorted. "Oh, I know you are. But you did the right thing bringing us here, and you have more to do, while I need to go."

"If you're sure, Tiffany, we have to do this soon. The window of opportunity is closing." Kate nodded sharply.

"I'm sure. Thank you for all your help, Kate."

"All right then. In three, two, one—"

Kate widened her hands and a shimmering, pixie dust wolf leapt through the expanding square. Her front paws made no tracks in the sand of the beach as she dashed straight for Tad. His eyes widened to the size of dinner plates and he took a step back when Tiffany lunged. The pixie dust wolf crashed into his chest and disappeared in a puff of sparkles like a fireworks display.

Svanhild eased the draw of the bow as Tad dropped to one knee, curling his body into a ball while he absorbed Tiffany's presence. Kate brushed her hands together as if ridding them of dust and the crowd around them relaxed some of its hostility. Svanhild dropped the bow to point the arrow at the ground and shifted her stance so she could see both the werewolf and Balder.

He stood with his feet braced shoulder-width apart, his hands down, and his shoulders slumped like someone who'd dropped a huge weight. He wore both exhaustion and relief in equal measure, but when he raised his gaze to meet hers, she found acceptance and contentment in his eyes.

"Tiffany says she'll make sure we find our Luna and Alpha, and the Goddess will come back to our pack." Tad looked like he'd rather be saying anything other than those words, something more manly, perhaps. But Svanhild suspected Tiffany remained a force to be reckoned with.

"I'm glad to hear that, Tad." Kate nodded with a smile. "Take care of yourself and your pack. It's late. Stop by the Gitchegumee Inn and get a room before you get something to eat. No point in driving home hungry and exhausted. I think you're gonna need your strength."

Balder snorted so softly only Svanhild heard it.

Tad nodded and whistled to the gathered wolves. They shot looks at Svanhild and Balder before retreating into the trees back toward town. Svanhild only relaxed when she saw their backs disappear in the darkness beyond the light of the fire. She dropped the arrow back in the quiver and threw her bow over her shoulder before resuming her human disguise. It always felt like stuffing herself into a corset or a mummy sleeping bag one size too small until she got used to it again.

"Oh, thank the Goddess that's done." Kate sighed and brushed off her hands again. "Who's up for some chocolate cake?"

"Would that be your very special uber chocolate cake from your Aunt Sue, Kate?" Anya sounded hopeful.

Gemini laughed. "She's never been able to resist that cake."

"Yep, and Gemini made some of her special Sangria." Sheriff Boulderson rumbled a laugh.

Murmurs of approval echoed through the assembled guests and they all headed for the house except Svanhild and Balder. As one they glanced down at the wolf's body lying on the bloody sand, before meeting each other's gaze.

"What about the body?" Svanhild shot a look toward Kate and Jayson. "Shouldn't we bury it or something?"

Iris approached and stood beside her, her head tilted in consideration. "Leave it for now. The dryads will take care of it and give him a proper internment."

Svanhild bit her bottom lip. "Do you bury your dead? Or do you let them rot?"

"A little bit of both. Since we're part of the trees, we put our dead in shallow graves with their trees over them so they may nourish the next generation. We will offer him the same honor. The breakdown of his carcass will help nourish the land."

Svanhild understood the whole 'circle of life' aspect to things, but it still sounded creepy as hell. *At least I don't have to dig a grave.* That was sweaty, dirty, disgusting work and she'd just as soon spend time with Balder instead. *I have to tell him how I feel.*

"Okay, then. Thank you for your help." She gave Iris a smile.

"You're welcome, Svanhild. We have to stand up for our friends and citizens." Iris returned her smile.

"Even if they are former Sword of God?"

Iris's gaze slid to Balder. "That makes it harder, for sure. But Balder seems to be trying to get better, and the *Morukai* thinks he's okay. I'll give him the benefit of the doubt."

Svanhild nodded. "Fair enough."

"Coming for Sangria and chocolate cake?"

Svanhild shot a look at Balder before shaking her head. "No, I think we'll head on home. We've had a rather exciting end to the day. End of the week, actually, and we could both use the rest."

Iris nodded and touched her shoulder. "Makes sense. Have a good night and may the summer breezes rustle your leaves but gently."

Svanhild waved as the dryad Queen caught up with her husband before they retreated to the house. She envied them their connection and love. *Helvete*, she envied all the couples the ease with which they showed their emotions and affection. She wanted something like it. With Balder.

I'm a fool.

****

Balder stood looking down into the quiet lake water and wished he could find the same stillness. While the programming voices had retreated enough that he could ignore them, his past still posed a danger to the residents of his adopted town. He didn't want to leave, but he stood alone in the aftermath of death. Even Tiffany had gone to continue her path as a teacher and guide.

He shot a look at the cooling body on the sand and grimaced. *Death seems to follow me everywhere.*

"Are you all right, Balder?" Svanhild appeared beside him back in her human disguise. No matter which form she wore, his heart always swelled with her beauty.

He'd never appreciated the female form before he came to Three Lakes. They were either targets or background decoration. But Svanhild made his heart race when she walked by. Hell, she could be sitting in her chair reading and drinking tea, and he'd be drooling from her beauty. Seeing her in her true form had been a treat.

"I'm good enough."

"I thought we might head to your place for some private time now that Tiffany's gone. I, uh, have something I need to talk to you about." She touched his elbow hesitantly, her eyes concerned. "How are you doing? Did this bring back bad memories?"

He shook his head, but shrugged as well. "Not memories, but regrets. Another death on my record."

"He only died because he couldn't let go and he would've done more damage than help. You're a part of this community now, Balder." She hesitated a little longer. "I couldn't let you be killed."

"Why not?"

It was a question that had been bothering him a long time. What worth remained in his life? He'd killed and harmed so many people just because they weren't human. And now another had died because of him.

"Because I want you."

All his thoughts and worries shattered, leaving behind stunned silence. He gaped at her. *Did she say she wants me?* He'd never expected her to feel anything close to the sentiment he'd felt for over a month. Not for a man like him.

"Come on. Let me take you home. It's been a rough night."

"I don't want to go home." He shook his head.

"All right." She dropped her gaze to her feet. "What do you want to do then?"

"I want to be with you. Alone. Safe and secure."

"I could take you home with me. We'd be alone, safe, secure and…"

"And?" He hoped she meant more than just sitting and talking.

Svanhild shot a look back toward the house then scanned the trees before she returned her gaze to him. "And I'd like to touch you. To know you're all right and uninjured."

"Oh." He let a half-smile curl his lips. "Yeah, that would be good."

She smiled back at him and they waved to the others on the deck of the house as they strolled to the car. He climbed in the passenger side and wondered if this was their last night together. Would she get the last piece to her bike, fit it together, and ride off in to the sunset? He tried to rein in his aching heart. He didn't deserve her or her love. Not really. He had his skills and he'd made friends, but he'd always be subject to suspicion.

"You okay? You're kinda quiet over there." Svanhild pulled onto the main road and headed back toward town.

"I was just thinking about your bike and what will happen once it's fixed." He kept his gaze out the window at the darkening trees passing by. "Will you leave the moment it's ready?"

She was silent as they drove through the gathering dark, only the hiss of the tires on the pavement breaking the quiet. He smelled the wet humid woods and the hot pavement, but instead of distracting him, it only made his worry deepen.

Svanhild still hadn't answered his question by the time they turned onto her driveway off the road. His heart dropped and sadness damn near stole his breath. With Tiffany gone, he couldn't really leave Three Lakes. He didn't feel safe in the world without her or Angelina or Kate around to steady him. *Or Svanhild.* If she drove off because she needed to move on, he had nowhere to go. Besides, he liked Three Lakes. They understood him, even if they didn't fully trust him.

She pulled the car up in front of her cabin, the porch light coming on sensing their motion, and sat for a few moments when she turned off the ignition. The silence stretched and his hope slipped away like sand through a sieve. Crickets chirped in the evening gloom, singing their hopeful 'fuck-me' songs. He wished he knew the tune for the human 'love-me' version.

But she's not human. I'm so screwed.

"Let's go in and I'll start some tea." She patted his thigh before she got out of the car.

Balder followed more slowly, his heart in his shoes. He took a deep breath and squared his shoulders. If she planned to hand him rejection, he'd face it like an adult. He didn't know much about love, but he wanted more of it from Svanhild. Only Svanhild. He sighed and shook his head as he headed into the cabin.

The scents of cookies and freshly cut wood filled his nose as he stepped into the warmly lit room. Svanhild's braid had fallen down her back as she set two mugs on her rough hewn table. He admired her curves, from the taut round ass to her glorious breasts held in linen. Goddess, she turned him on like no one else ever had.

259

And I'm losing her.

"Come sit down."

"All right." He settled himself in one of the chairs and wrapped his hands around the mug. The temperature outside was high, but a chill ran through him and he craved the heat of the tea. He had to make her understand at least how he felt.

"Balder—"

He held up a hand to stop her. "Before you say whatever it is, let me tell you something so you're clear on where I stand. I should've told you this a week ago, but I was too worried it would be too much for you. Especially from a man like me." He took a deep breath. "I love you, Svanhild, as inconvenient as it may be. And as corny as it sounds, I do go to sleep thinking about you and wake up the same. You've given me hope and strength when everyone else turned their backs."

He sighed and rubbed his hands together before meeting her gaze. "I know my past is riddled with horrors and unforgivable crimes, and I'm working at atoning for them. I know I'm human and not the first choice of a Valkyrie for a partner or mate. But if I have any choice in this, I want you to know I love you more than I've ever loved anyone and I want to be with you. Please stay here in Three Lakes. With me. And not just to translate any warnings I have to the community. I know I asked before, but this is my heart speaking. Please."

There. He'd said what he needed and submitted his request. His faults made it unlikely, but he had to put forth the effort.

"Done?" She raised an eyebrow as she sipped her tea.

"Yes, ma'am. For now." He nodded.

"Good." She set down her mug, but held it in a mirror image to him. "The reason I didn't answer your question right away is I had to figure out how to say it as clearly as possible."

Oh, Heavens, she's going to let me down easy. His gut sank.

"As you know, I'm a Valkyrie, and we're known for fighting and valor, but not really for speaking our hearts." She gave a one-shouldered shrug. "So I'm just going to say this and hope for the best." She paused again and he swore the suspense would kill him.

"I love you with all my heart in ways I shouldn't, being a Valkyrie."

When he raised his eyebrows in surprise, she grimaced. "Valkyries aren't supposed to love. We judge who's worthy of Valhalla and who should be given pride of place, but love has nothing to do with it. And to be brutally honest, when I first saw you, I didn't find you worthy."

He nodded, resigned to her assessment. *She can love me, but not find me worthy.* He suspected that would always be the case.

"I understand."

Svanhild blinked. "You understand what?"

"I understand you love me, but can't see yourself with me because I'm unworthy."

"What? No. Sweet Freyja, that's not what I'm saying at all. Be patient and let me finish. I told you I'm not good at speaking my heart."

He opened his mouth to speak, but thought better of it when she shot him a dark look. He closed it again and nodded.

"Okay." She nodded as well and looked down at her hands as if gathering her thoughts. "I've never loved anyone before, but after I met you and Kate asked me to help you understand how to be part of a community, I found I liked you."

"Like is good." He snorted, but smiled.

"For me, it's important. I've discovered I have to like someone before I can love them. It may not work for others like this, but it works for me." She raised her gaze to his and he read the uncertainty in her eyes. "I didn't know I loved you until the moment the librarian nearly killed you. When I heard the news, I almost vomited in my panic. I can't lose you and be whole." She swallowed hard and took a deep breath. "I love you and like you, Balder, and I want to stay here in Three Lakes with you, be your lover, be your friend, and be your protector for all time." She looked like she wanted to say more, but she closed her mouth and nodded sharply.

"Done?" He gave her a half smile to hide his thundering heart. *She wants to stay!*

"Yes, sir, for now." She grimaced.

"Good." He set his mug aside and rose to walk around the table. He knelt beside her chair and grasped her face in his hands. "I accept." Then he tilted his head and kissed her.

A relieved and needy moan erupted from her as she wrapped her arms around him. He opened his mouth and caressed her tongue with his, giving her all his love and desire. This was the woman he wanted beyond reason or time. His life had been monochromatic up until he met her, but she stepped in, bringing color and life with her. And he wanted more.

When they pulled apart, he met her eyes and swallowed hard. "I love you, Svanhild."

"I love you, too, Balder."

"Thank you for defending me against the werewolf. I really didn't want to kill him myself." He shook his head. "I'm sure that sounds cowardly, but I've worked so hard to give up that lifestyle. Killing him would've destroyed all my efforts."

"I will defend you with my words, deeds, and skills." Svanhild held him close to her chest, her gray eyes serious. "I may have lost my sisterhood when I defied Odin, but the Goddess brought me to Three Lakes where I have a new community to stand with."

"And me."

She chuckled. "*Ja*, and you. I wasn't expecting a lover. Or a community. *Helvete*, I wasn't expecting any of it. My bike simply broke down here."

Balder tipped his head. "Did it? I don't think things simply happen anymore. At least not here in Three Lakes. Tiffany and I were drawn here, probably for the *Morukai*, so she'd help us find what we needed. I needed a home and family. She needed to be freed from me." He dropped his gaze and shook his head with a smile. "I thought that meant she'd be free from the life of being a ghost, but it meant she'd be haunting someone else to get them in line."

Svanhild snorted. "She was very good at keeping you focused."

"Yes, she was." He laughed, but lost his smile as he met her gaze again. "I was afraid if she left that I wouldn't be able to hold off the voices in my head. But you, and Angelina, and Kate help me ignore their prompts, and they're fading away. I hear them less and less now."

Svanhild cupped his cheek with one hand. "This is good news. So the more time you spend around strong women, the less the voices capture your attention?"

He blinked then laughed. "Yes, that's about it. Thank heavens for strong women." He nodded, but a grimace worked its way onto his face as his knees whined about being on the floor. "I need to get up. This kneeling thing looks cool in movies, but isn't comfortable long-term."

She laughed as he levered himself up using the table and sat in the nearest chair. But he grasped her hand and met her gaze again, hoping all his sincerity filled his face and voice.

"I want to make this work, Svanhild, even if I'm an old, retired, messed-up assassin who works in a shelter as a handyman."

"Old?" She snorted. "I think I have you beat in the age department. I've been around since the Romans got their asses handed to them by that Hunnish upstart."

Balder blinked again. "In this world?"

"Oh. No, I was exiled around the time of the Ottoman-Hungarian War."

"Wait, you mean the time that produced the legend of Dracula?"

"That's the one. Brutal time, glad it's done. But the point is, it's you I want, and who you are now is based on all the experiences you've had." She leaned forward so he couldn't see anything but her face. "I want you, Balder, with all your flaws. We can both work on our flaws together. Here in Three Lakes."

"So you'll stay?"

She nodded. "I'll stay as long as you're with me." She spread her hands over the table. "Besides, Bart offered me a partnership with him in the Fix-It Cave. I signed the papers a couple of days ago."

Balder raised his eyebrows. "When did this happen?"

"The night you first saw the wolves around the cabin. I was all ready to tell you, but your delivery of your reasons for me to stay kinda derailed my thought train." She waved her hand near her head. "I'm sorry I didn't mention it after that. The preparation for taking on the invading pack and keeping you safe took precedence."

"So, you're going to stay. When were you planning to tell me?" He couldn't quite keep the hurt out of his voice. He'd worried for nothing?

"As soon as the threat was dealt with, which it is now." She shrugged uncomfortably. "I'm sorry, Balder. I didn't think you'd mind. I didn't know the extent of your feelings, and that's my failing. I should've said something earlier."

He nodded to show her he was listening, and to keep himself from saying something stupid. Anger flickered through him at her reticence, followed swiftly by chagrin. He hadn't told her how he'd felt either.

"I guess we both have to work on our flaws,

particularly communication."

"*Ja*, you're right." She met his gaze again, her face contrite. "I promise to make more effort on that score if you stay with me." She pointed to the table. "Here."

"Here in this cabin?" His heart started to lift.

"Yes. I don't think Bart will mind as long as the rent's paid and I show up to work. He said I could live here as long as I liked and he knows how I feel about you."

"Wait, he knew before I did?"

"*Helvete*, I've done this all wrong, haven't I?" She rubbed her face with her hands. "I didn't tell him, but he figured it out. Then he offered me the partnership in the Fix-It Cave and I was all ready to tell you when you came over." She sighed and studied her hands around her mug. "But then you only wanted my help as a message translator and I wasn't sure you felt the same. I was a coward. I couldn't make the first move and tell you how I felt when you seemed to only want me for my friendship. And I could do friendship, but that's not what my heart wanted."

"Why didn't you tell me? It's been over a week."

"I know. I should have, but I was scared."

"A Valkyrie, scared?" Balder shook his head. "Scared about what?"

"About the feelings I had for you, about giving away my heart to someone who didn't want more than friendship." She shrugged again, the corners of her mouth pulling down. "Valkyries don't have lovers or soul mates or whatever. We're warriors and defenders of the weak, but we don't give away our hearts. I've never felt anything like this and it frightened me."

He gazed at her and wondered if maybe he wasn't as messed up as he thought. "Will you let me in, Svanhild? I can teach you what I know about love and emotion, but not if you hide from me or shut me out. Can you do that?"

"*Ja*, I can, and I want to." She grasped his hands as relief loosened her shoulders. "Please teach me how to love, Balder. Stay here in this cabin with me and teach me the best of your human heart."

"I don't know if I have the best human heart, but I'll give you the best of mine. Are you sure you want to stay in this cabin?"

"*Ja.*" A coy smile curled her lips. "That way we won't have to worry about breaking the rules on having sex at the shelter. Because I plan on have a lot more sex with you."

He raised an eyebrow. "Oh, do you, now? Making up for lost time?"

"Yes, sir, I am. It helps to have a dedicated lover."

"I'm happy to be dedicated to you, Svanhild." He nodded and met her gaze. "I'll stay here with you, every night, until I'm done with this life."

"*Jeg elsker deg*, Balder." *I love you, Balder.*

His eyes widened. She'd used her first language, the language of his mother, and the one closest to his heart where the voices and programming couldn't reach. Light exploded outward from his heart, flaring brilliant enough in his mind's eye that he had to close his real eyes. Energy burst through his body, scouring the dark corners, and the voices wailed in distress as another one of their anchors in his mind broke free.

He gasped and bowed his head, reeling from the giddy sense of joy and freedom that one statement brought to him. Three little words, but they meant more to him than any praise he'd ever received.

"*Jeg elsker deg*, Svanhild." He raised his head and met her gaze. "And I'm yours, forever."

She clasped his head and pulled him close until they sat nose-to-nose. "Good."

Then she kissed him to seal the deal.

THE END

L.T. DALIN'S DEILIG COOKIES
RECIPE

225 grams (1 cup) butter at room temperature
150 gr (3/4 cup) white sugar
150 gr (3/4 cup) brown sugar
3 large (4 small) eggs
1 tsp vanilla
1 tsp baking powder
340 gr (2.5 cups) flour
400 gr (1 1/4 cups) dark chocolate cut into chunks

Set oven to 180 C (350 F)
Whisk together butter and sugars
Whisk in eggs, beating until smooth
Add vanilla and mix
Add baking powder to flour and sift into butter mixture before stirring in chocolate chunks
The cookies swell with baking so only nine fit on a sheet, about a Tbsp's worth of raw dough for each.
Bake for 10-15 mins until a golden brown, elevation permitting.
Let cool on sheets for two minutes before transferring to a wire rack.

ORDER OF THE DRAGON
WARBLER PENINSULA, BOOK 1
SNEEK PEEK

Drake MacGregor always adhered to the adage 'let sleeping dragons lie', until he slept with one.

In an effort to make up for his past as Vlad the Impaler, Drake has been living a small, quiet life in Three Lakes. As the town's archivist, his knowledge of history and his place in it weigh on him. Drake has one desire—to rectify the atrocities committed in the name of his knightly order. Too bad he can't keep his hands, or his fangs, off the local doctor, especially when he discovers she's an actual dragon.

Aliandra Cantora del Viento is old enough and wise enough to ignore her attraction to the handsome historian, especially when her heart suggests he might be something more than he appears. Drake stokes her fires and curls her tail, and after a hot night in her clinic, the game is on. But he avoids her and nothing she tries breaks through his reserve, despite his obvious interest. He turns her on then apologizes for it, repeatedly. Not exactly the kind of relationship she'd hoped for yet she can't walk away.

When a mysterious researcher arrives with his son, Drake becomes more edgy and irritable, and Aliandra must decide if she's willing to fight for him. Especially when he might be her True Mate.

OTHER BOOKS BY SIOBHAN MUIR

Her Devoted Vampire (from Three Lakes Books)
Queen Bitch of the Callowwood Pack (from Siren Publishing)
Not a Dragon's Standard Virgin (from Siren Publishing)
Second Chance Succubus (from Three Lakes Books)
Darwin's Evolution (from Amazon)

Cloudburst Colorado Series
A Hell Hound's Fire (from Three Lakes Books)
The Beltane Witch (from Three Lakes Books)
Christmas I.C.E. Magic (from Three Lakes Books)
Cloudburst Ice Magic (from Three Lakes Books)

Rifts Series
Take the Reins (from Three Lakes Books)
A Centaur's Solstice Wish (from Three Lakes Books)
In Death's Shadow (from Three Lakes Books)

Bad Boys of Beta Squad Series
Bronco's Rough Ride (from Three Lakes Books)
The Navy's Ghost (from Three Lakes Books)
Rimshot's Hard Target (from Amazon)
Bam-Bam's Inked Hart (from Three Lakes Books)

The Ivory Road
A Walk in the Sand (from Three Lakes Books)
Outback Dreams (from Three Lakes Books)

Triple Star Ranch Series
Rope a Falling Star (from Three Lakes Books

Star Light, Star Bright (from Three Lakes Books)

Warbler Peninsula Series
Order of the Dragon (from Three Lakes Books)
The Valkyrie's Sword (from Three Lakes Books)

Coming Soon
Deli's Take Out (Bad Boys of Beta Squad #4)
Wildfire's Heart (Elemental Hearts #1)
Loch'd Hearts (Elemental Hearts #2)

ABOUT THE AUTHOR

Siobhan Muir lives in Cheyenne, Wyoming, with her husband, two daughters, and a vegetarian cat she swears is a shape-shifter, though he's never shifted when she can see him. When not writing, she can be found looking down a microscope at fossil fox teeth, pursuing her other love, paleontology. An avid reader of science fiction/fantasy, her husband gave her a paranormal romance for Christmas one year, and she was hooked for good.

In previous lives, Siobhan has been an actor at the Colorado Renaissance Festival, a field geologist in the Aleutian Islands, and restored inter-planetary imagery at the USGS. She's hiked to the top of Mount St. Helens and to the bottom of Meteor Crater.

Siobhan writes kick-ass adventure with hot sex for men and women to enjoy. She believes in happily ever after, redemption, and communication, all of which you will find in her paranormal romance stories.

Connect with Siobhan online at:
http://siobhanmuir.com
http://www.facebook.com/siobhan.muir.35
http://twitter.com/SiobhanMuir
http://siobhanmuir.com/siobhans-blog
http://pinterest.com/siobhanmuir.35